TOPPERS

AAYUSH

PENGUIN BOOKS

PENGUIN BOOKS

USA | Canada | UK | Ireland | Australia
New Zealand | India | South Africa | China

Penguin Books is part of the Penguin Random House group of companies
whose addresses can be found at global.penguinrandomhouse.com

Published by Penguin Random House India Pvt. Ltd
7th Floor, Infinity Tower C, DLF Cyber City,
Gurgaon 122 002, Haryana, India

First published in Penguin Books by Penguin Random House India 2016

ISBN 9780143428077

Typeset in Adobe Caslon Pro by Manipal Digital Systems, Manipal
Printed at Replika Press Pvt. Ltd, India

www.penguinbooksindia.com

How much can you know about yourself if you've never been in a fight?

—*Fight Club*

CONTENTS

PROLOGUE

*T*wo silhouettes stood against the moonlight on the roof of the country's toughest school. A gigantic neon-white banner towered over them. Placed on a raised platform, it illuminated the night sky with the words 'Woodsville Scholars International'. The 200-acre school campus, located in the Central Ridge, almost seemed to be a part of Lutyens's colonial-era design of the Rashtrapati Bhavan, which was visible in the distance. Both structures had the old-school charm of red sandstone on the outside.

'I am going to kill you,' one of the shapes said, shivering with anger, its voice hushed with fear.

There was an involuntary bark of laughter from the other figure. 'You know what the problem with being a topper is? There's always someone waiting in line to beat you.'

A moment later, the two shadows merged in a scuffle. A part trying to wriggle free and the other intent on engulfing the struggling captive.

'Let me go' . . . 'What're you doing?' Two rasps punctuated the short but intense fight. The finale, however, came with a *dull thud on the unfeeling concrete below. The shadow had been split once more, right down the middle. One half stood leaning forward at the edge of the roof, seemingly reeling from the shock of the abrupt separation, while the other lay immobile on the ground.*

Fifteen-year-old Nabil, who had been dutifully cleaning the banner a few minutes ago, could do nothing but stare on in shock, the neon light behind him outlining a third silhouette that went completely unnoticed.

THE TOPPERS

A deathly silence blanketed the cricket ground and the stands of the jam-packed stadium. Nature herself seemed to be in harmony with the palpable tension of the spectators: there was no breeze, the grass had stopped fluttering and the clouds seemed to have stood still, as if to watch—all eyes fixed on the player at the crease. Slowly, but steadily, the hush was broken by a chant that rose like a wave, unsynchronized at first, then gradually settling into two intelligible words, repeated with increasing frequency and amplitude.

'Dev! Woodsville! Dev! Woodsville!'

*

Inside the three-storeyed pavilion, Dr Athar exited the washroom for the sixth time that afternoon and walked across the lobby, avoiding eye contact. Athar clutched his stomach and groaned as he had another cramp. He was here only because Director Walia had felt that the student counsellor should be giving pep talks to the school team. He cursed the roadside vendor who had served him salmonella and diarrhoea along with his morning lassi. He was dying to head back to the washroom, but the rising chorus from the stands drew him towards the club lounge.

On a chintz sofa, right in front of the glass panel, Director Walia sat next to Headmistress Shonali Chhaya of St Peter's School, surrounded by players and faculty members. It was a mark of the importance Woodsville gave to inclusive excellence that an inter-school tournament was concluding in the very first week of the new term.

'Seems like it's the last ball already,' Dr Athar exclaimed. Director Walia motioned him to come closer.

'Dev's on the crease,' Walia informed him, his voice tense. Walia was around sixty-five; his scarce but wavy white hair bore witness to that. A pair of old-fashioned glasses, deep, majestic wrinkles and a boyish curiosity adorned his face. It was hard to believe that he was the founder of Woodsville and the foremost educationist in the country.

'So, what do you say?' Walia chirped, unconcerned about keeping his voice down. 'What's going to happen?'

As Woodsville's student counsellor, Athar had never known what the exact nature of his job was. While in most schools a counsellor mentored the academically weaker students, Walia insisted that he keep his eyes on the best of them, class five onwards. Dev, the head scholar, was one of the fiercest Athar had come across.

Athar grimaced. 'I don't think I am the right person to predict—' he stopped short as he spotted Dev through the glass. Even at a radial distance from the pitch, there was no mistaking it—Dev was injured. 'When did that happen?' Athar asked, pointing.

Director Walia's face split into a grin. 'Last ball hit him straight in the face. Probably broke his nose, but the boy set it straight without a flinch . . .' He seemed reminiscent. 'I must remember to mention it to his grandfather.'

Athar concealed his frown. Surely, as the director, Walia should be more sombre about a student getting hurt? But Athar knew Walia was an unorthodox man; his single-minded drive for competition had propelled Woodsville Scholars International to the helm in the national arena of education.

Dr Athar didn't like to share details about his patients with the administration, but at thirty, with just an MBBS degree and his two years of junior residency over, Walia pretty much owned him.

'How many runs do we need?' Athar asked quietly. Although it was April and it had been a month since Athar last spoke to Dev, he knew what drove the boy.

'Four.'

Athar experienced a particularly alarming cramp in his stomach. 'He'll hit a six.'

*

Dev Bhushan
Topper in: VIII
Motto: Trust No One
Current: XII/ Science

3

Dev never saw the people in the stands; they were a blur as soon as he'd walked on to the pitch. Had he been able to, he would've seen Director Walia in the pavilion, up on his feet, both his hands in the air, including the one that held his walking stick. He could hear all right, though, and right now he could hear the spectators' roars getting louder.

He smirked.

As if he needed more encouragement. He knew he was going to hit a six as soon as the last bouncer had made him look weak in front of his fans. It was his fault . . . he'd been careless.

Most of the bowling side seemed elated. Surely, being hurt as badly as he had been, even this muscular batsman would be pretty disoriented? But having bowled six overs to the guy, the bowler knew better. Dev always formed a bond with the bowler. It was akin to the bond between a master and his pet. Right now, the bowler knew that the master was angry. And there wasn't much the master forgave.

Dev didn't even spare a glance at the fielding set-up. Because it didn't matter. It was just him and the bowler.

After the last bowl, it would be just him.

*

Aniket Jain
Topper in: X, XI
Motto: All Means Necessary
Current: XII/ Commerce

The huge cheer from the stadium, constrained by the speed of sound, reached the student residences of the campus a second later. Aniket Jain could tell that they had won. He scowled. *What a waste of time.* An enthusiastic answering cheer from their own little villa told him that his housemates didn't share his thoughts.

Although he understood the jubilation of winning better than anyone else, he had never understood how people could be so happy at the triumphs of others. Did they think that Dev gave a shit about them, or even Woodsville, for that matter?

He grunted and slid aside his copy of *Advanced Mathematics* on to the floor in frustration. It wasn't that he had anything against the sport; he liked cricket as much as any self-respecting Indian, but Aniket couldn't stand the fierce obsession with it—especially since he had failed to make the team last year.

Aniket hated losing—which is why he didn't do much of it. He had been the school topper the last two years, as well as the all-India topper in his tenth boards. He competed harder and meaner than any of his peers. The head scholar, however, was a guy whose only discernible ability was that he knew how to hit a piece of leather with a bigger piece of wood. Sure, Aniket had been made a house captain, but he didn't work this hard to be the second best.

Woodsville was a school for toppers, and being the head of the student body meant being recognized as the best among the best. Aniket knew he *was* the best, but he wanted it to be recognized. Moreover, Woodsville sponsored the head scholar's higher education.

And Dev was a *science* student! Aniket snorted at the thought of how ridiculous it all was. Woodsville Scholars was renowned for its commerce department; it was a base for the bureaucrats of tomorrow, the most powerful people in the executive, legislature and judiciary. The best of them went on to study at Harvard Business School. The science and arts streams were considered irrelevant in comparison.

At this moment, Aniket loathed Dev more than he did Rikkhe Rajput, and he considered Rikkhe Rajput his mortal enemy. He started pacing around his unkempt room, ignoring the music blaring from the adjoining quarters, ignoring the seemingly unsolvable equation Dr Sinha had assigned him.

All those people should be cheering for *him*, not for Dev Bhushan! This was his last year in school, and Aniket didn't believe in inaction. He would show them all tomorrow, at the inaugural assembly of the year . . . but first, he needed to write a speech.

*

Himanshu Pathak
Topper in: V
Motto: Head Down, Eyes and Ears Open
Current: XII / Commerce

Himanshu reeled from the blow. The left side of his face was buried in the dirt, and the right was throbbing with pain. He could hear jeers mingling with the cheering. The cheers were for the winning six Dev had just hit, and the jeers were directed at the loser who had been hit by the ball—Himanshu. He groaned as he got up from the ground, trying to look as nonchalant as possible. Fortunately, he hadn't been wearing his frameless spectacles.

As he saw a number of people pointing and laughing at him, he cursed himself; he should have stayed home and studied. This is what came of lying to his mother.

'Hey, you all right?' the fielder nearest the third man called out.

Himanshu nodded vigorously, which only made his head scream in protest. 'Yes . . . yes, I'm good.'

'Pity about your camera,' the fielder remarked.

Himanshu's eyes immediately dropped to the ground. He had been standing right outside the boundary as the official photographer for the bimonthly Woodsville Scholars magazine. Now he stood on the wrong side of the white rope, and behind him lay the DSLR the guy from the magazine had arranged for him, its 150–500 mm telephoto lens shattered.

'Shit!' said Himanshu, dropping to the ground and cradling the camera, all pretence of nonchalance forgotten. If they asked him to pay for the damage, he was in deep trouble. He shuddered at the prospect of telling his mother about his passion for photography. Between the driver dropping him off at school and the closely supervised home tuitions, he had had to move heaven and earth to buy his own camera—an ancient Kodak that shot thirty-six photos per reel, and which he'd secretly acquired by trading two of his birthday gifts and seven old silk shirts. Himanshu then cringed at the thought of having owned seven silk shirts.

He should have covered Rikkhe Rajput's polo match in the adjacent ground instead, although he wasn't sure he would have been let in. At least Rikkhe was careful enough not to hit the ball at the spectators. Himanshu let out a sigh as he saw that the LCD display of the camera was also broken. This didn't stop him, though. He replaced the lens with a normal one, searched through the viewfinder, zoomed in as much as the lens allowed, and got back to clicking pictures of Vishakha Sahdev, the magical girl in the crowd, who was cheering for Dev Bhushan as hard as she could.

*

Vishakha Sahdev
Topper in: VI
Motto: It's Who You Know
Current: XII / Commerce

Vishakha stopped the obligatory cheering almost as soon as she began, and made her way through the stands, back to her original place in the pavilion with the organizing committee.

'Vizac! Where have you been?' exclaimed Shikhar, as she entered the lobby, leaving the sound of cheers behind. 'Walia Sir called for you ten minutes ago!'

Vishakha smiled. *Finally*. She didn't let on how it irked her that Shikhar had called her Vizac after just one date.

'What are you smiling about?' Radha, another member of the committee, asked her. 'He didn't seem pleased with the preparations.'

The smile widened. 'I know,' she said, and promptly left, while they stared after this cavalier, provisional member of the organizing committee, which was otherwise filled with people who were responsible for maintaining Woodsville's—or rather Walia's—levels of excellence.

Vishakha made her way to the club lounge, a spring in her step. Right outside the half-open door, she could hear Walia's irritated voice: 'Where's that girl? We won, and the radio station wasn't even transmitting!'

Vishakha donned a straight face and approached the director, who was on his feet, probably getting ready to go down to the award ceremony. 'Good afternoon, sir. I heard you were looking for me . . .'

Walia looked sideways at Vishakha, and without preamble, said in a dry voice, 'Why wasn't the radio commentary up in time for the match?'

A few of the faculty and team members stopped what they were doing and turned to watch.

'I am extremely sorry, sir,' Vishakha replied without a hint of regret. 'There were some technical snags.'

Walia flared up. 'The only reason you were made the acting in-charge of the organizing committee was because you'd said to me, and I quote, "We need to integrate sports events with the campus radio, and we have to do it in the presence of an *outdated* OC."'

Despite herself, Vishakha was impressed by the man's eidetic memory.

'You know how many strings I had to pull to get a radio built right in the central government's backyard?'

Walia's left hand, along with his walking cane, shook with outrage.

Vishakha sneered inwardly. *Not more than it took to build the campus in the Central 'Reserve' Forest.* She didn't reply, though, letting Walia continue his tirade. She couldn't help but notice that the members of the cricket team, most of who tried to hit on her every now and then, were all squeamishly averting their eyes.

Walia pointed to a man beside him. 'You know who this is?' Everyone looked at him with such interest that the man became self-conscious. 'He is the joint secretary at the ministry of information and broadcasting. I invited him to see what we've been working on for all these months. All you had to do was coordinate with the technicians from the station. Why was that a problem?' Walia paused, expecting an explanation.

Dr Athar spoke up nervously. 'Sir, I am sure Vishakha is sorry for the botch-up. But she's a sincere student, and I am also sure she must've done her best—'

'Sir,' Vishakha addressed the director, unabashed, 'one thing I have learnt from this school, and you, is a certain regard for perfection. As discussed, I had handled the logistics of setting up a fully functioning commentator's box in the stadium. The inaugural christening, according to me, required a commentator who matched Woodsville's pomp. I had approached Shri Sunil Gavaskar for the honour.'

There was derision in everyone's face except Director Walia's, who now seemed bemused. *A schoolgirl offering a job to the cricketing legend?*

'All Mr Gavaskar's aides needed was a letter from the director's office, a request which I forwarded to you,' Vishakha paused as Walia looked dismayed.

'But I received no such request!'

'I am sure, sir,' Vishakha said quickly, 'you were much too busy to peruse all the student requests.'

Walia frowned, looking at her closely. Vishakha's heart was racing from lying to the director to his face, but she controlled her trepidation. There had been no letter, no invitation to Sunil Gavaskar and no intention on her part to send one.

Walia went back to looking thoughtful and remarked, 'So you left the commentator's box empty . . .'

'Yes, sir,' Vishakha said. Before Walia could interrupt, she pointed out from the glass wall. 'Do you see those men with the cameras, sir?'

Walia—along with Mrs Shonali Chhaya and the others—looked to where she pointed. And sure enough, a group of three men with a professional-looking video camera were following Dev Bhushan and the losing team on the field.

'Yes.'

'Seven groups like that have been shooting today's match . . .' Vishakha noticed the ministry man get even more self-conscious. 'They belong to a production house from Defence Colony. I hired them to document the match. I am afraid a substantial amount of the organizing committee's funds was used up for it . . .'

The man from the I&B ministry remarked, 'And what are you going to do with the footage?' There was no mistaking from his tone that he was still ready to pull some strings—for a price.

'It will be telecast on ESPN tomorrow, followed by the India–Australia ODI.'

There was a stunned silence. Vishakha mulled over the ordeal—a date—she'd had to endure with Shikhar to get that time slot from his father. Walia was more adept at bribing bureaucrats than worming his way into the house of the national head of an MNC.

A faint smile appeared on Director Walia's face. He understood why the girl hadn't come to him directly with such good news: she'd wanted to get one over on the director of Woodsville in front of his influential friends. Nothing gave him more pleasure than to find such a rare specimen of a student. The girl might even be duping him about calling Gavaskar! He hid his pleasure and said softly, 'I must say, I am impressed.'

Vishakha betrayed a faint hint of pleasure herself. Event management wasn't her thing; she had only wished to be acknowledged by the director and the important people he surrounded himself with.

'Thank you, sir,' she smiled curtly. Turning to the ministry official, she said, 'And thank you, sir, for all you have done to promote the school.'

Walia's personal assistant approached him and spoke softly, 'Sir, the ceremony is about to start. Your presence is required down there.'

Walia nodded promptly, leaned on his cane and made his way out of the lounge along with everyone else. As they left, Vishakha could hear Headmistress Chhaya's voice: 'A bold student you've got there, Walia Sahib.'

Athar was left alone with Vishakha. He shook his head disapprovingly. 'Nicely played . . .'

'Sir?' she said innocently.

Athar gave her a piercing look. He knew what the girl was capable of. 'We'll talk about this in the next session.'

Vishakha mused. Athar was practically her psychiatrist; what was the point of pretending?

'Do you know what the floors are laden with here at Woodsville?' she asked abruptly.

Athar shook his head, thrown by her seemingly random question.

'It is Makrana marble, the stuff the Taj is made of.'

'Your point being?'

'I am not from an elite family like the others here, Doc,' she said simply. 'My father is a government servant . . . "servant" being the operative word. And servants have to learn to make do in their lives. But these people here?' she pointed through the glass wall. 'They will *matter* in a few years, courtesy either of their parents or their talent. What matters right now are appearances . . . like this white marble. And since I am no royalty like Rikkhe Rajput, I make do with what I have.'

Athar sighed. Vishakha was the bitterest girl he'd ever come across, but he hadn't given up on her yet. 'Today. After school. Be on time, Vizac.'

*

Rikkhe Rajput
Topper in: VII, IX
Motto: I Am King, What I Behold, My Kingdom
Current: XII / Commerce

Everyone could hear the din from the cricket stadium, but there was something serene and illustrious in a game of polo that told its audience that they were better off here. Anyway, this was a family affair.

Even though the match was going on in the grounds, there was no mistaking the real contest taking place in the vanguard of the spectator stand. The maharaja of Chaseer and Rana Dhananjay of Jahalgarh sat next to each other, faces closed and pride flexed. The maharaja, clad in a formal, three-piece business suit, was hunched forward, his left eye squinting at the proceedings, while his right eye tried to catch a glimpse of the idiot from Jahalgarh sitting beside him. The rana, a title for kings in Rajasthan, was one in every sense of the word. He might very well have been riding into war; resplendent in his royal white *bandhgala*, a jewel-studded red turban, handcrafted shoes and a recently polished sword.

The maharaja snorted silently at Dhananjay; what a bloody cliché. The royalty, after decades of banishment, still found ways to enthral the commoners. The polo match, other than being an ego clash between two ancient families, was also an exercise in networking. And although Dhananjay still thought of himself as a king, it did give him an opportunity to conduct a little business. Jahalgarh, earlier known for its rare diamond mines, was now primarily a cement-manufacturing district, with the rana's family playing a major role in it.

The stakes of the game were simple: whoever lost would reimburse the cost of this newly built ground—the size of nine football fields—to Woodsville.

Meanwhile, on the field, the rana's son, Rikkhe Rajput, soared on his chestnut-brown horse, adjusting his team's strategy lightning fast as he moved. He almost felt pity for Prince Shekhawat, the maharaja's son and his opponent; there was no greater shame than to fail one's king. It was the last chukka—seven-minute play—of the game, and Jahalgarh had scored the only three goals.

Rikkhe always believed in motion and unpredictability on the field. He had the body of an athlete, the mind of a military strategist and the conscience of a philosopher— the combination made him a born leader.

However, he stayed in the background by choice, always in the minds of people, but rarely ever in front of them, which was a source of great frustration for Dhananjay, who knew Rikkhe had the tendency to hold back his true potential. Even now in the field Rikkhe hadn't truly let go yet.

'Number three is open!' Rikkhe called out to a teammate. 'Take him.' He then signalled another teammate, Karan, to take control of the ball, who, after a few moments, passed it back to Rikkhe with an expertly carried offside belly shot.

'Ride out!' cried Rikkhe, and Karan rode clear from the onslaught of entangled horses before Rikkhe sent him a back shot, leaving him free to score.

Prince Shekhawat was visibly desperate. Changing gaits, he galloped on his thoroughbred horse to bump into Karan, almost at a right angle. Karan raised his mallet to call a foul, but Rikkhe checked him before the umpires saw it.

'We are on the king's errand,' he said quietly, approaching Karan. 'There will be no crying for help.' He could see from Karan's face that he disagreed. '*Nor* will you pay Shekhawat back in kind. Just play the game. I'll take care of it.'

So far, Rikkhe had refrained from humiliating Shekhawat, but he had also been taught that a Rajput never let an insult slide. As he got in position for the bowl-in by the referee, he caressed Nandini, his horse, and started humming the war song of Jahalgarh.

In the stands, a spectator seated behind the kings, and unacquainted with the sport, spoke up hesitantly, 'What did Shekhawat just do?' The question was addressed to the man sitting beside him in traditional Rajasthani attire.

Karamveer Singh, who had zealously guarded Rikkhe since his birth, leaned in to answer with a smile, 'A mistake.' On very rare occasions, Rikkhe was a living embodiment of something that Karamveer's father, who had served the royal family as well, had described to him as 'the king's wrath'. After seventeen years of service to Rikkhe, Karamveer instinctively knew that he was about to witness one such occasion.

The rana's face, too, broke into a grin as he watched the familiar look of determination settle on his son's face, and he knew that the prince of Chaseer was in trouble.

Almost as soon as play resumed, just as Rikkhe had wanted, Shekhawat was in possession of the ball. Rikkhe effortlessly intercepted him near his position at number three, and rode off with the ball towards the enemy goal, Shekhawat's faster thoroughbred vehemently bumping into Nandini from the left.

Shekhawat's mallet found a clear swing to the ball, but Rikkhe cut him off mid-shot, hooking Shekhawat's stick away. Using Shekhawat's brief moment of frustration, Rikkhe swiftly swung an offside tail to Karan, simultaneously slowing Nandini down to a trot.

As soon as the prince realized the ball was on the other side of Rikkhe, he tried to slow down and fall behind him. However, Nandini now blocked the way, and in a desperate bid to cross over, Shekhawat tried to overtake them. It was all Rikkhe needed.

In the stands, the maharaja gasped, half rising from his seat. A murmur of shock and cheer went through the crowd. As Shekhawat foolishly tried to cross Rikkhe from the front, Nandini charged forward with the wrath of a lion, sending Shekhawat and his thoroughbred reeling into the grass.

Karan brought down his mallet, gently changing the line of the ball towards the goal. He turned to his teammates just in time to catch a glimpse of the rival captain falling. The next moment, umpires signalled the end of the game.

The spectators might just have witnessed a battle.

Dhananjay raised a thoughtful eyebrow. This usually quiet boy might yet prove to be the answer to all the troubles of Jahalgarh . . . and his own.

THE CHALLENGE

The morning after he had broken the camera, Himanshu reflected on how much he didn't want to go to school. Unfortunately, he wasn't a boarder, and couldn't do as he pleased. So he hurriedly hid his mismatched socks under the frayed edges of his blue jeans, picked up his bag and took a nervous look around his huge, circular room.

'Bhaiyaji,' called Monu, the domestic help, from outside the door, 'madam is calling you for breakfast.'

'I'm coming!' said Himanshu, quickly checking the bed, his study table and the windowsills. He hated forgetting anything he might need at school, and that seemed to happen to him quite a lot. Teachers didn't usually reprimand him as he was 'one of the good ones', but he hated the negative attention. At least he didn't have to worry about the uniform—Woodsville didn't have one. Like always, he ensured that the door right next to the windowsill was locked.

He ran downstairs to the dining room, the house unusually quiet at eight in the morning. His father probably wasn't back from Toronto.

His mother hadn't eaten yet. She, unlike Himanshu's father, was tall and stately looking. Clad in formals, she was ready to leave for office. They usually left home at the same time, even though Woodsville's timings were fixed—from nine to five—while her working hours were anything but predictable.

'Cheenu, you're late,' she said softly. 'Now sit and eat something.'

'Cannot, Ma,' Himanshu replied, running past her. 'I *am* late.' As usual, he'd lost track of time, practising accounts all morning.

'HIMANSHU!' Her voice rang with authority—more Geeta Pathak, CFO, than his mother now.

He stopped immediately. He knew when not to mess with his mother.

'Eat your breakfast now,' she said, her voice quivering. Himanshu noticed her eyes were red and her hair a little dishevelled. 'Maybe next time you'll remember to get ready on time. And wear something besides your stupid T-shirts tomorrow.'

Himanshu obligingly sat down on the seat next to his mother and looked at her with concern. Ever since her promotion last year, he could see that the stress was wearing her out.

'Is everything okay?' he asked timidly.

She flared up. 'I thought you were getting late?'

*

Each two-storey villa at Woodsville came with a helper, and provided single-sex housing for four students. When

Vishakha left her little building in the student residential area, their housekeeper, Kirthi, was still serving breakfast to her three housemates. Stepping out, she spotted a few neighbours and classmates emerging from their red-sandstone villas, briskly crossing their yards. Vishakha quickened her pace; she had learnt long ago that despite what the Constitution said, opportunities were usually dished out on a first-come-first-serve basis. Equality was like utopia. A myth.

Normally Vishakha was the first to reach the main building, but she'd been busy socializing the night before; Dev Bhushan had thrown a party at the campus mall to celebrate his victory. By the time she had finished studying to make up for the time lost, it had become late.

Walking past the stone amphitheatre, Vishakha lamented the fact that students weren't allowed to use the two dozen golf carts that had been bought for the teaching staff recently. Of course, had they been allowed, it wouldn't have been as much fun to ride in them.

'Good day, ma'am!' she called out to Ms Jyoti Sharma, her economics teacher. Ms Jyoti was fresh out of Harvard, prior to which she had been a student at Woodsville. She was still new to teaching, but there wasn't a single person on campus who didn't already adore the tall, good-natured woman. Vishakha was no exception. It helped that economics was Vishakha's favourite subject; one she always got a perfect score in.

'Good morning, Vishakha,' Ms Jyoti replied from her cart. She put a hand on the driver's shoulder, signalling him to stop. 'What are you doing this side of the amphitheatre?'

The amphitheatre and the green cover surrounding it were what separated the student and teacher residences.

Vishakha smiled. 'To tell the truth, ma'am, I was hoping to catch a ride.'

Ms Jyoti looked hesitant. Vishakha knew the cause of her hesitation—being new at the job, she was afraid of overstepping her bounds.

'Of course, Vishakha, hop on . . .' Ms Jyoti shifted to make space; she wasn't new at being awesome.

Vishakha and Ms Jyoti reached the oval marble atrium together. While the teacher went on towards the admin office, Vishakha thanked her and took the escalator on the left, leading to the indoor auditorium.

'Hi, Vizac . . .' A shy guy standing ahead glanced back at her. Shyly.

'Hey, you,' Vishakha said shortly, pretending not to know the guy's name. If he was going to 'Vizac' her, she knew how to be doubly annoying.

The boy turned to the front once more. Vishakha felt satisfied; she could tell his face was red—the back of his neck and his ears definitely were.

As soon as she reached the auditorium, she left the horde of ordinary students behind her, heading backstage to where the real action took place every morning during assembly.

And as she entered the green room, she felt the atmosphere change. Whereas the auditorium would by now be filled with sleepy-eyed kids looking for the most comfortable chairs, the green room was pulsing with energy. Everyone here was focused on conquering the day ahead instead of reeling from the night before. Vishakha felt right at home. They were all Villeans here.

'Villeans' was what the best at Woodsville called themselves. When sentimental, they marked their bond with the school by the affectionate moniker 'Woozies'.

One Villean, standing alone in the corner, past the mirrors, past the chit-chatting groups and the fretful, twitchy teachers, drew Vishakha's attention. Aniket Jain. The topper for the last two years.

His eyes were closed, his mouth was moving soundlessly, and in his hand was a tightly clutched piece of paper.

'Hey,' Vishakha spoke quietly, approaching him.

Aniket came out of his reverie with a start. 'What? Is it time?'

'Time for what?' asked Vishakha, frowning. Aniket was acting strange . . . the 'backstage people', as Vishakha called them, were never nervous about facing the 'auditorium people'. Especially not Aniket Jain.

Aniket collected himself. 'My speech . . .' He was almost muttering to himself!

'Oh, yeah,' said Vishakha coolly, as if she'd forgotten about it, 'the topper's speech. You topped last year, no?'

Aniket gave Vishakha a piercing look. She could tell that her feigned indifference had irked him.

But he wasn't some shy boy she could intimidate so easily.

'Yeah,' he said just as coolly, 'I did. To be honest, I was a bit worried about you trumping me in business studies, you know . . . but Rikkhe came closer than you. Then there was some other guy, I think. *Then* you.' Aniket gave her a condescending smile. 'But there's always next year. So, good luck and do the best you can, okay?'

Vishakha narrowed her eyes. She and Aniket were among the few scholarship students at Woodsville; their tuition fees came out of the pockets of all the rich dads paying for the overpriced education of their mediocre offspring. And this had formed a sense of camaraderie between them over the years. They knew each other well enough to know that they had much in common, and that they could never be friends. He envied her savvy, while she secretly admired his grit.

'Seems we are both short in the luck department,' she said with barely concealed anger. 'Otherwise the topper would have been the head scholar. Instead, Walia's boy, Dev Bhushan, is strutting around with the honour.'

Aniket's nostrils flared. There it was again. No victory was complete at Woodsville without the title of head scholar pinned to one's chest.

'Well, he just got it a week back; let him enjoy it for now. Then we'll see if we can do something about it,' Aniket said innocently. 'Now you'd better go welcome the people out there . . . and announce *my* name!'

*

'Now that's what we call a *pataka*!' Himanshu heard Vivek enlighten a couple of British students. He looked to where Vivek was pointing and saw Lisa Chauhan with her gang of prima donnas enter the auditorium.

Himanshu shook his head slightly. A week from now the exchange students would be singing 'Sheila ki Jawani', if left in Vivek's charge.

Vivek, who was sitting next to Himanshu, gave him a wink and got back to the Brits. One of them—Jacob—let out an involuntary whistle as he spotted Lisa, and Vivek chuckled.

'Don't get your hopes up, boys,' he said, 'she's taken.'

As if on cue, Himanshu saw Rikkhe Rajput enter the auditorium, give Lisa and her friends a courteous nod, and walk past them. His elegantly embroidered kurta, white trousers and black Jodhpuri jacket were a drastic contrast to Lisa, who donned a red haute couture dress.

'Good morning, Himanshu,' Rikkhe said with a smile as he crossed them.

'And to you, Rikkhe,' Himanshu replied with a grin, adjusting his glasses. Rikkhe had always been cordial with Himanshu, but then, he was cordial with everyone, even his enemies. Despite this, Himanshu somehow felt that Rikkhe was the most trustworthy person on campus.

'That's whom she's with, guys,' Vivek continued, pointing at Rikkhe. 'Or, at least, whom she's going to be with. There's a rumour she's interested in Rikkhe. He won't be able to resist once he gets to know of it . . .'

Himanshu looked at Rikkhe thoughtfully. He didn't believe Rikkhe could be interested in anyone as naive and practically blank as Lisa, no matter how beautiful she was.

'Naah . . .' Himanshu joined the gossip, addressing Jacob, 'he's a loner . . . he's everyone's friend, but no one's *his* friend. Get it?'

They shook their heads.

'It means he talks to people just for the sake of being polite,' Himanshu said impatiently. 'What is he going to do with a girl who can't put two intelligent sentences together?'

The four of them turned to look at Lisa once again—she was giggling away madly with her friends, while blocking the entrance to the auditorium. Himanshu marvelled at what a perfect human specimen she was—tall, lean, fair, uncaring, stupid.

'If Rajput doesn't want her, you keep your hands off, boys,' Vivek said to the Brits. He added with a wistful sigh, 'You are here for a week; I'm going to take care of her forever . . .'

A couple of girls sitting nearby threw Himanshu dirty looks, and he squirmed. He could do nothing about Vivek's exuberance, though, for he was the only friend Himanshu had.

*

While everyone crowded the auditorium, Dev Bhushan had sneaked into the counsellor's office for his session. He shifted nervously, acutely aware of the tic in his eyes—every third second they closed and momentarily blurred the person sitting across the table.

Athar felt sorry for the pitiable state of the school champion sitting in front of him. Dev's involuntary throat-clearing and eye-twitching gave off a sense of helplessness that somehow infected Athar as well.

'Calm down, Dev,' Athar spoke gently, 'and tell me . . . why do you come to me? Think before you answer.'

Dev was in no state to think clearly. He was playing a very risky game, but it was his only chance—Athar must believe that the school star was having a nervous breakdown.

'To talk, what else!' he said irritably. He was growing impatient with all the soul-searching, but he wouldn't get a chance to talk to Athar again until the next assembly . . . it was the only time Dev felt comfortable doing so—when everyone else was looking the other way.

'Exactly,' Athar replied, 'and why do you talk?'

This one made Dev think. However, he didn't like the answer he had come up with. He lied instead.

'Because Director Walia made it compulsory for all the top students to attend counselling sessions,' he grunted.

Athar gave a bark of laughter. 'I doubt *anyone* can make you do something you don't want to do.' He paused. 'No, wait. Someone *is* making you do something; that's why we're here.'

Dev scowled. His scarlet–silver head-scholar badge shone against his pale, milky complexion, but as he grew more agitated, the contrast seemed to lessen.

'You talk because you *want* to, Dev,' Athar said earnestly. 'You talk because you know that sharing your problems with another person gives you another mind to solve it. Why not share it with your grandfather as well?'

Dev stood up abruptly, upsetting his chair as he did, and it went crashing down. 'Because he *is* the problem!'

Athar sighed. 'He isn't, Dev, you are.'

Dev glared at Athar. Athar was a little wary of the unpredictable brawny young man in front of him, despite himself; Dev's tics had vanished as soon as he'd taken control. Athar's upset bowel started gurgling once again.

'Why don't you just tell him that you do not want to enlist in the army?'

'The air force,' Dev corrected him dully. 'God, man, do you even listen to what I say?'

Athar's eyes narrowed. 'I do, Dev, but do *you*?'

'What are you talking—?'

Athar stood up as well, slamming his hands on the table. 'It shouldn't matter that your grandfather served in the Indian Army! That he wants you to go further and join the air force! This is about *you*, not him. Talk to him, tell him what you—!'

'That I what?' Dev snapped back. 'Want to be a cricketer? He'll laugh in my face. Again.'

'So what? You'll fight for your country, and you'll get the rewards that come with it. That's what you want, right?'

For an instant, Dev was amazed at how well Athar knew him. He wasn't selfless enough to be a true patriot; he needed his bonuses. He *was* loyal, though, and to openly rebel against his grandfather, who'd supported him when nobody else had, was unthinkable.

'I can't.'

Athar controlled himself. 'I know you are strong, Dev, perhaps the strongest of all those who come to me.' He said that to everyone who came to him.

'*You* don't understand,' Dev said quietly. 'He's got my balls in a vice-like grip.'

Athar wrung his hands in exasperation. 'He's your grandfather! How can he control you?'

'I am not talking about my grandfather,' Dev said shortly, turning to leave for the assembly, hiding the deception on his face.

Athar stopped short in surprise. 'Then who?' he called after Dev.

Just before Dev shut the door after him, Athar distinctly heard his defeated voice say, 'His old fart of a friend, Walia, who else?'

Dev smirked as he calmly walked away from Athar's office, convinced that the director would get the message—Walia's star student wouldn't be winning any more accolades for Woodsville unless Walia could convince his grandfather to let him do as he pleased.

*

A blur of colours and faces was all Aniket could see from backstage. There wasn't an empty seat in the auditorium. The entire school, from the cowering fifth-standard sheep to the swaggering class-twelve hyenas, was present. As Vishakha theatrically welcomed-them-*all*-to-the-*morning-assembly!* Aniket closed his eyes and started muttering under his breath. He hid it expertly, but public speaking made him nervous as hell.

Mrs Swaminathan, his English teacher, put a hand on his shoulder.

'Ani, what are you doing backstage?' she said in her throaty voice. 'Head out to the wings! Vishakha is about to announce your name.'

Aniket made his way to the side of the stage, walking past the other students, all of whom seemed strangely relaxed in contrast to his light-headedness.

He moved to the front of the line and saw Vishakha on stage, animatedly addressing her peers in the audience. He spotted Director Walia hobble in on his cane and take a seat on the sofa right in front of the stage. A technician attached a cordless mic to Aniket's ear and tapped the cushioned speaker.

Aniket had half a mind to tear up his carefully concocted speech and run away from the stage, when he spotted Rikkhe, who'd casually walked up to Walia and begun a conversation. Walia got Vice Director Kaul to vacate his chair and beckoned Rikkhe to sit by his side.

Aniket's blood boiled as he saw Rikkhe discreetly withdraw something that looked suspiciously like a cheque and present it to Walia, who passed it to Admin Kumari with a smile.

Afterwards, Aniket wouldn't be able to say for sure, but the last sane thought in his head at that moment seemed to be something along the lines of—*screw these bastards.*

*

Rikkhe didn't like being in anyone's debt, and he'd been in one since the time Director Walia had had the polo ground built for him. It was a burden off his chest as he handed the sizeable cheque from the maharaja of Chaseer to Director Walia, for an amount that was more than the cost of the polo ground. Rikkhe earned his keep.

Something caught his eye, and the eye of everyone else in the auditorium too. Aniket Jain, without ceremony, had stormed up to take centre stage in the middle of Vishakha's address.

A wave of muttering swept the hall. *Probably couldn't wait to give the topper's speech . . .*

'What is that boy doing?' Kumari spoke up, frowning.

At the podium, Vishakha, too, had seen Aniket come striding on to the stage. It had given her a moment's pause, following which she'd realized that it also gave her an opportunity to humiliate him.

Something stopped her, though. She was the closest to Aniket, and his face told her that something more interesting was about to come. She immediately went back to her address.

' . . . And the term shall begin with a word from last year's topper . . . Aniket Jain.' Vishakha paused and smirked. 'As usual.'

There was a murmur of bitter laughter that Aniket knew only too well. He braced himself; more of it would follow in the next few minutes. Everyone hated toppers; *toppers* hated toppers even more. For all he knew, there wasn't a single person here who was sympathetic towards him.

Sitting beside Walia, Rikkhe Rajput felt an uneasy sense of foreboding. Aniket's rude gesture had turned every person in the auditorium against him. Despite the well-known fact that Aniket detested 'silver-spooners' like him, Rikkhe was worried for him.

'Ladies and gentlemen,' Aniket spoke, undeterred, his voice quivering a little. 'Welcome to a new year at Woodsville Scholars International.' Everyone listened closely; it was clear from Aniket's voice that he was bursting to say something. 'Having topped my batch last year, it is apparently my responsibility to "enlighten" you with the ways of my brain, and what it takes to be the best of the best.' Aniket's voice grew stronger. 'Well, the first thing you must do is stand up for what's right, no matter the cost.'

Dr Athar, who had just entered the auditorium after having finished his session with Dev, snorted involuntarily. Aniket was many things, good and bad, but he stood up only for himself. Nothing and no one else.

'And the issue that I take up today is of grave importance. It challenges the very principles this institution has been built upon. We all know that at the end of every year, a student from class eleven is chosen to be the head scholar of Woodsville for the next year. This person is also the de facto head of the student body, and gets a full scholarship for their higher education.'

There was a hush. No one was thinking about Aniket's rudeness now. Only his words . . . words that openly, unbelievably challenged Dev Bhushan, the school star and current head scholar.

Aniket, too, seemed to have sensed the effect of his words. His voice instinctively went down to a whisper. 'Is it *fair* then, that the representative of all the students of the school is a person handpicked by the director alone?'

The question hung in the air, staring at open mouths, shocked eyes and blank faces, echoing over and over. Not even Vishakha, who believed Aniket to be capable of anything in order to win, could believe that he had just challenged Director Walia in the inaugural assembly.

'Who the hell does this boy think he is?' Vice Director Kaul exclaimed, infuriated. He made to get up, but stopped at a gesture from the bemused Walia. Admin Kumari, Director Walia's right hand at Woodsville, had her dangerous, hawk-like eyes trained on Aniket's face.

Standing in the far back, Dr Athar seemed unfazed, as though he had been waiting for this to happen. He felt oddly proud of Aniket, who he knew wasn't naive enough to believe that he could ever win this face-off, but obstinate enough that he would try nonetheless.

'DO WE WANT ELECTIONS?' Aniket shouted into the mic, his voice infectious enough to make many of the people who despised him get up on their seats and cheer.

No one noticed a figure slink in from the wings and displace Vishakha at the podium.

'I turn my head for two seconds, and look what happens . . .' a voice rang out drily, cutting short the echoes of Aniket's question.

All eyes turned to the podium to find Dev Bhushan holding the mic, his stance casual and playful.

Aniket froze for a moment, but he had his script prepared for this eventuality.

'Oh, Dev, glad you could join us,' he said calmly. 'We were just talking about you.'

There was a bout of laughter as Dev smiled.

'It seemed to me,' Dev said, 'like you were about to tell us why *you* should be head scholar.'

Himanshu Pathak, like many of his peers, sat up straighter in his chair. It was a slugfest.

'I don't like this, sir,' Rikkhe spoke quietly to Walia. 'This is not the appropriate place.'

Walia snorted. *Most certainly not.*

'May I take care of this?' Rikkhe inquired.

'Take care?' Walia asked, confused.

'There cannot be elections, sir, you know that,' Rikkhe said simply. 'It would completely undermine your authority. There would be mayhem.' He didn't say it, but he felt there was already enough unhealthy rivalry at Woodsville.

The director's face was inscrutable. Rikkhe couldn't place it but he would have guessed that it was rage. What it really was, was regret. There was just one thought in Walia's mind. *A bunch of kids tearing the school apart with their desire to win? Why didn't I think of that?*

On stage, Aniket was out of pre-planned responses and one-liners.

'Yes, I know why the idea would be indigestible to you,' Aniket spat at Dev. 'But we live in a democracy—not some monarch's fiefdom!' There was a collective gasp as people turned to Rikkhe at this barely cloaked attack, but he was still busy conferring with Walia. 'We have a right to choose our leader.'

'Please tell us why you should be our leader.'

Aniket opened his mouth but not a sound came out. 'I—I topped—'

'So did I.' On the surface, Dev was calm. 'What have you done for anyone except yourself?'

Aniket, who had never done anything for anyone but himself, blurted out, 'What about *you*, Mr Head Scholar?'

Which seemed to be exactly the question Dev had been waiting for. 'I captained the Woodsville team last year, and it won the country's first National Young Cricket Championship. While you were busy being a topper, I arranged remedial classes for all the new transfers to the school. I've personally chauffeured and hosted half the guests Woodsville has had in the last six months. I have assisted Dr Athar with counselling three young students in the last two years, kids who were on the verge of a nervous breakdown. You want more?'

Aniket didn't want more, so he stayed quiet.

Dev now looked genuinely furious—at his loyalty and allegiance being doubted. He struck the top of the podium with his fist. 'Does anyone want Aniket Jain to be the school leader?' he barked into the microphone. Dev knew from experience that people preferred not to raise their hands, no matter what the question was.

Aniket's speech was over, and not a single student or teacher seemed inclined to stand up for him now. There was, what teachers called, a 'pin-drop silence'.

From where he sat in the last row, Athar saw Rikkhe Rajput stand up and approach the stage purposefully. And he had to admit that he had no idea what Rikkhe had in mind. Despite weekly sessions with him, Athar had never been able to know him as he did the others. The hour they had together was usually spent discussing topics that ranged from the non-essential to the immaterial. Indeed, Athar suspected that Rikkhe knew more about him than he did about Rikkhe.

Dev made way for Rikkhe as he walked to the podium. Aniket blanched at the sight of his sworn enemy, a poison more potent than even Dev Bhushan. As usual, there was an awed silence when Rikkhe took the stage, not because of what he was, but the way he carried himself. There was an understated dignity and authority in his manner. When Rikkhe spoke, people listened.

Yet to be acquainted with him, the new lot of class-five students was amused by his traditional attire. By nightfall, they would be as awed as the rest.

'Friends,' said Rikkhe calmly, 'although I didn't top last year, I am still going to say a few words.' There was light laughter; he was easy to like. 'The history of this school is as formidable as it is well known.' Rikkhe paused, and then added with a smile, 'And it certainly didn't come from wasting time in the assembly. Off you go to your classes.'

THE CONTENDERS

A week into April, the atmosphere in the campus was tense. Everyone knew through the grapevine that some big announcement was coming. For the first time in anyone's memory, classes were occasionally suspended, impromptu faculty meetings were called at odd hours, and the usually outgoing Walia was rarely seen. Another rumour had it that the first rumour had something to do with Aniket Jain's audacious speech. The question everybody was asking: was the former all-India topper going to be expelled?

Anyone who wasn't in the assembly that day had heard wildly distorted versions of it. The perpetrator, Aniket Jain, was lauded for his guts by the younger kids and scorned for his foolishness by his peers. There was no way he was getting away with it.

None of this came in the way of lessons, though. Most students were clocking in eight hours of study daily, with the complete-the-syllabus-first race very much on. The weaker students weren't bothered, the average and above-average ones tried to study by themselves, while the best took expert coaching.

There was just one student who knew that this yearly routine was going to hit a road bump, the only one who knew of Walia's real intentions . . . but he was mum and impenetrable as usual—for everyone but his father, the king.

'You are absolutely sure?' asked Rana Dhananjay. His eyes were fixed on the glass of spicy-red wine he held, his legs making his chair swing in little arcs.

Rikkhe sat up straighter on the sofa and sipped his own Shiraz. They were sitting in the dim-lit study of their bungalow in Chanakyapuri, where Rikkhe usually lived alone—with the exception of his guard, Karamveer Singh, and the housekeeping staff. The rana was in Delhi for a day on work. Both father and son were dressed in white kurta-pyjama.

'Director Walia has been working on the written draft of "The Constitution of Woodsville Scholars International", the cornerstone of which will be yearly elections for the post of head scholar, who will chair the student council of Woodsville,' Rikkhe recited from memory. 'The council will consist of—besides the head scholar—the four house captains. The council will be allotted funds, which will be dispensed as per the members' discretion, through a democratic, constitutional process.'

Dhananjay narrowed his eyes and shook his head in annoyance. 'Constitution! What a joke!' He grabbed some peanuts from the plate in front of him. Rikkhe cringed as some masala fell on his mahogany study table. Rikkhe had noticed that his father had had an unfavourable disposition throughout this visit.

Rikkhe put down his wine glass. 'There has been some opposition by the faculty, but Admin Kumari has been persuaded to see director sir's viewpoint: the more tedious administrative duties will now be handled by the students themselves. It'll certainly make Mrs Kumari's job easier.'

Dhananjay gave his son a piercing look. 'How were you made aware of this?'

'Director sir forwarded a copy of the constitution to me for . . . *student feedback*.'

'Constitution, huh? A bunch of rules that can be twisted around whenever they wish . . . damn hypocrites!' Dhananjay grew sombre. 'Elections, Rikkhe, they have proven to be the bane of our existence.'

It was a little comical to see the rana utter these words in his 10,000-square-foot bungalow, with its contemporary, opulent interiors, but Rikkhe understood what he'd meant . . . what his family had lost.

'A king doesn't need the mandate of his subjects to rule,' Dhananjay said aggressively. 'All he needs is their presence.'

Rikkhe nodded his head. He didn't mean to contradict his father, but he carried on in the vein of a discussion. 'He needs an army as well.'

Dhananjay glared. 'The commoners don't know what's good for them; those morons never have! If they did, Jahalgarh wouldn't be at the beck and call of some corrupt parliamentarian, someone who made a deal with the capitalists to hand over our—*our*—diamond mines, of which not a paisa has been given to the people.'

Dhananjay had got so worked up with his rant that he was now on his feet and his voice rose in anger. Rikkhe didn't react except to stand up as well, so as not to be disrespectful to the king.

'Tell me,' Dhananjay continued, 'do you think that these *people* of yours know what's good for them? Will the students of Woodsville elect the right person?'

'No,' Rikkhe replied softly, after a pause. 'They'll elect whoever *seems* right.'

'And what will you do about it?'

Rikkhe thought about it for a long time. Finally, he bowed his head. 'Once I am through with it, it won't be a democracy any more, genuine or otherwise.'

Satisfied, the rana stalked out of the room, leaving the young prince to ponder over their conversation. Rikkhe withdrew from his pocket a small, green booklet, entitled 'The Constitution of Woodsville Scholars International'.

Rikkhe crushed the booklet with his hand as he recognized the truth in his father's words. Left to themselves, the students of his school were sure to elect Dev Bhushan, the only person at Woodsville whom Rikkhe genuinely disliked. He was a bully, an uncontrolled, wilful force. Being the elected leader would give him a free rein over the entire student body. Elections, as his father had pointed out, could be the bane of everyone's life.

Rikkhe closed his eyes as he realized that he was probably the only one who could prevent this from happening. There was one problem, though—a king didn't run for election.

The dilemma gave rise to a more fascinating question: when Walia's decision was relayed to everyone tomorrow, who *would* run for election?

*

'What will the management do then?' asked Dr Dheer.

Vishakha's hand shot up, quick as lightning, among a few others. 'Reduce cost.'

Students belonging to one section each of classes eleven and twelve of the commerce department were sitting in Lecture Theatre 1. Dr Dheer, their teacher for business studies, was conducting a practical exercise.

Dr Dheer had formerly been a professor at MIT. He disliked what he called 'Indian answers', and Vishakha's was definitely one, for he seemed irked.

'Not the result! The process!' Dr Dheer exclaimed from the stage. 'What will the management *do*?'

Aniket raised his hand. This time, his was the only one. He closed his eyes as he spoke, as though reading from a parchment inside his head. 'The management will direct the production head to work out ways to reduce cost. In addition, to counter the negative attitude that price reduction brings to the market, a marketing plan should be etched out to sell this cheaper product so that it doesn't come from a point of disadvantage. Or the cheaper product can be presented as a completely different alternative to the existing product.'

Dr Dheer seemed pleased. 'Sublime,' he commented, his highest praise.

Vishakha grunted as Aniket took the commendation in his stride. It was over a year since she'd been trying to impress Dr Dheer, but with people like Aniket and Rikkhe in her class, it had been next to impossible. Dheer was part of the Prime Minister's Planning Commission; his mandate alone could propel Vishakha to her dream job.

Himanshu, sitting in the front row, took a deep breath to calm himself. Although he'd known the answer—even the 'Americanized' one—he hadn't been able to muster the courage to raise his hand. Public speaking was not his forte.

'ANNOUNCEMENT!' the public-address speakers in the theatre blared. Everyone looked up as they heard the director address the entire school.

'Students,' said Director Walia, 'it is my great pleasure to announce that from this year forth, elections for the post of the head scholar will be held annually. Each one of you from the senior secondary will have a vote, as will the teachers. The elected person will head the student council, the other members of which will be the four house captains. A constitution has been drafted to decide the jurisdiction of the same, and is available at the administration office. Voting will begin in the last week of April, and campaigning for the same may commence immediately.'

There was excitement and confusion in equal measure at this statement. But most of the students in Lecture Theatre 1 were looking at Aniket Jain, whose heart had started racing the second he'd heard the word 'elections'. He hadn't let it show, but he'd been living in perpetual terror this past week; he couldn't afford to be expelled or, worse, lose his scholarship.

'Applicants,' Director Walia continued and everyone held their breath, 'must be from class twelve only. Registrations are also open at the admin office.'

There was a groan from the class-eleven students in the theatre, and a general, shocked silence from their seniors.

At the same moment, the atmosphere in Lecture Theatre 2, where a physics class was under way, was somewhat different. The class there was less bothered about the announcement and more interested in the reaction it elicited from Dev Bhushan, their enigmatic classmate.

Dev sighed. When he had confided in Dr Athar, he'd had no doubt that Walia would hear of it. In fact, that's why he had faked the nervousness; Walia couldn't afford to have his prize student go loony. Dev had hoped Walia would somehow try to convince his grandfather to let him choose his future himself. *This*, however, wasn't the reaction he had anticipated.

Dev got up and his teacher looked at him warily, aware that he was facing a person who'd just had his title of head scholar taken away from him.

'Yes, Dev?'

While everyone in LT 1 just stared at each other, in LT 2 Dev gave his teacher a cocky smile. 'Didn't you hear, sir? Registrations are on. I am going to get my post back.'

Without so much as a pause, Dev Bhushan strode out the door amidst loud hurrahs from his classmates, and rushed towards the administration office.

*

It was the one o'clock recess, and the corridors were bustling with people. Most of the crowd flitted around the usually neglected admin office. Dev Bhushan, after registering, had planted himself right at the entrance of the office. Rikkhe watched with increasing anger as, one by one, many potential candidates retraced their steps to their classes after spotting Dev and his intimidating posse. The couple who actually made it to the door were ridiculed and taunted by Dev's friends to the extent that they never ended up registering.

'So . . . seems like the election has already begun,' Rikkhe heard someone muse.

Rikkhe turned to see Yash Malik grinning at him, and quickly suppressed the contempt he was feeling for the entire electoral process.

'Yes, it does,' Rikkhe replied guardedly. Everyone suspected that Yash Malik was Director Walia's eyes and ears in the student body; Rikkhe was the only one who knew it was true.

'You know, I don't think anyone's getting past him,' Yash nodded at Dev. 'I heard he randomly burnt down a building, back in the United States.'

'Someone serious enough will stand up to him,' Rikkhe said firmly.

'You aren't going to register?' Yash asked innocently.

Rikkhe leaned on the corridor wall and carefully watched Dev and his friends, a little further ahead, near the office door. 'No.'

'Pity,' Radhika said, joining them. 'You are the only one who can beat him.'

Rikkhe smiled; he had always been fond of Radhika. Of average height and slim build, she was a fighter, though not in the way Aniket was; she stood up for what she thought was right. It hadn't won her many friends in school.

'Hello, Riddhi,' Rikkhe said, ruffling her short hair, at which she yelped and backed off. 'What about you, any thoughts of participating?'

Radhika sighed theatrically. 'I'm afraid I cannot trust myself with power,' she said as she reset her hair.

'Why not?' Yash asked, bewildered.

'I am Dumbledore, see?' Radhika frowned, seeing that no one had understood her joke. 'From *Harry Potter*?'

'I am afraid I don't follow,' Rikkhe said apologetically.

'Aargh!' Radhika burst out, 'I am . . . well, I'm Caesar. Get it?'

'Ah . . .' Rikkhe said, nodding. 'Actually, Caesar's power had deep socio-political issues behind—'

'Oh, spare me the lecture,' snapped Radhika, and Rikkhe shut up. 'Um . . . everyone's looking.'

He glanced around and saw she was right. He was getting stared at as much as Dev. Everyone was expecting him to go out there and confront Dev Bhushan. Rikkhe, however, was waiting for a messenger.

*

While the rest of his classmates thronged the administrative side of the building, Himanshu sat in the unusually inert cafeteria. He was surprised; he had expected it to be abuzz . . . Was *everyone* busy registering? He proceeded with his lunch tray to a corner table and sat himself down. A minute later, Himanshu's ears reddened as he noticed Vishakha and some of her friends take the table right next to his.

'I have no intention of participating,' Vishakha announced loudly to the nearly empty hall. She turned to look at everyone there, one by one, and even spared Himanshu a glance.

'But you could do so much for the school,' Nidhi said earnestly.

Vishakha stamped her foot dramatically. 'Enough!' she said in the same loud voice. 'I have more important things to do. Now can we stop talking about this?' She suddenly abandoned her lunch and said she had somewhere else to be.

Himanshu couldn't help but smile.

As soon as Vishakha crossed that invisible line of earshot, Nidhi snorted.

'Who's she fooling?' she said mockingly to the rest of the table. 'As if she's going to win!'

Himanshu hid his scowl as all of Vishakha's 'friends' made noises of agreement. He wanted to give an invigorating speech and stand up for Vishakha right that instant, but he kept quiet.

'Actually, I'm thinking about joining the race,' Nidhi continued conspiratorially.

At this, Himanshu *had* to snort. Everyone at the adjacent table turned to stare at him, and he hurriedly disguised his laughter into a coughing fit. He got up and quickly exited the cafeteria, cursing himself.

He was barely out, when Vishakha planted herself firmly in his path. Himanshu lost his balance trying to avoid her, and grabbed her arms to steady himself so he wouldn't fall on her. Surprisingly strong, she was able to bear his weight.

'Get a grip on yourself, boy,' Vishakha said, frowning.

Himanshu immediately let go of her, stammering his way through a sorry. Simultaneously, a word resounded in his head. *Boy?*

Chagrined, he sidestepped her and sprinted towards the lift, back to his class on the third floor.

'Wait!' Vishakha called out and Himanshu froze. He had seen her humiliate a lot of people before, and while he had enjoyed watching, he very much doubted he would enjoy living it.

'I am sorry, Vishakha,' Himanshu said again, turning to face her. 'I was going too fast—'

Vishakha wasn't interested in his apologies. 'What did they say after I left?'

Himanshu stopped short and stared at the fascinating creature in front of him. Medium height, lean, oval face, shoulder-length black hair, black eyes, dusky skin, fake smile. Her features were ordinary . . . then why was she so captivating to look at?

They were so close that, for the first time, he could see her eyes without his camera's zoom lens, and suddenly he had the answer. It was the eyes! They were the reason he was enthralled by Vishakha Sahdev. And right now, those eyes weren't pretending; they reflected their owner's nature—cunning, hawk-like.

'Well?' she pressed.

Himanshu shook his head and came back to his senses. 'Uhh . . . um . . . nothing, nothing at all. Anyway, I was too far away, I couldn't hear—'

'It was Nidhi, wasn't it?' Vishakha cut in. 'She wants to be head scholar?'

Himanshu stared at her in awe. 'Yes. She does.'

A satisfied smile crept across Vishakha's face as she became oblivious to Himanshu's presence. 'I knew it . . .'

The lift door opened behind them.

'I told you to go to the campus mall, not the canteen, man!' Vivek shouted, leaping out of the lift.

'I didn't feel like walking the distance today,' Himanshu said, frowning, 'besides, Rohan's friend said he wasn't looking for me.'

'GODFATHER, man! It was a ruse; I saw him downstairs.' Vivek was beside himself. 'Guess what, he was looking for you.'

'Wait,' Vishakha interrupted them, 'you're the guy who got hit by Dev's winning shot, aren't you?'

Himanshu avoided her eyes. *Shit.*

'Wha—? No. Course not. That fellow, he was someone else . . .' he laughed nervously. 'That dumb shit.'

Vivek had just noticed Vishakha, and he gaped at her.

'Hi, Viz—Vishakha!' he blurted, giving Himanshu an inquisitive look and trying to hide behind him at the same time. She had a fearsome reputation.

Himanshu was about to introduce Vivek to Vishakha, then realized he hadn't introduced *himself*. 'I am Himanshu.'

'Himanshu Pathak?' Vishakha asked, sizing him up.

Himanshu was elated. 'Yes, the very same.'

No one noticed, but the lift doors had opened once again and two tough-looking bums got out.

'Hey, look who it is,' one announced with a laugh. Both of them lunged for Himanshu, while Vivek got out of the way. Himanshu stumbled back just as Vishakha planted herself between them.

'What is this, Rohan?' she demanded from the bigger one.

Rohan had never dared to cross her. 'It's personal business, it doesn't concern you,' he said with a scowl.

Vishakha raised an eyebrow. 'It doesn't? When the editor of the school magazine instigates a fight in the cafeteria, it is everyone's business. Provided he still *wants* to be the editor, that is.'

Rohan glared at her, then at Himanshu. His bulging muscles strained to reach out for him, but his gut told him to steer clear for the moment.

Himanshu leaned a little to the side, so that he could get a better look at Vishakha's face. The face and the eyes never stopped speaking, even when the words ran out. Right now, they were clearly saying, *Just try me.*

Rohan backed off, but pointed a finger at Himanshu before leaving. 'It was my father's camera, you son of a bitch. And you will pay for it.'

Vishakha turned around slowly. 'So it *was* you who got hit that day.'

Himanshu sighed and nodded.

Vishakha grinned while Himanshu squirmed. She already knew him as 'the guy who stood third in the commerce section last year'; she'd stood fourth, and she always kept track of the people who beat her.

'Yeah . . . I was under the illusion that I was tracking the ball with my camera, but it was really the other way around,' Himanshu mused drily.

Vishakha laughed. 'And it was Rohan's camera?'

Himanshu nodded. 'Unfortunately.' Vivek was looking on from a distance, incredulous.

'So why don't you pay him back?' Vishakha knew he came from one of the richest families in Delhi, though he was more modest than even Rikkhe Rajput.

Himanshu hesitated. 'It's worth fifty thousand.'

Vishakha frowned. She knew he didn't brag about his wealth. Hell, he wore clothes as casual and cheap as hers. But she also knew a Mercedes dropped him to school each morning. 'So?'

Himanshu wished he'd had a camera with him right then. This genuinely inquisitive expression on Vishakha's face was something he hadn't seen before. He cleared his head and replied, 'It's complicated.'

Vishakha scrutinized Himanshu Pathak. He didn't look like much—a little awkward, a little chubby, spectacles slightly lopsided. But it was his attitude that had previously made her dismiss him. He was a brilliant student, no doubt, but he wasn't a go-getter. He was, and would remain, one of the 'auditorium people'.

Vishakha hadn't cared enough to talk to him before. Now that she had, he seemed full of contradictions.

'So you're a photographer?' she asked.

Himanshu blinked. 'Well, yes.' He sounded more confident than he did during class. He was probably good with a camera. Vishakha was good at posing for one.

She nodded appreciatingly. 'Cool.'

Himanshu smiled. 'Thanks for coming to my rescue.'

'Don't worry about it,' she replied shortly, impressed that he hadn't felt too 'emasculated' to acknowledge it. 'Anyway, see you around.'

'You too, Vishakha,' Himanshu said sheepishly, grinning stupidly at her retreating back.

Vishakha didn't stop or turn. 'Call me Vizac.'

*

Aniket didn't want to seem desperate. He also didn't want to face Dev. He therefore spent most of lunch hour eating at the campus mall, some distance away from the main school building. As he walked back, he drew a lot of eyes. Some looked at him with admiration and awe, while some held derision, anger and contempt.

Being the self-professed best student at Woodsville, Aniket was used to negative attention. But the occasional encouraging smile now gave him hope that he might actually stand a chance of winning the election.

'Way to go, man!' someone commented, passing by Aniket as he entered the atrium.

As he reached the corridor that led to the admin office, he saw that the place was still crowded. He didn't care. If this was how it was going to be, then this was how it was going to be. What he didn't realize immediately was that most of these people were, in fact, waiting for him.

Including Dev Bhushan.

There was a bout of hoots, whistles and claps when the crowd realized that Aniket had arrived. Just a week ago, all of them had witnessed him challenge the authorities, and today he had come out on top. This victory had even pushed aside their general dislike of him. Unaccustomed to such positive feedback, Aniket couldn't help but grin widely, suddenly confident.

Although he had nothing but contempt for most of the silver-spooners here, he needed them. He needed votes. And for that, he would exploit every opportunity he got to be in the public eye.

Rikkhe watched uneasily as Aniket smiled widely and took a bow, while his classmates cheered even louder. Rikkhe was now convinced—they did *not* know what or *who* was good for them.

Dev had been keeping a furtive eye on Rikkhe ever since he'd got here. He was the only person who worried Dev, but all through lunch hour Rikkhe had remained glued to his spot. Dev had a strong feeling that he, too, was waiting for something . . . or someone.

The sudden noise distracted Dev from his thoughts. He tilted his head up to see the tall, lanky figure of Aniket walking towards him, towards the office. Dev grinned. *Finally.*

'It's the moron, Dev,' one guy from his cricket team said quietly. 'Let's get him.'

Even though Dev felt fully inclined to, he sensed something was amiss.

'Are they *applauding* for him?' Dev asked his cronies incredulously.

Rikkhe watched closely. Aniket gave him a smug smile as he walked past, and Dev broke away from his gang to meet him halfway to the office. The applause quickly subsided to a watchful silence.

'Yash,' Rikkhe muttered, 'do me a favour. Just go and stand somewhere Bhushan can see you.'

Yash, initially confused, caught his drift. 'You want to help Aniket?' he asked, an eyebrow raised. 'He hates you.'

'Just do it.'

And so Yash joined the crowd thronging around Aniket and Dev, and slowly, deliberately entered Dev's line of vision.

Aniket stopped at arm's length from Dev Bhushan's muscular figure, his self-assurance halved. Dev's posture made Aniket wish he'd brought protective gear to safeguard his vital organs.

Dev was seeing red. This pretentious son of a bitch had diminished his image as the infallible champion. And Dev never forgave . . .

Aniket flinched as Dev extended his hand. Everyone laughed.

'To a clean and fair race,' Dev said loudly. 'For Woodsville.'

Aniket, red in the face, quickly grasped and shook Dev's hand. He gave a cocky smile. 'I am sure it will be.' It was a barefaced lie, but everyone appreciated the superficial show of sportsmanship.

Rikkhe had always thought of Dev as the worst kind of bully. Where other bullies were usually guided by just emotion and instinct, Dev always assessed the environment before making his move. Despite his anger, he wasn't stupid enough to hit Aniket, not when the voters thought him to be a hero.

Moreover, Walia's lapdog, Yash Malik, was watching them and Rikkhe knew Dev wouldn't chance upsetting Walia further. The man had just announced elections to put Dev in his place; there was no telling what he might do next.

Aniket, smiling nervously, had no clue that Rikkhe had just saved him from a fair bit of humiliation, and maybe a broken nose.

Nobody noticed a quiet figure move through the crowd and slink into the open doors of the admin office. His face looked harassed, his hair ruffled, and his jaw hurt like hell.

'Really, what do you think you are doing?' Vivek hissed, trying to keep up with Himanshu.

Himanshu couldn't bring himself to face Vivek, who had just witnessed him get manhandled by Rohan. As soon as Vishakha had left, Rohan had accosted him again. A resolute Himanshu had made it clear that he wouldn't steal the money from his parents, which caused Rohan to proclaim Himanshu to be his punching bag forthwith. *I am going to make you piss blood every time I see you from now on*, he had said.

'Being invisible hasn't worked, in case you hadn't noticed.' Himanshu's eyes were a little wet at the injustice. But this time he intended to fight back. 'I am going to make sure no one screws with me.'

Vivek clutched Himanshu's arm before he could reach the registration counter.

'Think about it!' Vivek said insistently. 'No one even knows you properly. Why would they vote for you?'

Himanshu shrugged free. He didn't want to think about that. He had spent his life searching for reasons not to do things. Not today. Vishakha had spoken to him today, and if he wanted it to continue, he'd have to grow a spine.

Himanshu looked him straight in the eye. 'It is all right for you, Vivek. When you wish to stay invisible, people let you. Not me, though, not once in the seven years that I have been at Woodsville! You know why? Because I topped the first year I was here. Now I either actually start behaving like a vicious competitor so nobody messes with me. Or I try and be docile for these pea-brained thugs, so they don't feel bad that someone's better than them! These fuckers landed me in therapy, Vivek!'

Himanshu's voice had risen to a shout. Vivek's eyes were wide. He was finally letting out all the hatred, all the pent-up frustration. The admin staff working at their desks had stood up to watch.

'For years I have tried to be normal! To just blend in, be average. I keep my head down and I leave a question unanswered in every paper to make sure I don't ever top again! Guess what? Hasn't helped. They'll always find an excuse to punish me for something *they* couldn't do.' He leaned in closer to Vivek and added in a whisper, 'Never again. Not now, when Vishakha actually knows I exist. If I am to make a fool of myself one way or another, I will do it my way. I'm done being a sitting duck.'

Himanshu was panting heavily. His hands were shaking and his heart raced. He heard Dr Athar's voice in his head, telling him to breathe. *Just breathe.*

Aniket, who had just entered the office, glanced at Himanshu near the registration counter and smirked derisively. He walked over to them, swaggering all the way to the counter.

Get back in line, bitch! Himanshu wanted to bark at Aniket, but Athar's words came back to him, as they did in moments of great distress. *Breathe. Just breathe.*

*

'Sir, you can't possibly be thinking of doing this,' Athar said gravely.

'Thinking?' Walia exclaimed. 'It's already in motion!'

Walia turned his back to Athar and hobbled to the end of the gigantic office he occupied on the top floor of the main school building. Unlike the rest of the school, Walia's office had a futuristic look, and the interiors were severe and almost clinically immaculate. The traditional white marble used for the rest of the school wasn't used here; the floor and walls were made of smooth, black tiles, accentuated by sparse but effective furniture. One side of the room was pure glass, which gave Walia a direct view of the entire front plaza of the building.

Athar, agitated, shook the paper in his hand.

'But this is madness, sir,' he said. 'The names on this list . . . these children cannot be allowed to participate in such a stressful task! Dev Bhushan! Himanshu Pathak! Nidhi Somania! Aniket Jain! Niraj Singh!'

Walia, wearing his trademark golf cap, turned to face Athar. 'Is there something about any of these students that you wish to tell me?'

Athar blinked and quickly backtracked. 'Just their general mental condition, sir. Three of them are previous toppers who already have a lot to deal with.'

Walia walked back to his desk and sat down with a groan, massaging his bad leg.

'Why do you think these children come to Woodsville, Athar?' Walia asked.

'To study,' Athar replied with a frown, 'not to engage in dangerous—'

'Wrong.' Walia's voice was loud and contradicting. 'They can go to other schools to study. They come to *Woodsville* to be the best. And being the best is no walk in the park.'

Athar shook his head at Walia's callousness. 'With all due respect, sir, I am the student counsellor here. I do spend more time with these students than you do, and I think it's fair to say that I know them better. I know where they are vulnerable. And I feel that an election will have a deteriorating effect, not just on the candidates, but on the entire student body.'

'I lost my faith in your *abilities* as student counsellor when you failed to forewarn me of what that boy would do in the assembly,' Walia said coldly.

That stung. There was no way he could have predicted Aniket's actions.

'And I admit, you know the students better than I do.' Walia took off his golf cap. 'But you know them for what they are *now*. I know them for what they'll be when they leave this place.'

Athar sighed. He had to give it a last shot. He knew he couldn't prevail over Walia, but for the sake of his conscience, he had to try.

'Sir, I am sorry, but I will have to go to the board with my recommendation.' Athar avoided Walia's eyes as he said this.

Walia slammed both his hands on the desk with all his might, propelling himself into a standing position. He cut a forbidding figure.

'The world is watching this country, Athar!' Walia bellowed. 'We are supposed to be the next superpower, but the current breed of bureaucrats can never make that happen. And what happens when they don't? China, USA, Brazil? They'll devour us!'

Athar was bewildered. How did they go from Woodsville to world politics?

Walia smacked his thigh in frustration. 'This damned leg . . . you know how it became useless?'

Athar hesitated. 'When you were in the army?'

Walia gave a dry laugh. 'Yes. Shrapnel. Shrapnel from a stray enemy grenade. And you want to know when it happened? Peacetime. They thought it would be good fun to strike at our regular patrols in the area. Two of my men died, another lost an eye. And the only reason they had the guts to do it was because they knew that our government wouldn't let us retaliate. That there would be no consequences.'

Athar was adept at handling teenagers, but he had never had a patient like Walia. He was at a loss for words.

Walia smiled bitterly. 'The next day, other men replaced the dead ones in the patrol. Nothing changed.'

'I am sorry, sir.'

'Don't be. You are part of the change already.'

'Sir?'

'Woodsville.' Walia's eyes stared into the distance, proud. 'The next generation that will run this country. And I am going to make damn sure that they are up to the task before I let them out of here. You see now? They *have* to be the best. They *have* to be the toughest individuals of our society . . . because one day, they'll make sure the world fears *us*.'

Athar gaped. He could only lament the fate of the students studying at Woodsville. They had no idea that they'd signed up for someone else's dream.

'The election is nothing, I have something better planned for them.' Walia eyed a thick, bound folder on his desk. 'These students don't need protecting. They need something that pushes them to perform better than they humanly can . . . Oh, I'll get him here . . .'

Walia was practically talking to himself, as Athar hadn't a clue as to what he was on about. The phone on the desk rang, bringing Walia out of his reverie. He picked it up.

'Yes, send him in.'

The door opened behind Athar, and Rikkhe Rajput walked in.

'Evening, sir,' Rikkhe greeted Walia. He smiled at Athar and shook his hand. 'How are you, sir?'

'Fine . . . fine,' Athar mumbled.

'So, Rikkhe, have you thought about it?' Walia asked, his eyes narrowed.

Rikkhe looked dubious. 'Sir, as I said before, it really would be an honour, but I want to focus on my studies at the moment. Campaigning for an election would be too time-consuming. Still, I'd like to help. I'll take your alternative offer.'

Walia peered at Rikkhe, slightly disappointed. He had never seen more potential in a student. From among the secret nicknames Walia had for some of the students here, Dev Bhushan was 'Youth Icon', Aniket Jain was 'Nobel Laureate' and Rikkhe had always been 'Prime Minister'. What he lacked was the will.

'Very well, then,' Walia said, nodding. 'Dr Athar, if you could please give the list to Rikkhe.'

Athar was confused as he handed over the sheet of paper.

'I thought we were letting the participants announce their candidature themselves? Are we letting other students know beforehand?'

Walia laughed amicably. 'He isn't just any other student.'

Athar wasn't sure he'd heard right. Walia had favourites, but even he never admitted it in front of them.

'What do you mean, sir?'

Walia waved his hand towards Rikkhe, showing him off like a horse-trader would his animal.

'Athar, meet our first chief election commissioner.'

THE ELECTION

The fervent atmosphere that Woodsville usually had in the first month of the year was somewhat punctured by the wait—the wait for the candidates to announce themselves. Only Dev Bhushan and Aniket Jain had openly declared their candidature, and neither had commenced campaigning. The biggest disappointment everyone was preparing themselves for was that they'd only get to see these two names on the ballot paper.

For the first time since Athar had joined Woodsville, he found that students were actually being kind to each other; candidates, even undeclared, needed goodwill, and the rest wanted information about the rumoured candidates. Only Vishakha remained untouched by this atmosphere of temporary brotherhood.

'You do know our sessions are weekly?' Athar asked her in his room, three weeks after he'd seen her last.

'I know, Doc,' Vishakha said innocently. 'Don't worry, you won't see me more than once a week.'

Athar raised an eyebrow. 'This is your first session this term. I can report this, you know?'

'If it'll do you any good.'

Athar sighed. 'I thought we were past the hostility.'

Vishakha jerked her head in a non-committal manner.

'How's your mother?' Athar asked tentatively.

Vishakha, like every other time this subject arose, avoided his eyes. 'The usual.' Athar knew better than to try and press the matter, so he changed tack.

'So tell me, what is new in your life?' Athar prodded gently.

'Well, you know Nidhi, that spineless Judas?' Vishakha asked with relish.

Athar knew her only too well. Nidhi 'the spineless Judas' had been their topic of discussion so much that sometimes this felt less like therapy and more like a bitching session.

'Turns out, she actually is just that pathetic and shallow.' Vishakha continued, amused. 'She backed out of the election.'

'And why is that?' Athar asked with a sense of foreboding. He was damn sure Vishakha had something to do with it.

'Well,' Vishakha smiled like a pixie, 'I convinced her that Dev would make sure that no boy would hit on her for the rest of our school life. Believe it or not, it actually matters to her.'

Athar raised an eyebrow. 'And she believed that?'

'Not really. But then I got Dev to say it to her.'

Athar reclined in his chair. *So the election had already begun . . .*

'One other thing, Doc.' Vishakha was looking at her nails casually, trying not to give herself away.

Athar instinctively knew that she wanted information from him. *Maybe she wants to know who the candidates are . . .*

'That guy, Himanshu Pathak, he comes to you for sessions, no?' Vishakha said, still inspecting her fingers.

Athar was thrown. He hadn't been expecting that. Himanshu did come to Athar for sessions, and half the time he talked about Vishakha.

'Yes,' Athar replied slowly, 'what about him?'

Vishakha tilted her head and caught Athar's eye. She held his gaze for a brief moment, and then went back to her nails. 'Just wondering what he's like. He beat me in the exams last year.'

Athar relaxed a little. 'He's a good kid. Hard-working, a talented photographer, brilliant at singing and the flute . . . a bit of an introvert, though.' Athar tried to be as casual as he could. He couldn't believe he was actually being Himanshu's wingman; it felt unprofessional and pleasantly thrilling.

Vishakha looked up from her nails again. 'Really, an introvert? I was under the impression he had registered for the election?'

Despite himself, Athar blinked and his mouth parted in surprise. That was all the confirmation Vishakha had needed. She smiled and peered through the windows behind Athar's chair.

'The little chick's coming out of his egg, then . . .' she remarked.

Athar cursed himself. How could he have been so foolish? Vishakha's interest in Himanshu had been totally utilitarian.

'You think he's up for it?' Vishakha asked him point-blank.

'You mean being head scholar?'

'I mean the campaign. I am asking that if you put him in front of an audience, is he gonna piss himself?'

Vishakha's harsh words made Athar feel sorry for Himanshu. However, it was at moments like these that he tried to see something in Vishakha that even she didn't believe existed.

'Not if he has the right motivation.'

'The right motivation?'

'It could be anything.' Athar paused, and then added, 'Incidentally, he registered the day you met him. Isn't *that* a coincidence?'

It was Vishakha's turn to be disarmed. 'The day that we—he told you about me?'

Athar shrugged. 'Just in passing.'

Vishakha narrowed her eyes. 'What did he say?'

'Nothing much, I assure you.'

Vishakha stood up and glared at Athar.

'Tell me!'

Athar suppressed a smile. Vishakha was obsessed in this regard; she *had* to know what people said about her, even if she didn't care.

'Just that you were charmingly cunning and deviously heroic,' Athar said, watching closely.

Vishakha's anger vanished. In fact, all emotion was wiped off her face. Himanshu had once told Athar that

Vishakha's face always had something to say; this was the first time Athar saw it completely speechless. Just for a moment, though.

She regained her haughtiness. 'Don't play with me, Doc.'

'His exact words.'

'And he registered *that* day?'

Athar nodded vigorously. 'Right after he met you.'

A slight smile appeared on Vishakha's face for a fleeting second. The next instant, she was searching Athar's face for signs of lying. She was pretty good at it, and so Athar immediately lowered his face and decided to write something in his notebook.

'Why are you telling me this?' Vishakha asked him sharply. 'You are more discreet than that.'

'Was that a compliment?' Athar smiled widely, looking up. Then catching her eye, he answered hurriedly, 'Himanshu wouldn't mind.' *Oh, he would so, so mind.*

Vishakha sat back down. 'I don't think he'll win,' she said with contempt.

Athar nodded. 'Probably.' He caught a fleeting expression of anger before Vishakha hid it.

'So your interest in him is purely superficial? Nothing romantic or friendly?'

Vishakha had to fake the anger this time, and rolled her eyes. 'Of course not.'

Athar shook his head slightly. 'Then why, Vishakha Sahdev, did you ask him to call you Vizac?'

*

The English class had just ended. As usual, Aniket took his time gathering his stuff so he could 'have a word with the professor' before he left.

'Ma'am,' Aniket said, approaching her with a book, 'thank you for this. You were right, this edition is infinitely better.'

Mrs Swaminathan kept the book in her bag. 'Chekhov was a genius, Ani, never forget that. The more you translate him, the more disarrayed his thoughts appear. We wouldn't want that, would we?'

Aniket laughed politely. He had read the 300 pages overnight, getting barely two hours of sleep. He didn't mind, though. He usually didn't sleep for more than four or five hours a day. That way, while the rest of the students managed seven hours of study time, he got at least ten after school, including all the extra-curriculars.

'Of course not, ma'am. One question, though.' Mrs Swaminathan loved questions, and Aniket loved impressing his teachers. And so he asked questions even when he didn't have any.

Mrs Swaminathan looked at him expectantly.

'"The Death of a Government Clerk." Why did the clerk die in the end?'

Mrs Swaminathan gave a rare, small smile. She'd heard the question before. 'If we knew that, all of life's secrets would reveal themselves.' Aniket waited. Mrs Swaminathan never deflected a query. 'Ah! Well jokes apart, look at the theme of the story, Ani.'

'Forgiveness? Resolution?'

Mrs Swaminathan shook her head. 'The clerk sneezed on a general, Ani. The continued apologies and the final, unresolved death were only the manifestations of the theme.'

Aniket thought hard. 'Obsession?'

Mrs Swaminathan considered it. 'In part. He was obsessed all right. With what, though?'

Aniket hated it when he couldn't answer something. He tapped his toes in frustration and closed his eyes, getting it immediately.

'Acceptance.'

Mrs Swaminathan nodded sagely. 'When the general wouldn't satisfactorily forgive him, the clerk, in the social significance of the story, didn't have the validation of society. Without that social acceptance, an individual perishes.'

Aniket was almost bursting with joy. This was why he loved being a student at Woodsville. Brilliant as he was, the teaching was sublime. It even made up for being among other kids his age.

'Much like you, Ani.'

Aniket came out of his reverie. 'Ma'am?'

'With you, the need for social acceptance is slightly augmented.' Spotting the puzzled expression on Aniket's face, she went on, 'You are currently running for an election. Validation in the form of votes.'

Aniket nodded slowly.

'Which is something you need to work on. Upgrade your wardrobe, Ani. Your clothes are your first impression. Make it good.'

Aniket came out of the lecture theatre staring at his cheap striped shirt and grey pants, bought in the weekly local market. He had never minded what his mother had got him to wear. Assured as ever in the superiority of his intellect, he had always looked down on his peers. Suddenly, though, he didn't feel good at all. The only thing he could think of was tearing these clothes off and stealing Rikkhe's majestic polo pants.

He approached a group of his well-dressed classmates in the corridor.

'You'd think that after that dramatic beginning, he'd actually *do* something . . .' Aniket overheard Radhika saying.

Mohit, another annoying classmate of Aniket's, spoke up. 'Forget about him, he's too busy schmoozing teachers. Dev's the real surprise. He's doing nothing at all.'

Charu, an extraordinarily rude human specimen, laughed shrilly. 'Probably because he knows he doesn't need to, in front of that Ladyfinger.'

Aniket's face reddened as he slumped back against the theatre door. 'Ladyfinger' was what people called him when they were being kind.

'What about the others?' Radhika said hopefully.

Mohit snorted. 'No one's showing their scared little faces. The only student who even knows who all the candidates are is Rikkhe, and he's not going to give it up.'

Everyone nodded in agreement.

'Chief election commissioner,' Radhika said quietly.

Mohit and Charu gave adulatory looks. Aniket was livid; Rajput wasn't even participating, and here they were, acting as though he was somehow above the candidates.

'He left the announcement to the candidates' discretion,' Aniket remarked loudly.

They all jumped. Mohit and Charu were among those who begged him for notes every year.

'Any idea why no one's campaigning, Aniket?' Radhika asked with a smile.

Aniket shrugged. 'I honestly cannot say.'

'What about you?' Charu burst out.

Aniket grinned. 'I don't know how.'

Radhika stared hard at Aniket. It was the first time he'd said he didn't know something. She didn't know Aniket was just following Athar's advice till the election got over. *Don't say you know more than the others—even if you do.*

'Well, talk to people, prepare a manifesto, give speeches, make posters . . . the works.'

Aniket nodded. 'Thank you. I certainly will.' He had to struggle hard to seem likeable. He kept reminding himself that these were three votes standing in front of him. After the votes were cast, they could go fuck themselves.

He simply bid them farewell and walked away.

Damned silver-spooners. Aniket was fuming, but he realized that he'd been an idiot as well. He'd counted on the goodwill from his daring challenge to last for a few weeks at least. He had also become complacent because of Dev's seemingly quiet demeanour. Aniket had believed, foolishly, that Dev had been cowed by his sudden 'popularity'.

Momentarily dragged away from his own problems, Aniket wondered something he'd never had to wonder before. If not him, who was Dev afraid of?

*

At six-thirty in the morning, Dev sat in his customized Thar jeep, the flap down and adrenaline coursing through his veins. He'd woken up at four and proceeded to Woodsville for his daily practice session. Instead of getting back home to change, he had turned the jeep towards the DND Flyway, and stopped when he was on the other side of the Yamuna.

Dev drummed his fingers on the leather-padded steering wheel, indifferent about the hour he had wasted today. He never needed too much study anyway; a cursory reading, and he was done, ready to move on to bigger and better things. Despite this, his teachers were confident that he would easily crack the IIT-JEE. He didn't care. Everyone had some plan for his future, none of which coincided with his own.

Dev looked through the open window and finally spotted the train on the Blue Line taking the curve from Ashok Nagar and coming up parallel to his car. Dev revved and heated the engine, waiting for the shining, silver metro to pull up to him. And as soon as it did, he let the clutch go and started the race.

His face gleamed with satisfaction when the metro didn't stop at Mayur Vihar Extension. His contact at the DMRC had delivered, again. A report of a 'technical glitch' was forcing the train to proceed straight towards Yamuna Bank Depot.

The jeep didn't have the acceleration to keep up, though, and Dev was soon half a kilometre behind. The alloy wheels further reduced his speed, but Dev wasn't worried. As long as the road stayed clear, he would make it.

As though in response to his thoughts, he spotted a number of cars at the traffic signal a hundred metres ahead. Grateful for the alloy wheels now, he swerved sharply and jumped the signal from his left. He grinned as he crossed the Delhi Police Apartments, head to head with the metro.

Lost in the exhilaration, Dev didn't notice as he jumped yet another signal. A car hit his jeep's rear on the right, and he went into a skid. He panicked; he had been cruising at over a hundred kilometres an hour and now steered frantically to regain control of the jeep.

The wide wheels prevented the jeep from toppling over, but the railing on the left loomed dangerously close. Praying fervently, Dev flipped the switch to the nitrous oxide. In a fraction of a second, he had pulled out of the skid and gone back to chasing the silver bullet. He knew he should be making himself scarce now, but he didn't scram until he overtook the metro near the Akshardham Temple.

It was eight by the time he reached the modest bungalow he lived in with his grandfather in Delhi Cantonment. A black vintage Chevrolet parked alongside his grandfather's Ambassador told him that Walia was inside. Dev scowled; the old man's penchant for chaos was messing with his life.

'Come here, boy!' Dev's grandfather, General (retd) Brij Kishore Bhushan, called out from the front yard.

Walia and his grandfather were drinking tea and playing chess, while a servant watered the plants by the fence.

'Morning, sir,' Dev said, first to his grandfather, then to Walia. His grandfather was stocky and well built, and had the same intense look in his right eye as Dev did, although it was more disciplined than aggressive. His left eye he had lost the day Walia had become a cripple.

'What is this I'm hearing?' he asked sharply, his eyebrows drawn together in clear disapproval.

Dev was confused.

'Oh, I was just telling your grandfather about the race,' Walia interjected jovially.

Dev froze for a moment, and then realized that Walia was referring to the election.

His grandfather frowned. 'Ballu tells me you haven't been making an effort?'

Dev looked reproachfully at the director—Balvinder Singh Walia. 'Sir, that's not fair. I have been doing a lot of groundwork, making personal appeals to students. Granted, I have not prepared a directed, large-scale campaign for the post of head scholar, but I think a more focused, personal approach should be sufficient.'

Walia had a thoughtful smile on his face as he nodded. 'Well, we can't ask for more than what a man feels is right.' Dev cringed as he realized that Yash Malik was Walia's informer; he knew Dev was lying.

Dev's grandfather still looked sceptical. 'There's just a week left . . . are you certain you are prepared for it?'

Dev was not certain, but there was nothing he could do, except find solace in his belief that Woodsville wouldn't betray him. 'I am, sir.'

'Oh, and your father called,' his grandfather said after a brief pause. 'Something about them wanting you back in Chicago with them. Give them a call.'

Dev's face was expressionless. 'Yes, sir.'

Both Dev and his grandfather knew that Dev was never going back to his parents; that ship had sailed. Dev's parents, settled in the States, abhorred his naive patriotism for India as much as the general tried to cultivate it. The only reason they'd agreed to let Dev go was because he had set fire to an abandoned factory a block from their home and been convicted of arson in the state of Illinois. He had been eleven at the time.

Now they wanted him back. His mother was running for mayor in Chicago, and needed to counter her detractors for having a less-than-perfect record as a mother. But Dev had an election of his own to worry about.

Walia inspected him through his glasses. 'Go and change, then, Dev. Have breakfast. I'll finish this game and give you a ride to school.' Walia winked. 'They even let me park my car inside.'

Dev laughed politely. He was sure that Walia was going to grill him further about the election in the car. But the thing that no one, including Walia, seemed to know about Dev was that he was cautious. He had everything. And to keep it that way, he *had* to be cautious.

'Thank you, sir, but I have to visit a friend before I go to school.' Dev looked apologetic. 'And you know how women get when you break a promise.'

Dev proceeded back to his jeep and surveyed it; his baby was tough. The dent wasn't too bad. He discreetly removed the black cover he always put on the number plates before racing. As always, he was cautious.

Dev would die before he admitted it, but he was also wary of the chief election commissioner. Rikkhe could, and *would*, disqualify him for no reason at all; they'd loathed each other since the day they'd first met. The only way he would let Dev even reach Election Day was if Dev gave him no excuse to disqualify him. So instead of covering his tracks, Dev had made no tracks at all. For the first time in his life, he had done nothing.

*

Himanshu had spent the last couple of weeks in a state of constant fear. He felt like a spy on the verge of getting caught. After his reckless registration on the day of the announcement, he'd become even quieter, dreading the day people would see his name on the ballot paper and laugh.

The only person whom he'd told of his participation, besides Vivek and Athar, was Rohan, the editor of the school magazine. Himanshu had promised him more funds for the magazine if he came to power; he'd felt like a real dirty politician. It hadn't helped when Rohan offered to run a story on him in the upcoming issue.

Himanshu slunk into the assembly hall late that morning. Pretty soon, the article in the magazine would be out, and he'd be getting almost as much attention as Aniket Jain. Thankfully, people were still focused on finishing the syllabus as fast as possible.

Himanshu was searching the crowd for Vivek, when someone sat down next to him.

He turned towards the newcomer and jumped. 'Rikkhe! Uh . . . hi.'

Rikkhe smiled. It was one of those rare occasions when he was wearing normal—if one could call Armani 'normal'—clothes: a dark blue shirt and black trousers. Himanshu always felt a little underdressed in front of him. But then, who didn't?

With a jolt Himanshu realized that Rikkhe was chief election commissioner; he would be aware of everyone who was participating. Himanshu squirmed and avoided Rikkhe's gaze.

Students were still trickling into the auditorium when Vishakha came running towards them.

'Himanshu!' she sounded out of breath.

Himanshu's heart jumped with joy. For a second he debated whether to be a gentleman and stand up. But then he tried to play it cool instead.

'Hey.'

'Will you save me?' Vishakha said, panting. A couple of rows ahead, he spotted Vivek, who was grinning appreciatively at Himanshu.

All pretence gone, Himanshu immediately stood up. 'What happened?' he asked urgently.

'Walia Sir had asked that the school song be played before each assembly session. Today was supposed to be the first time, but the piano player bailed on us. Kumar Sir said you are the best player in his class. Can you please fill in?'

Himanshu's jaw dropped. He couldn't speak. Was she actually asking him to go on stage? Didn't she know that he'd rather jump off the roof of the school building?

Rikkhe had stood up as well, his face grim. 'I suppose director sir has invited a guest today?'

Vishakha shrugged. 'His courting never stops. Just can't stop showing off. So, what do you say, Himanshu?'

Himanshu's mouth was dry. Rikkhe seemed to understand.

'He'll be along,' Rikkhe said, pointedly nodding at Vishakha, who took the cue and left them alone.

Rikkhe placed a hand on his shoulder.

'I know it must be unnerving, but try not to look at the crowd. Just concentrate on the keys.'

Himanshu was panicking. 'I can't do this, man.'

Rikkhe gently pushed him forward. 'Yes, you can. And as head scholar, you'll have to face other situations like this. Consider it target practice. There'll come a time when you'll look your audience in the eye, but for now, just go and be a Villean.'

Himanshu felt light-headed as he walked towards the stage and took his place at the grand piano behind the curtain. He nodded at his fellow players, recognizing many of them from music class. All of them were surprised to see him. He went over the piece with them as Vishakha took the podium.

Himanshu noticed a mic placed near his face, next to the lyrics of the song. He tilted it downwards, towards the piano.

'Hey! What are you doing?' the girl on the harp called out to him. 'That mic is for vocals only!'

Himanshu looked at her, frozen. *Vocals?*

The curtain rose and light flooded the stage. In his peripheral vision, he could tell that the spotlight was on him. It was either a very bad dream or a very bad joke.

There was polite clapping. Himanshu could vaguely hear Vishakha announcing the names of the musicians.

'And the pianist, as well as the lead vocalist, is Himanshu Pathak!' Dazed as he was, Himanshu was conscious enough to register the hint of enthusiasm in Vishakha's voice as she shouted his name. She nodded at him, mischief in her eyes.

Himanshu's insides calmed a little. It was just a game. And the girl of his dreams wanted to play it with him. He cleared his throat.

Although he played flawlessly, his voice quivered in the beginning. Despite Rikkhe's warning, Himanshu's eyes wandered into the crowd. He saw Vivek looking dumbfounded. And suddenly, Himanshu found his voice. He abandoned caution and lost himself in the music, coordinating with his fellow players when he had to. They were all good musicians, and enjoyed the challenge as Himanshu moulded the tempo and varied his enunciation for greater impact.

By the time Himanshu reached the last refrain, the crowd was humming with him. Nor did anyone miss the way Himanshu had had his eyes on Vishakha almost the entire time.

'And the king of the woods roars in his land! A conqueror, he, a vanquisher, he!'

Like the school itself, the song of Woodsville was notorious for the competitive spirit it evoked.

Himanshu couldn't believe what he'd done when the song ended. He stood up with the rest of the team, walked forward and took a bow. In the first row, he saw Walia sitting with Mukesh Jha, an upcoming satirist—and a former student of Woodsville.

'And incidentally, Himanshu would like to say something to all of us . . .'

Himanshu couldn't understand what was happening even as Vishakha approached him with a mic. The game was still on. He'd never flirted before, and had no idea how protracted or how painful it was.

It was only when Vishakha handed him the mic and muttered, 'Announce it,' that Himanshu realized that this was no flirting. Vishakha had conned him into declaring his candidature. The fact that she cared enough to do it to him and no one else was enough for Himanshu.

He kept it short and simple. 'Hello, friends. I wanted to take this opportunity to announce that I'll be running for head scholar. I cannot say that I am better for this job than the other contenders, but I *can* assure you,' his eyes found Vishakha, 'that I am the most motivated.'

As he continued, it struck Himanshu how serendipitous the timing of Rohan's magazine article and Vishakha's ploy had been. 'As for my vision for our school and its student body, please take a look at today's issue of the school magazine. You can get in touch with me for any further queries and suggestions.'

Nobody realized it, but the thing they'd been waiting for had finally happened. Someone had declared their intention to fight for the honour of being declared the best of the best. And somehow, he'd chosen a truly appropriate time and place to do it—in the assembly, right after singing the invigorating school song. While most people lauded the gesture, Aniket Jain and Dev Bhushan sat in silence, fuming. The underdog had just kick-started the race. And left them blinded in the dust.

*

The week after Himanshu's declaration witnessed intense, albeit scattered campaigning by the other participants. There was no doubt in anyone's mind, however, that Himanshu Pathak's way had been the most organized and dignified. Nevertheless, not many thought he'd actually win.

The excitement had managed to disrupt the grave air of academia, and few people talked about lessons in their free time. Aniket Jain, whose determined hard work had forced several peers to increase their study time, threw himself entirely into his election campaign. He was doing whatever he could think of to win, although there was not much that he could think of. But just the fact that Aniket Jain was wasting his hours on the election lent it more importance than before.

Other participants revealed their candidature after Himanshu, although not on a similar scale. The clear favourite even now was Dev Bhushan, and he was still mysteriously dormant.

When D-Day finally arrived, students were out of their beds and scurrying towards the voting booths like wild mice. It was the day of the election, the day of the result; it was everything people had waited for, and everything they feared would end; it was the twilight of tradition, it was the dawn of change. Like all good things, though, it too had to be let go of. The afternoon after the voting was one of the laziest ones anyone remembered.

'Why'd you do it?' Vishakha asked curiously, sitting in the deserted cafeteria. She had just finished voting. The results were due to be announced at the end of the day, at five. 'You don't seriously believe Himanshu's going to win.'

Rikkhe disliked talking while he ate, but there was no way he was getting away with that in school. He finished the bite of his home-made lunch before he spoke.

'It doesn't matter what I believe, I just hope he's up for the job.'

Vishakha knew Rikkhe was keeping something from her, and it was driving her mad. Like Aniket, she despised people born with a silver spoon in their mouths, yet here she was, helping one.

'I just spoke to the people outside the poll booths,' Vishakha said doggedly, 'and more than half said they voted for Dev.'

'Well then, he'll win, I suppose.' Rikkhe was stubbornly cryptic.

'Why then did you so meticulously plan for Himanshu to announce his candidature like that?' Vishakha could be stubborn too. 'Unless you're just screwing with him.'

Rikkhe looked up from his lunch and stared at her. Vishakha immediately regretted accusing him.

'Listen, Vishakha, I believe that Himanshu is the best candidate for head scholar; I respect him. We cannot have any immature, self-serving person being the school's face. I got Himanshu up there on the stage because I believed that he could handle it, not because I thought he'd make a fool of himself.'

Vishakha didn't believe Rikkhe. Or maybe she didn't want to. His reasons were all too noble for her to continue loathing him.

'You are the election commissioner . . . Isn't it considered cheating to help a candidate?' she asked, determined to cut him down.

Rikkhe was unperturbed. 'I didn't break any rules. I just gave moral support and some general advice to a friend.'

Vishakha couldn't argue with that. Talking to Rikkhe Rajput often frustrated intelligent people; he was like a wall against their barbs.

'Now, I *am* grateful for your help,' Rikkhe said pointedly, reminding her of her complicity in the plan. 'I couldn't have made it happen had you not been on board. And as I promised you before, this puts me in your debt.'

A favour from Rikkhe Rajput. That was the price she'd agreed to help get Himanshu on stage for. Now that there seemed to be little chance of Himanshu winning, she was questioning Rikkhe's motives. No matter how noble he was, Rikkhe certainly didn't deal in the futile. He either had to actually believe that Himanshu stood a chance, or he was completely sure of his victory.

'There's no way he's winning this. No one voted for him,' Vishakha said firmly.

For Rikkhe, the conversation was over. He stood up, grabbing his lunch box.

'Whom did you vote for?' he asked with a smile.

Vishakha reddened. Himanshu, of course.

'Well, so did I. Let's just hope there are more like us.'

Rikkhe proceeded to the lockers on the second floor. Along the way, he was accosted by Rohan.

'Hey, Rikkhe!' Rohan beamed. 'What's happening, man?'

Rikkhe quickened his pace to find a secluded area. 'I am good, Rohan. How about you?'

'A little worried, to be honest,' Rohan replied animatedly.

Rikkhe pursed his lips and entered the temporarily closed restroom on their right, and Rohan followed him in. As soon as they were inside, Rohan rounded on Rikkhe.

'Are you sure you didn't just make me run a completely useless errand for you?' he asked.

Rikkhe just had time to muse over how inappropriate Rohan was for his job as the editor before he answered.

'Yes, I am sure.'

If anything, it made Rohan angrier. 'The magazine just did an exit poll for the website. It heavily favours Dev Bhushan, with Jain following, substantially behind. *Then* it's Himanshu.'

Rikkhe pursed his lips. 'If I were you, I'd stop that exit poll from going online. It may make you look bad when the final verdict is out.'

Rohan shook his head. 'You are living in a fantasy land, Rajput. Himanshu Pathak won't win, and I won't get more funds for the magazine—as *you* promised me before I ran that pretty flattering article on him. Pathak owes me more than money now.' He turned to go.

'Rohan.' There was something in Rikkhe's voice that made him stop. His face was grim and his voice dead serious. 'I don't involve myself in anything if I cannot control the outcome. I know that Himanshu won't get the votes, but believe you me, he'll win. All I needed from that article was for his win to look credible. So I say once again, don't jeopardize that credibility; do *not* let that exit poll go online.'

Rohan licked his lips and nodded half-heartedly.

Rikkhe's mind was in overdrive as he walked out of the restroom. He had still not cheated . . . he still had a chance to back out . . . everything up till now was justifiable. But Rikkhe wasn't thinking about that. He had weighed the pros and cons before he'd set out on this quest. He was just hoping he hadn't given the conspiracy away to his co-conspirators, Vishakha and Rohan.

Rikkhe wrote a mandatory note to his teachers and left it in the staffroom. He was going to be absent for the rest of the day. Rikkhe would be busy carrying out the incriminating part of his plan, the one that he had to take care of personally. The note was a single line, and a valid excuse for his absence.

Sir/Ma'am, I will not be able to attend any more classes today as, being the chief election commissioner, I am supposed to report to the admin office in order to count the ballots and prepare the announcement of the verdict.

*

It was six by the time Himanshu wandered out of the main school building. Everything seemed unreal. As he had done throughout the day, Himanshu avoided company. Most of the school had gone out to the vast ground that separated the campus mall from the main building. Himanshu had been waiting for just that; he wanted to slink out the back while everyone was looking the other way.

Instead, curiosity got the better of him, and he cautiously inched towards the ground and saw the huge crowd that had completely engulfed the stage. Going closer, he spotted Rikkhe, Vishakha, Walia, Admin Kumari and the vice director in the middle of the throng. But something was amiss.

Himanshu moved closer still, and suddenly realized that there was no noise. There were hundreds of students surrounding the stage, but not one of them made so much as a peep. Not even Walia, who held the mic. Whatever the result had been, Walia was shocked, and his silence had infected everyone else.

Himanshu was close enough now to be recognized. One by one, he saw the students turn to face him, and pretty soon everyone—including those on the stage—was staring at him. He saw Vishakha peer at the name in Walia's hand and take the mic from him.

'Yes, my friends,' Himanshu heard Vishakha say from the stage, 'you heard right. Your new head scholar . . . HIMANSHU PATHAK!'

And then there was pandemonium. Himanshu almost shat his pants when the mob abandoned the stage and swarmed over to him. There were shouts, cheers, roars, curses, but most of all, adulation. At the head of the crowd, running towards him, was Vivek.

'You lucky bugger!' he heard Vivek shout, before Vivek lifted him slightly off the ground. The crowd roared harder. With people pressing down on him from every side, Vivek had to shout into his ear. 'Where the hell were you?'

'Just where you left me this morning,' Himanshu yelled back in the din.

Vivek laughed. 'Don't tell me you spent the entire day hiding in an out-of-order toilet?'

Himanshu had. Initially ashamed of it, he was now glad that he had. If he hadn't hidden there, he'd never have overheard the two people who had come into the bathroom and discussed how they'd played Himanshu Pathak.

Rikkhe watched as the crowd carried the new head scholar over its shoulders, and sighed. He had kept his promise to his father. *Once I am through with it, it won't be a democracy any more.* In the process, he'd managed to keep the throne from the likes of Dev Bhushan.

He'd just given the school the shock of its life. But one thing he didn't know—*couldn't* have known—was that there was a bigger shock in store for him. The summer vacations would start in a few more days. And someone was waiting for Rikkhe on the other side of summer break. Someone was about to come and topple his carefully contrived kingdom and the crown of his dummy regent, Himanshu Pathak.

RAMANUJAM

'I told him. Use a razor and go bald; it helps save time. These kids never listen,' Mr Kumar growled.

The hairdresser nodded vigorously and addressed the thirteen-year-old pasty-skinned kid he was giving a haircut to. 'It does save time.' The kid wasn't going to pay the bill; the father was.

Mr Kumar continued with his rant. 'Tenth, eleventh, twelfth. These are big years. You should stay home and study, not waste time getting haircuts.'

The boy seemed too young to be in senior secondary, but the man let it slide. The boy, too, disregarded Mr Kumar's sagely advice and ordered the hairdresser. 'Be a little light with the scissors, man, I'm not joining the army.'

Mr Kumar ignored the boy's words as thoroughly as the boy had his. 'Leave the scissors, take the trimming machine. The number one for the sides and four for the top. And be quick.' Mr Kumar growled louder, 'He's got a test to prepare for.'

The boy's face reddened visibly. Everyone in the waiting seats was watching intently. Even the guy getting the blackheads ripped out of his face was looking hard from the corner of his eyes. Most of them seemed irritated with the loud Mr Kumar.

'Okay, Uncle, as you wish,' the boy spoke up innocently. 'After that, will you take me back to my parents? They must be worried.'

The three hairdressers at work simultaneously stopped working to stare questioningly at Mr Kumar, who still seemed impervious to the attention.

'What parents?' Mr Kumar barked.

The boy looked down and replied quietly, 'The ones you took me away from.'

Although everyone was listening, most thought that the kid was playing a prank on his father. That is, until Mr Kumar opened his mouth.

'They are not your parents any more. I am.'

The customers, already restless at having to wait this long, stood up in unison, rounding on Mr Kumar, who seemed to have just realized the situation he was in.

'Wait—I *am* his father—I got him from somewhere—'

But Mr Kumar's feeble attempts at an explanation were drowned by the boy's sobs, now crying earnestly into the damp towel tied around his neck, spattered with cut hair.

'He . . . took me from . . . my mother a year ago, and he hasn't let me see her even once,' the boy managed between sobs and hiccups. He pointed at his face. 'He attacks me with a knife when I talk about her.' Sure enough, a closer look revealed faded scars on the sides of his face, his neck and on his arms.

Mr Kumar's face contorted with anger. 'You lying bastard, I have only had you for three months!' he snarled, grabbing the boy by what was left of his hair and yanking him up from the chair.

This seemed to be all the provocation anyone needed. Bristling at the word 'bastard', which someone in the back said meant a person with no family, and the idea of shortening the waiting line by one, the customers grabbed Mr Kumar and pushed him to the floor. Soon, imitating their clientele, the hairdressers, too, joined the pummelling.

So busy was everyone that they never noticed the boy who had turned them into a mindless mob disappear, not even when he snatched the cell phone from Mr Kumar's hand. Not even when Mr Kumar yelled, 'RAMANUJAM! Ramanujam!' at his retreating figure.

Ramanujam ruffled his wet hair and hurried out into the busy market, dialling as he did.

'Hello, Mr Kumar,' a raspy voice answered. 'I suppose this is about Ramanujam?'

Ramanujam got right to the point. 'I just got rid of my eighth adoptive family.'

There was a sigh on the other end.

'If you still want me, you'll have to sign on as my legal guardian. I am done with parents.'

There was a long pause. 'All right then, Ramanujam, welcome to Woodsville.'

That was the answer he'd expected. It was what had given him the courage to get his last (hopefully) parent beaten up in a barber shop. Ramanujam didn't betray any hint of the glee he felt.

'Good doing business with you, Mr Walia.'

*

Aniket caressed the fabric of his grey business suit with his right hand while trying to steady himself with his left. The DTC bus was swerving dangerously, but Aniket didn't sit in the many empty seats around him. He stood right in the middle. He wanted people to see him.

He put his hand in his coat pocket, and withdrew a cell phone and put it to his ear.

'Yes, Mr Oberoi?' Aniket kept his face impassive, though his voice was urgent. 'Yes, of course. I'll be there in half an hour. My car broke down, you see—yes, yes, you can have a copy of the presentation from my assistant. Thank you.' Aniket put down the phone.

Slowly and deliberately, Aniket buttoned up his coat, adjusted the tie and pushed back the zero-power spectacles up the ridge of his nose. Then he made an impatient clucking noise, while smartly checking his wristwatch. Throughout this performance, he was aware of the curious eyes on him.

After some time, having had his fill of the attention, Aniket bent down, picked up his briefcase and walked towards the door.

'Mayur Vihar Phase II!' the conductor yelled, slapping his abnormally large hand outside the window, a little too close to a dried patch of vomit.

Aniket alighted from the bus, and once outside, he exhaled. He felt rejuvenated.

Walking with a little spring in his step now, Aniket proceeded towards a nearby restaurant.

He entered and nodded to the guy at the reception.

'Lunch here today, Aniket bhai?' the guy asked.

Aniket shook his head. 'Just need to use the bathroom, Gullu.'

Gullu nodded. He was used to this.

Aniket went into the toilet, placed his briefcase on top of the cistern and withdrew a pair of jeans and a shirt from it. Once he'd changed, he folded his suit with great care and placed it in the briefcase.

He nodded at Gullu and even gave him a little smile on his way out. Aniket had never had a problem being nice to people who posed no threat to him.

He knew he was going to be late for lunch; he quickened his pace. Despite his erratic schedule at Woodsville, the summer months he spent at home were always quite disciplined. His mother was a stickler for rules.

For the past two months, Aniket hadn't had much to do . . . except brood about the verdict. He had no idea how or why Himanshu Pathak had won, nor did he care. What he cared about was that he'd lost. And that now there was *one* more person people would consider better than Aniket.

Mrs Swaminathan's voice rang in his head every now and then. *Upgrade your wardrobe, Ani. Your clothes are your first impression. Make it good.* Was it maybe because Aniket wasn't presentable enough that he'd lost the election?

Aniket couldn't know for sure, but playing the successful businessman in public places helped him regain an iota of his self-esteem.

When he finally reached his apartment building, it was already a quarter to two. He ran up the two flights of stairs and knocked on the door to his house. Through the steel grille, Aniket saw his mother hurriedly come out of the kitchen, unlock the door and run back in.

Aniket heaved a sigh of relief. So the food wasn't ready yet.

He walked through the corridor and saw his mother busy arranging her precious tea set. Immediately suspicious, Aniket hurriedly walked across the corridor—and stopped short as soon as he was in the dining area.

'Aniket,' Athar said, smiling at him from the dining table, 'so good to see you. How're you doing?'

Aniket's voice got stuck in his throat. He put down the briefcase. 'I—uh—fine. I mean, I am good.'

Aniket's father, sitting next to Athar, looked awkward. The aroma of tea, followed by Aniket's mother, spared him from having to say anything.

'Here, Atharji, your green tea.'

Athar smiled graciously and picked up the cup. Aniket's mother sat down as well and motioned for Aniket to do the same.

'So, Aniket, how are things?' Athar asked kindly.

Although Aniket knew why Athar was there, he got the feeling that he didn't really want to be there.

'Everything's fine,' Aniket replied shortly. He wasn't going to make it easy for him.

Aniket's father interjected. His voice, deep and baritone, reflected a hint of concern.

'Aniket is really well, actually. He's been so busy with the syllabus that we've barely seen him since he got back from school.'

Aniket's mother nodded. 'He works so hard, never listens. The independence of hostel life has spoiled him, I think.'

Athar responded with an engaged nod. 'That's understandable. After all, Aniket's one of the best we've got.'

As soon as he'd said it, Athar cringed. Aniket hated being *one* of the best.

'Ma, Dad, could sir and I talk alone?' Aniket said.

His parents gladly left them alone, and Athar took a deep breath. Aniket knew, though, that they would be listening keenly from the next room, waiting to come to his aid at a moment's notice.

'It won't happen again. You can tell Walia that. Anything else?' Aniket spoke briskly.

Athar frowned. 'To be honest, Aniket, I have stopped believing that I can tell what you are planning to do. And that diminishes my ability to assure Director Walia of anything.'

'Take my word for it then,' Aniket said simply.

'The incident made the papers, Aniket,' Athar said after a pause.

'I know,' Aniket replied bitterly, 'my father reads them.'

'Then you know how it might worry people at Woodsville when one of its brightest students climbs to the top of the water tank, inebriated, and nearly instigates a mob to violence?'

Despite himself, Aniket grinned. The day he'd lost to Himanshu Pathak, he'd bought himself some liquor from Sid Malhotra and climbed atop the water tank in the middle of the student residential area. Frustrated, he'd thrown the empty bottles down, one by one, all the while abusing Walia, Himanshu, Rikkhe, and anyone else he could think of. Although he'd only been letting off steam, as soon as he'd started targeting the administration, a number of other students joined him on the water tank, throwing empty coke and ketchup bottles themselves. By morning, crews from various news channels were thronging the campus gate, eager to cover the 'student protest' happening inside.

'I didn't intend to,' Aniket said defiantly.

'Aniket, I know for a fact that the director will take a personal slight over letting a student like you leave the school . . . but what he *will not* tolerate is the besmirching of Woodsville's name.'

Aniket felt ashamed but he didn't show it. 'It was an isolated incident.'

'You'll see Himanshu Pathak at school tomorrow. And he'll be wearing the head-scholar badge,' Athar said harshly. 'What will you do?'

Aniket flared his nostrils. 'I'll take him up to the roof and throw him off the building, what do you expect?' he said scathingly.

Athar relaxed and gave a dry chuckle. 'Okay, Aniket, take it easy on the studying, though. Spare some time for your family.'

Aniket nodded without really listening. As he saw Athar out, he noticed the doctor was thoughtful. At the main door he put a hand on Aniket's shoulder.

'Being the best isn't everything, Aniket,' Athar said urgently. 'What you must learn is to be yourself. You have no control over others and their abilities. So . . . if someone . . . someone beats you, don't forget that you are still the same person.'

'What are you saying?'

Athar looked worried. 'Just remember, Aniket, you can always be beaten, but no one can take from you who you are.'

'No one's taking anything from me, Doctor,' Aniket grinned.

Athar shook his head in desperation. Aniket probably felt that what he'd done two months back was an isolated incident because he didn't think Himanshu could beat him again. But *someone* could, and sooner than he might expect.

'All I am saying is that if someone beats you again, Aniket, don't lose it this time.'

*

'And this is my room,' Himanshu said nervously, his heart pounding strenuously.

Unlike with the rest of the house, which she had barely noticed, Vishakha inched slowly into the room, taking in all of it.

'Oh my God,' she said in revulsion, and Himanshu's insides churned, 'it's circular!'

Himanshu laughed. 'Welcome to my nightmare.'

'How do you live here?' Vishakha was still in shock. 'It's like a villain's lair.'

Himanshu led her inside. 'It's easy once you get used to it.'

Although it had repulsed her initially, once she entered the room and took in the sunlight streaming in through the windows, which spread across half the circular wall, she felt a bit better. On the right, in front of the window, was a cute little study table and a low bookshelf that ran along the wall, ending only when interrupted by a teak door. On the left, away from the windows, was a piano.

'At least your bed is normal,' Vishakha quipped, before jumping on it, face down.

Himanshu walked gingerly towards his bed and sat down, looking down at Vishakha, her face buried in one of his pillows. They had spent the better part of the summer vacation constantly talking on the phone, and had even met each other a few times. This was the first time she'd come over to his house.

'So? What do you think?'

Without moving, Vishakha mumbled indistinctly, 'It's depressing.'

Himanshu grinned. '*I* am depressing.'

Vishakha turned over on her side and looked at Himanshu. 'I know that, but your room is, too.'

Himanshu chuckled lightly.

Vishakha sighed. In the time it had taken her to get to know him, she'd found him adorable . . . He was *so* not her type. After some deliberation, she leaned forward to straighten Himanshu's spectacles. She then cradled his face; Himanshu stopped breathing.

'So you two are getting comfortable!' a shrill, lively voice called out.

Vishakha withdrew her hand as though she'd been burnt. In the doorway stood a pixie-like creature, wearing a bright floral-print dress. Her hair was cropped short and her skin was the same caramel as her brother's.

'You must be Vishakha,' the girl said, coming forward. She turned towards Himanshu and said reproachfully, 'You sneaked her up here.'

'Vishakha, this is Sana, my troublesome little sister,' Himanshu said, grimacing.

Sana jumped on to the bed, nearly knocking Himanshu down. 'I am sick of you, Vishakha.'

Vishakha was usually very confident around people, but something about Himanshu's sister threw her. 'What?'

Sana slapped her shoulder amicably. 'This guy—' she pointed at Himanshu, 'cannot stop talking about you. My entire vacation has been nothing but a Vishakha-centred vortex.'

Himanshu froze. His sister was the most wilful person he knew, and right now she seemed to be in a mood to spill his innermost secrets. And according to her, she would be helping Himanshu 'get the girl'.

Vishakha gave Himanshu a quick glance before gathering herself. 'Sorry about that.'

Sana waved the apology aside. 'To tell you the truth, I was looking forward to meeting you. I must say, I am impressed.'

Himanshu breathed a little as Vishakha smiled.

'Why is that?'

'You broke into a prison, girl!' Sana exclaimed conspiratorially. 'And the jailer never even noticed.'

'Sana,' Himanshu said warningly.

Sana's eyes were cold as she said, 'What? She should know what she's getting herself into. No?'

Himanshu was practically begging her to stop. 'We don't need to burden her with your unresolved issues.'

'*My* unresolved issues?' Sana shrieked.

'Please, stop.' It was Vishakha who spoke. 'Both of you. And Sana,' she said firmly, 'if Himanshu has something to tell me, he'll do so himself. There's no need to embarrass him.'

Sana frowned at Vishakha, long and hard. Then she snorted, 'I like her.'

'Thank you for the seal of approval,' Himanshu said tersely. 'Now will you leave?'

Sana scowled as she left. 'See you around, Vishakha. Take care, *Cheenu.*'

Himanshu flinched.

'She's something,' Vishakha remarked.

Himanshu sighed. 'She's the bravest person I know.' Vishakha's inquisitive gaze prompted him to continue. 'It's not—easy—living in this house, you know,' Himanshu said, squirming, 'and Sana fought like hell to get out. She lives in Kota now, and is preparing for her tenth-standard boards.'

Vishakha remained quiet. She could hear the longing in Himanshu's voice.

'I could have fought too,' Himanshu muttered. 'I could have left.'

'So why didn't you?'

Himanshu looked down at his hands. 'I don't like fighting,' he mumbled, chagrined. 'And I didn't want to leave my mother alone . . .'

Vishakha could see he was unwilling to discuss it further. She changed the topic.

'So, you're crazy about me, huh?' she said playfully.

Himanshu was about to deny it, when he changed his mind, sighed and shrugged. 'Like you didn't know it already.'

Vishakha was surprised by Himanshu's answer. She hadn't expected him to actually own up to it. Himanshu was unlike anyone she'd ever met, but she was always wary when it came to boys. They were too fickle. Like her.

'What is it that you're crazy about, then?' she asked, curious.

Hesitantly, Himanshu took her hand. He led her, slowly at first, then hurriedly, through the door next to the bookshelf.

Inside the small, dark room, Vishakha's eyes started adjusting to the dim, red light. Her mind registered about half a dozen threads criss-crossing the length of the room, with row upon row of photographs hanging from them. On either end of the room were a couple of slabs, with rectangular metallic containers placed evenly upon them.

'*This*, actually, is my villain's den, my darkroom,' Himanshu said nervously. 'This is where I develop the film from my camera. And this,' he added, gesturing at the scores of photographs suspended from the threads, 'is what I am crazy about.'

Vishakha gasped. Her face loomed back at her from every single photograph. Happy, sad, inquisitive, angry, proud, calculating, Vishakha saw her many selves.

There was a click and a flash.

'Sorry, but I have never seen you dazed,' Himanshu said apologetically, putting his old Kodak down. 'I just had to capture it. Besides, it feels so freeing not to have to hide when I am clicking you.'

Vishakha had never known she had such an ardent admirer. She was lost for words.

'It's just that there are so many faces to you,' Himanshu said imploringly, 'and I couldn't help but capture every one of them.'

She cleared her throat, trying to shoo away the emotion. Her eyes became teasing. 'Does your sister know that the head scholar of Woodsville is also a peeping Tom?'

Himanshu flinched. 'No one at home even knows that I am the head scholar.'

Vishakha didn't know what to say. Himanshu Pathak baffled her, and there weren't many who did.

'Why not?'

Himanshu looked her straight in the eye. 'Because I didn't earn it. It was Rikkhe Rajput who did it, not me.'

There was a sharp intake of breath from Vishakha, but Himanshu didn't notice it.

'Why do you think so?' Vishakha asked cautiously.

Himanshu recounted what he'd overheard in the toilet two months ago. Vishakha grew more sombre with each passing sentence.

'It was just an article, Himanshu,' Vishakha said finally. 'It wasn't the only reason you won.'

'But what if he did something else?' Himanshu exclaimed in despair. 'He was the election commissioner, for heaven's sake!'

Vishakha's mouth was dry. 'But why would *anyone* do that, let alone Rikkhe Rajput?'

Himanshu shook his head. 'That's what beats me. What do you think?'

Vishakha shrugged. 'I have no idea,' she said truthfully.

'I feel like there's something coming for me,' Himanshu let his fear show, 'and I am completely unprepared for it.'

Vishakha got up and gingerly put a hand on Himanshu's shoulder. 'You know you can count on me, right?'

Himanshu looked at her, sad. 'Of course I do . . .' Of course he knew he couldn't.

After Himanshu escorted Vishakha down to the car and instructed the driver to get her to Woodsville, his mood was grim. He turned to go back inside, when Sana came out; she had obviously been observing them.

'*This* is the girl you can't get out of your mind?' she said incredulously.

Himanshu nodded and turned towards the estate grounds instead. He was in no mood for this conversation. But of course, Sana followed him.

'You know you can't take this further,' Sana persisted.

Despite himself, Himanshu felt irked. 'I thought you said you liked her.'

'Ha! Like it matters,' Sana snorted. 'All Mum will see in her is a social climber.'

Himanshu couldn't control himself. He rounded on Sana. 'You know, for someone who's always been so outspoken against mother, you've started to sound uncannily like her.'

Sana was taken aback. 'Sorry, bhai. I am just saying it'll be easier to let go of her now than after you give in to your feelings.'

'I already have,' Himanshu said, sighing.

'Given in?' Sana asked blankly.

'Let go, I mean. I'll not see her again.'

'What happened? What did she do?' she asked interestedly.

'I might not wish to engage with her any more,' Himanshu said firmly, 'but that doesn't mean I'll speak ill of her. Ever.'

Sana backed off. 'Chill, dude. Mr Romeo.'

Himanshu walked on while Sana went back to the house. He saw his parents with another couple, far off in the distance, lounging on the white chairs under the large umbrella by the pool. His parents were more animated with each other than they were with the guests.

He, too, turned back lest they saw him and asked him to join them. His parents loved showing him off—the exceptional, model student.

Himanshu's eyes were wet, and he fought back those tears with increasing frustration. He'd given Vishakha a chance and, in return, she had treated him like a complete moron. He had not a shred of doubt that Vishakha had helped Rikkhe put him on stage and announce his candidature. Himanshu could forgive that; he had been nothing to her then. But if she was unwilling to confess to him now, he could safely assume that he was still nothing to her. And she was still playing him.

He'd meant it when he told her that he was afraid, afraid of what was in store for him. The mantle of the best student in the best school of the country had been thrust upon him by Rikkhe Rajput. And Himanshu no longer believed that Vishakha was by his side.

*

School reopened on the first day of July, and Lisa Chauhan stood morosely outside the lecture theatre. Although there were plenty of appreciative stares, as usual, the person she was waiting for had still not appeared. Two months she'd spent thinking about him, and now she'd lost the will to socialize. She stamped her foot in irritation. Where was Rikkhe?

'Lisa,' said Dev, materializing out of nowhere. Like her, he too had dispensed with his posse today. 'How was your vacation?'

Lisa smiled. She was mostly kind to her many suitors, especially if they didn't stand a chance. 'It was good. How was yours?'

Dev grimaced fleetingly. A more perceptive person would not have asked that question. How did she think his vacation went after being so terribly humiliated? Losing the election had snapped something inside him. He no longer felt that the school was *his*, so to speak.

'Well, just completed the syllabus, and looking forward to the unit tests.'

As he'd suspected, Lisa looked a bit uneasy at this. 'You are done with the syllabus already? I always thought science was so tough,' she said innocently. 'What will you do for the rest of the year? Won't you get bored?'

Dev laughed. 'There are plenty of other things to keep me from getting bored.'

'Like what?' Rikkhe's voice floated over. Lisa and Dev immediately turned to look. Rikkhe, impeccably dressed, was walking towards them, Radhika by his side. Lisa narrowed her eyes as she saw that Rikkhe had his arm around Radhika. He caught sight of Lisa's face and immediately disentangled himself from Radhika, who looked amused.

He bowed a little before Lisa and her face flushed. He then extended a hand to Dev, who, for some reason, was looking triumphant. Dev took his hand in a firm grip.

'Rikkhe,' Dev said, 'nice to see you, buddy. I was just about to tell Lisa that a lovely girl like her shouldn't be standing alone looking so sad. We ought to be ashamed of ourselves.'

Dev tightened his grip but Rikkhe didn't flinch. He didn't even notice it; he was too busy reflecting on how much he loathed Dev Bhushan, who'd sent him a message that morning, dropped at his doorstep by one of his minions.

Lisa really likes you, eh? Let's play this game . . . see who gets there first.

The message, as intended, had sickened Rikkhe. He realized that Dev held him responsible for the election verdict. And now Dev was using Lisa to get back at him.

Rikkhe smiled at Lisa, who, he noticed, was visibly pleased by his presence. He already felt guilty about not being able to reciprocate her feelings for him. It was one of the few things he actively discussed with Athar in their sessions together. But it would be unbearable if someone hurt her because of him.

Himanshu, waiting in the corridor with the rest of the class, was dodging eyes and fielding sniggers from his classmates. However, his attention was diverted when Vivek elbowed him and pointed to the little soirée going on a little further ahead. Rikkhe, Dev, Lisa and Radhika stood together, looking awkwardly formal.

'Look at him,' Vivek whispered in annoyance, 'the little princely git, smiling at her and all. Get away from her, damn it! Go look for someone else for your harem!'

'He's just being polite, is all,' Himanshu reassured him. He didn't say it, but Vivek had as much of a chance with Lisa as he himself had of being with Vishakha.

'Why doesn't he come be polite to me, then?' Vivek shot back, raising a fist. Himanshu chuckled.

'Hey,' someone said, tapping Himanshu's shoulder, 'help me out, man. It's my first day here.'

Himanshu turned and saw a little kid with unhealthily pale skin and gleaming white teeth grin at him. The boy's hair was cut quite unevenly. Had such weird hairstyles not been in fashion, Himanshu might've thought the boy had got only half a haircut.

'Yes?' Himanshu said attentively, realizing that, as head scholar, he was *supposed* to help everyone out. 'What's your name?'

'Ramanujam, at your service,' the boy said confidently, extending a hand.

Himanshu found the name a bit odd but didn't mention it. 'Well, Ramanujam, I think you are on the wrong floor; these lecture theatres are only for classes eleven and twelve.'

Ramanujam waved that information aside. He had bigger fish to fry. He had been on the Woodsville campus since the previous evening, and he'd never felt more at home. Walia had personally enrolled him in the student residential area and shown him around the whole school. Ramanujam had never been happier in his life, but he'd learnt long back that happiness made people weak. He had to mould his state of mind accordingly.

'Say, you wouldn't by any chance know who the most threatening person around here is? Someone everyone else is scared shitless of?' Ramanujam's voice was excited.

Himanshu frowned. 'I am the head scholar, you know.' He'd meant it as a warning to the kid.

Ramanujam sized Himanshu up. He could tell a lot about a person from just a handshake, and head scholar or not, this guy certainly was a nonentity.

'Come on, man,' Ramanujam said lightly, 'I'm new here, don't you think I should know these things before I do something stupid, or step on the wrong foot?'

Himanshu blinked. He pointed to Dev. 'See that big guy?' he said in a low voice. 'Just stay clear of him, okay? You don't want to get caught around him when he's in a bad mood.'

For some reason, Ramanujam's face broke into a wide smile. The tiny white scars on his face stretched into prominence. 'Sure thing. Anyway, thanks, dear Sir Head Scholar.'

As Ramanujam started walking forward, Himanshu narrowed his eyes.

'That one's kind of odd, no?' he said to Vivek.

Vivek, who'd been watching with interest, nodded. 'He's part of your empire now. Just keep an eye on him.'

There must have been something in the kid's expression, or maybe it was just the fact that someone so little was among the big guys, but as he crossed the corridor, everyone turned to look at him.

'So what do you say, Lisa?' Dev was saying softly. 'Should we do a double date with these two lovebirds?'

Lisa looked hurt, while Radhika seemed to bristle with anger.

Ramanujam had everyone's attention except for the four people in the corner. Smiling gleefully, he walked up to Dev Bhushan, who stopped short as he felt all eyes on him.

'Yeah, kid?' Dev said, irritated at the interruption.

Ramanujam extended his hand. 'Sir, I have heard so much about you.'

Dev wanted to tell the kid to go hear about him someplace else. But when you were in front of Rikkhe, trying to wrench a girl from his grip, niceties had to be observed. He took the kid's hand.

Still smiling widely and shaking Dev's hand, Ramanujam drew his left hand as far back as it would go, and sprung a well-forced slap on Dev's muscular face.

Before the stunned silence that followed, Lisa shrieked and Radhika stepped back, gasping. Dev and Rikkhe, however, remained unmoving.

As soon as people found their voices, they started laughing, and as soon as they started laughing, Dev found the strength in his arms.

Forgetting all else, Dev picked the boy up by his collar and slammed him against the wall. Before Rikkhe could intervene, there was a shout from behind them.

'Dev Bhushan!' Mrs Swaminathan thundered. 'Unhand that boy! Now!'

With great difficulty, Dev made himself leave Ramanujam, who fell to the floor, the grin still plastered on his face.

'You're hurt,' Lisa said in alarm, bending down. Indeed, Ramanujam had hit his head when Dev had slammed him to the wall, and was bleeding profusely.

Lisa frantically searched for her handkerchief, while Ramanujam waved her aside. He didn't want sympathy or niceness from anyone; that would defeat the whole purpose of what he'd done.

With surprising agility, he jumped up. 'Get a grip, m'lady, 'tis but a scratch,' he growled.

'I bet you're regretting telling him you're the head scholar,' Vivek whispered in Himanshu's ear.

'You must be Ramanujam,' Mrs Swaminathan said.

'Right you are, ma'am,' Ramanujam said.

Mrs Swaminathan addressed everyone present. 'People, this is Ramanujam. He has just joined the class-twelve commerce section. If you look past his age, you might very well learn something from him.'

'I would like to learn where he got such guts from,' Radhika said to Rikkhe, who was looking at the newcomer very closely. Woodsville rarely accepted new students for class twelve, and now here one was, three months into the academic year, and a mere kid at that.

Aniket and Vishakha, who'd just got there, also looked at Ramanujam warily. The back of his shirt was now stained with blood. Aniket took a deep breath, feeling no sympathy. *A fucking prodigy?* This was what Athar had been warning him about. Aniket had to agree, if this little wimpy-looking thirteen-year-old topped over him, he might very well lose it again.

Ramanujam had fallen in love with Woodsville the moment he'd entered the premises, but love and happiness couldn't last if one wanted to win, and Ramanujam could never focus in that state anyway—he *needed* pain and humiliation to spur him on. His need to be detested was greater than his need to be admired. He needed enemies more than he did friends. Looking around the corridor, his head in a daze and hostile stares all around, he had to admit, he now had everything he could have asked for.

*

Rikkhe put the wooden pail of water down and wiped the sweat on his brow. He patted Nandini lightly; it was a tough job, bathing a horse, and though he couldn't personally care for all the horses in his stable, Nandini was special. He scrubbed and cleansed her until he felt satisfied.

Next to him and his gleaming, chestnut-brown horse stood Karamveer Singh, the man who cared for Rikkhe as thoroughly as Rikkhe did for Nandini. Indeed, Rikkhe was more influenced by Karamveer than by his own father.

It was evening, and the atmosphere was relaxed in the wake of the rigorous unit tests. It had been three weeks since Ramanujam burst on to the scene, although Rikkhe was trying not to think about that.

'So, what's Karan up to these days?' Rikkhe asked Karamveer in his native Shekhawati, placing the pail under the running tap. Karan, Rikkhe's childhood buddy, was Karamveer's son.

'Ranaji is initiating him into the business,' Karamveer said guardedly. 'He says Karan shows a lot of promise.'

Rikkhe frowned. Where he was from, experience was valued over education. He didn't want Karan to fall victim to that mentality. He was also confused as to what Karan could possibly be doing to help in the cement-manufacturing arm of their business.

'What business, *kaako*?' Rikkhe asked.

Karamveer, duty-bound to the rana, remained silent. Rikkhe wondered what his father would possibly want to conceal from him.

'Karan wrote to me about rani*sa*.' Karamveer deftly changed the topic. 'She's teaching him nowadays.'

Rikkhe stopped short, as he always did, when he heard news of his mother. He felt a little envious of Karan. Rikkhe hadn't seen his mother since he was twelve. It was a family tradition that the prince, from the time he hit puberty till the time he found his way in the world, would travel alone. The king was vehemently conservative, and Rikkhe, by default, had complied with his father's wishes.

'Did she ask me to visit?' Rikkhe said, faking nonchalance.

Karamveer bowed his head. 'I am sure she doesn't want to disturb you. She understands that what you are doing here is important. And anyway, this is your last year of schooling.'

Rikkhe nodded vigorously. 'Of course, of course.' He turned his face slightly, to avoid Karamveer seeing the frustration and anger there. Nothing about his father supporting the tradition hurt more than his mother's indifference. She had not tried to contact him *once* in five years.

He nodded curtly at Karamveer, who took that as his cue to leave. Rikkhe turned his attention to Nandini's long, silky, voluminous tail, which he believed she was as proud of as he was.

For years now, Nandini had been his only constant friend. As Karamveer left the bathing area and headed towards the lush green polo ground, Rikkhe reflected on how much time he needed alone with Nandini these days. She was the only one he could open up to without feeling vulnerable.

'Yeah . . .' he muttered to her, while applying copious amounts of shampoo on her tail, 'we are one of a kind, aren't we?'

Nandini turned her head back towards him and neighed softly. She had a beautiful face, with sparse mane. The fine brown coat gleamed on her long, slender back, her entire body devoid of any markings. At sixteen hands, Nandini was a stunner, but also a tough beast to handle. She was a horse worthy of a king, although that was hardly why Rikkhe felt such a connection with her. The reason was much deeper. Nandini, like Rikkhe, was the member of an extinct breed. Just as Rikkhe was the last living member of true Rajput lineage, she was the last living Turkoman horse in the world.

A trader, a couple of hundred years back, had gifted the then rana of Jahalgarh a stud of Turkoman horses. Hidden from the reaches of history, the stud had survived. The dwindling finances and tastes of the subsequent kings, however, had caused the line of Turkoman horses to taper off to the last of their kind—Nandini. Although she could breed, there would be no pure Turkoman horse after her.

'The last of our kind . . .' Rikkhe muttered. The Age of Kings, no matter what his father's pretences, was over. 'Where can we find companionship when there is no one like us?'

'Is that an Akhal-Teke?' an interested voice rang in the bathing area.

Rikkhe looked up to see Ramanujam, flanked on the right by a sombre-looking Karamveer.

'We cannot say for sure, although it has the characteristic traits,' Rikkhe said without smiling. There hadn't been another incident like the one with Dev, but Rikkhe was certain that there would be. Ramanujam, according to the rumour mill, had been very busy these past few weeks, studying twenty hours a day for the units, and confronting random people with questions about Woodsville.

Karamveer noticed Rikkhe's posture change completely on seeing the little boy in the knickers and T-shirt. And even though Rikkhe hadn't realized it, Karamveer saw his fist clench around the scrub he held.

Ramanujam was inspecting Nandini closely.

'You know much about its lineage?' he asked, approaching her. 'Because it *could* be a Turkoman . . .' he paused, observing Rikkhe's face, 'but of course, they are extinct.'

In his father's social gatherings, Rikkhe had had much practice confronting people of great wit. That experience was the only reason he was able to maintain his composure after Ramanujam's casual, calculated, chillingly correct guess.

Rikkhe bowed his head, letting go of the scrub. 'Yes, they are.'

Ramanujam seemed indifferent to Nandini now, and clucked his tongue impatiently. 'That head scholar didn't give me the right guy when I asked him for the most dangerous person on campus, you know. He gave me Bhushan,' he snorted, his eyes never leaving Rikkhe, 'but we both know it's you.'

Rikkhe debated whether to feign surprise, but decided against it. Instead, he folded his arms and spoke calmly. 'Why do you think so?'

'Come on,' Ramanujam said, almost bouncing on the balls of his feet, 'Dev Bhushan is a tough guy, but *you* crushed him without even lifting a finger. *And* no one knows about it. Certainly not that dim-witted head scholar. He doesn't know you made him the head scholar, does he?'

Rikkhe, for a moment—just a little moment—was speechless. Not even his co-conspirators knew the extent of his involvement . . . the only way Ramanujam could was through pure intellect and intuition.

Rikkhe nodded at Karamveer, who hesitantly left them alone.

'And what made you jump to that conclusion?'

Ramanujam rubbed his palms together. 'You're like a broken record. All questions and no answers; what kind of a topper is that?' He paused, as he had taken to doing, to gauge Rikkhe's response to the insult. Finding Rikkhe nothing but expectant, he continued with relish. 'I have been doing an exit poll myself, over the past few days, asking people whom they voted for. I know when I'm being lied to, and unless I am losing my grip, there's *no* way Himanshu Pathak made it without some inside help.' He winked.

Rikkhe smiled. 'We are all entitled to our opinions, of course—'

'Yeah, not like we're in a monarchy, no?' Ramanujam jibed.

Rikkhe wondered for a moment how Ramanujam knew all his weak spots. 'Of course not. This is a democracy where people know what's best.'

112

Ramanujam's expression hardened when he realized Rikkhe wasn't going to play along. 'Stop fucking with me, Rajput. Just admit I got to you.'

Rikkhe sighed exasperatedly. It was like dealing with an actual spoiled child. 'What is it you want, Ramanujam?' He had learnt some time ago that Ramanujam had just the one name—nothing before or after—probably because of his obscure parentage.

Ramanujam's thin upper lip twitched dangerously. He hated being talked to like a kid. He took a couple of steps towards Rikkhe, who stood his ground, unwavering. Rikkhe could tell that he'd struck a nerve.

'You're not too bright, are you, Rajput,' Ramanujam offered. 'I want what all of us want. To be the best. And for that, I need to beat the best, which, unfortunately for you, is you. For now.'

'Thank you for the compliment, Ramanujam, but I would advise you to concentrate on your studies instead. I heard you passed the class-eleven exams just a few weeks back . . . wouldn't a more productive use of your time be to catch up for the boards?'

Ramanujam shrugged. 'What do you think I have been doing since I got here? The syllabus is done. I gave the units and I'll top. But academics isn't the only thing that matters here, now, is it?'

'And you can only go so far by slapping people,' Rikkhe remarked coolly.

Ramanujam laughed. 'Right you are, my liege.' He made a deep bow. 'Until we meet again. Oh yes, do remember that *you* put Himanshu Pathak in harm's way, not me.

As Ramanujam left, Karamveer came back inside. He looked at the calculating expression on Rikkhe's face.

'Kaako,' Rikkhe said after a while, 'you have my grandfather's *murki* with you?'

Karamveer nodded and, from within the folds of his turban, drew something that he had carried around for years. It was a mark of his servitude that his most prized possession was merely meant for safekeeping.

Rikkhe headed over to wash his hands and when he was done, he walked over to Karamveer and extended a hand.

'I'll take it now,' Rikkhe said matter-of-factly.

Karamveer hesitated. He didn't think of Rikkhe as rash, but he was still just seventeen. 'That craven child? Are you certain?'

Rikkhe's face was grim. 'I am certain, kaako. And that boy was neither a child nor craven.'

Karamveer bent down on one knee and placed in Rikkhe's hand his grandfather's earring, which the then king had entrusted to Karamveer instead of his own son, Rana Dhananjay. The earring had been worn by the old emperor in the last battle Jahalgarh ever fought as a Rajputana kingdom.

Karamveer watched in wonder and pride as Rikkhe heated the needle of the earring till it was red-hot and shoved it into his earlobe without preamble. No sound of pain escaped his lips, though Karamveer could smell burnt flesh.

Ramanujam had just declared war. It was now up to Rikkhe Rajput to give him one worthy of his family name.

ALLIANCES

It was only six in the morning, but the first day of August saw the usual crowd near the oval atrium at the main school building; the names of the highest-scoring students in the unit tests would be displayed on the huge LED screen above the reception desk. As time passed and the crowd grew, so did the anticipation. There was a rising murmur of hope, derision and challenge.

Aniket arrived, and stopped at the entrance. He could feel the several gazes following him as he coolly tried to find a vantage point. On the day of a cricket match, Dev Bhushan was the star; the rest of the time, it was Rikkhe. But on each result day, Aniket was the centre of attention. It was the one thing no one could take away from him. But despite his unblemished record over the past two years, Aniket was more worried than usual.

The strain of the past month was quite visible on Aniket's face. His eyes were red, his face haggard and his hair unwashed. Since Ramanujam had started at Woodsville, Aniket had studied harder than he ever had in his life, unrelenting even after the units were over; he wasn't going to let anyone gain a second of study time over him. His fanaticism had shot through the roof when rumours of Ramanujam having completed the syllabus in ten days reached his ears.

A little further ahead, out of Aniket's earshot, a couple of guys sagely argued over his fate.

'There's no point betting about our result,' said Prakhar resignedly. He was a student of class twelve from the commerce department. 'It's going to be Ladyfinger again.'

Mohit nodded. 'I just wish *someone* would beat the sucker.'

'If anyone can, it's Rikkhe,' Prakhar shot back.

There was a laugh from behind them. It was Ramanujam.

'Don't worry, fellas, you, and Aniket Jain for that matter, are in for a surprise today,' he said calmly.

Mohit frowned, and so did Prakhar. Their expressions didn't escape Ramanujam—they preferred even the loathed Aniket Jain over him. Good.

'Aniket hasn't been outscored in a single subject in the last two years,' Mohit boasted, as though talking about his own achievements.

'Yeah, he's legendary,' Prakhar added condescendingly. 'He once argued with Mrs Swaminathan over his English paper and she had to award him a hundred!'

'He had to argue?' Ramanujam said smugly, laughing at the irate expression on their faces. And though he was smaller, neither of his classmates had the guts to say anything else.

Right on cue, the names and percentages of the top-scoring students from each class appeared before them on the screen. At the top was: XII—RAMANUJAM 100%.

There were audible gasps all around him, but Aniket was unable to utter a single word. He had dreaded this moment for the last four weeks, and now that it was here, he couldn't wrap his head around it; Aniket had given the exam everything he had. He heard an unfamiliar voice from the crowd sum up what he was feeling.

'He's just better,' the voice said. Aniket didn't know whether the comment was about him and Ramanujam in particular, or about someone else altogether. It didn't matter.

Academics had been his bastion and, within a second, he'd lost even that. Athar's warning rang in his mind, and as he made his way back to the residential area to change for another day of classes, he repeated it to himself over and over again.

Don't lose it, Aniket, don't lose it.

*

At the very moment that the toppers of the units were being announced at Woodsville, Vishakha stood twenty kilometres away, grumbling in her house in Shahadra. *Pigsty, not house,* she corrected herself. The two-bedroom ground-floor flat was ancient and, like most others around them, on the verge of collapse; every second spent in it alive was a miracle. It was where you sent atheists to convince them of the existence of God.

'Vishakha, beta,' the shrill voice of one such miracle-working neighbour rang out in the kitchen, where Vishakha was making tea. Lately unused to a neighbour's head poking in through her window, Vishakha jumped.

Mrs Kalra, Vishakha's next-door neighbour—more literally, her next-window neighbour—was leaning over from her own kitchen into Vishakha's, sweating profusely.

'Vishakha!' she said, panting, putting an empty bowl on the slab. 'So nice to see you after so long. Holidays at school? It's a good school, no? Your father says you are doing so well. Arré haan, is there some dahi? Just a little curd is all I need. Mr Kalra loves curd. You have curd?'

Vishakha might have been a bright girl, but these were just too many questions for her to answer. So she chose to answer none. Without a word, she headed over to the refrigerator and took out the curd, poured some in Mrs Kalra's bowl, smiled and said, 'Namaste.' When Mrs Kalra didn't budge, Vishakha quickly poured the tea into a cup and left the kitchen and the precariously balanced Mrs Kalra.

Tiptoeing around the cluttered drawing-cum-dining-cum-living-cum-guest room, Vishakha entered her parents' dimly lit bedroom. On the bed, as usual, lay her mother. Although only her half-burnt face was visible over the covers, Vishakha knew that 80 per cent of her body was covered with third-degree burns.

'Tea, Mummy,' Vishakha said colourlessly as she entered.

Her mother smiled through the oxygen mask; she always did when Vishakha was around. 'Sit by my side,' she said with difficulty, her voice slurred and hoarse. 'Tell me about school.' She slowly reached with her left hand and took off the mask, exposing her face entirely.

Vishakha hated sitting with her mother, and she was spared the ordeal when the doorbell rang. She set the tray down on the bed, accidentally spilling some of the tea on her own kameez, and her mother winced.

'I'll be back,' she said shortly.

It was her father. His eyes sleepy, his beard unshaven and his walk uneven, he dragged behind him his travel suitcase, which seemed even more worn and weary than him. Even so, he hugged Vishakha warmly. She could smell the distinct odour of the passenger train on him . . . it was the same whenever he went out for work.

'How's Mummy?' he asked, heading towards her room.

'She's drinking tea,' Vishakha said. 'Nothing major happened.'

Her father nodded absent-mindedly and headed for the kitchen. Vishakha nervously tapped her foot on the floor, dreading the thing she wanted to say so badly. Mrs Kalra's voice emanating from the kitchen interrupted her thoughts. Mr Sahdev came out a minute later, holding a piece of toast in his hand, his face grim.

'You should be more polite to the neighbours. They do a lot for us, Vizac—' he began firmly.

'It's Vishakha, please.'

Mr Sahdev contemplated his daughter's words. Ever since her mother's accident with the electrical fire a few years ago, his once lively, lovely daughter had been living in denial. Mr Sahdev knew that different people had different ways of coping, but choosing to forget about one's family could not be one of them.

Mr Sahdev was too tired to argue.

'Technically, I am on work-related travel till tomorrow,' he said, changing the topic, 'so we can spend the day together.'

'Actually, I can't,' Vishakha blurted out. 'I've already missed two days of school. Now that you are back, I really should go. It's seven already . . . I can make it to the campus by the time classes start.'

Mr Sahdev took a step towards her. 'But we need to talk, Vishakha. The doctor said your mother's contractures aren't responding to physiotherapy and that—'

Vishakha nodded instinctively. 'Yeah, all right. The doctors always know best, no? Anyway, I should be going,' she looked down at her old salwaar kameez, 'or I might not get time to change.'

Mr Sahdev held up the toast as Vishakha turned to leave. 'Next time you make her chai, whenever that might be, give her this too. You might not remember, but she always loved it.'

Vishakha didn't react. The usual blank look covered her eyes as she gathered her things and left.

Mr Sahdev sighed as he made his way to the bedroom. Over the years, his daughter had become accustomed to her mother gradually losing most of her motor functions. It was a way of life for her, a life she avoided as much as she could. Vishakha had moved on; was it then fair to tell her that her mother would soon lose the ability to breathe?

*

'Himanshu, um . . . sir,' a stuttering class-ten girl approached the new head scholar near the atrium. Himanshu turned his surprised gaze away from the LED screen to look at her. It was nine in the morning, and most of the crowd had proceeded towards their respective classes, leaving the atrium almost empty; the only other person there was the unmoving receptionist.

'Yes?' Himanshu said politely. He had found people being uncharacteristically deferential towards him lately. Admin Kumari, it seemed, through the newly drafted constitution, had conferred a lot of responsibilities on the student council. Therefore, in the first month of assuming his position, Himanshu had found himself unexpectedly busy.

The girl was fiddling with her long hair nervously. She seemed vaguely familiar. The next instant, Himanshu remembered—she was the girl on the harp. She had been next to him the day he'd sung the school song in the assembly.

She pointed towards the LED screen. 'The guy who stood first in tenth,' she said hesitantly, 'cheated.'

Himanshu raised an eyebrow. Even for the problems he had been approached with of late, this was quite unusual. But he'd learnt by now that his position gave him some influence among the students, and that influence warranted that the school administration listen to him.

'I'll be glad to take this up with the controller of examinations,' Himanshu said, 'but I'll need more than just your word on it.'

The girl pointed at three or four students standing right outside the atrium, looking nervously at him. 'They all saw him sneak in his cell phone. I would have gone to the administration, but people said Kumari would probably sweep this under the rug.'

Himanshu looked at the determined expression on the girl's face. The allegation was serious enough for him to intervene. Still, he would first talk to the boy in question. Himanshu looked at the screen again: X—LALIT NAGPAUL 96%. If Lalit wasn't convincing enough, Himanshu would have to go to Admin Kumari, something he heartily disliked.

Himanshu nodded. 'I'll look into it.' He turned to go, and then remembered something. He turned back, not noticing that the atrium door had opened and someone had walked in wearing a white-and-green salwaar kameez.

'I forgot to ask,' he said to the girl with a smile, 'but what's your name?'

Suddenly, the person who'd just walked in through the door materialized right behind the girl.

'Yeah,' said Vishakha with mock concern, 'tell him your name. Can't you see he looks so damn interested in you?'

The girl shuddered as Vishakha breathed down her neck. Ignoring her, she smiled at Himanshu and answered, 'Rina Singh, Himanshu Sir.'

'Ooooh!' Vishakha exclaimed. 'Sir! Well, sir, what say you? Isn't that a pretty name?'

Himanshu's ears reddened and he dreaded what he was about to say.

'Okay—uh—Rina,' he stuttered, avoiding their eyes, 'I'll need your contact number—in case—in case I need to . . . uh . . . contact you.'

From the corner of his eye, Himanshu could see the anger appear on Vishakha's face, while Rina immediately scribbled down her phone number on a piece of paper.

'Thank you so much, Himanshu,' Rina said boldly, handing him the paper, much less nervous now. 'I'll wait for your call.'

As she left, Himanshu felt rooted to the spot under Vishakha's gaze.

'Well, I think you finally got yourself a date,' Vishakha said icily. It was only then that Himanshu noticed that she looked tired and much less groomed than usual. He'd never seen her like that. He wondered with a stab of guilt whether he was the cause of it.

Himanshu gave a small nod and turned to leave.

'What the fuck?' Vishakha exclaimed incredulously, and Himanshu stopped. He hesitated for a second, and then turned back to face her. The receptionist busily tapping at her keyboard punctuated the tense silence in the atrium.

It was a few seconds before Vishakha continued. 'What happened to you?'

Himanshu gulped. 'Nothing.'

'Like hell!' Vishakha said, her voice a high-pitched shriek. 'You've been avoiding me for a month now! And you don't even care to explain why? That day I visited your house, what happened—what did I do?'

Himanshu couldn't bring himself to say it. He was afraid that Vishakha might apologize and try to patch things up with him. He couldn't let that happen. Sana had been right; their mother would not allow it. Geeta Pathak was too steeped in the ideologies of her own demanding father, and too delicate not to distrust the world. What was more, Himanshu couldn't place his faith in Vishakha again.

'You did nothing,' he said, looking down at the ground. 'It's just that I've been too caught up with the duties—'

'Yeah, I can see that,' Vishakha said scathingly, gesturing at the spot where Rina had stood a minute ago. 'Is that it? You can get your pick, now that you are head scholar?'

Her words stung Himanshu more than he could express. He opened his mouth in frustration, and then closed it without a single coherent sentence.

'We're done, Vishakha,' he said in anger. It was the only thing he could think of that matched her level of malevolence.

Vishakha could see that her accusation had hurt Himanshu enough to make him snap back at her, but she couldn't digest the words. *We're done?* She didn't know why it bothered her so much. She'd never even seen Himanshu as more than someone who just fascinated her enough to pique her interest briefly, then why should his absence affect her so? Maybe because he had no reason to be absent. She knew Himanshu was still hung up on her; she could see it in his eyes. *What's holding him back?*

'We're done?' Vishakha said derisively. 'We never even started, you fool.'

Himanshu huffed angrily and walked away.

A second later, he realized he'd underestimated how disturbed Vishakha was this particular morning. He heard a pattering of footfalls, and then felt a hard smack on the back of his head.

'Hey!' Himanshu shouted.

The receptionist was on her feet now. 'Hey, kids! Don't you have your classes to get to?'

Himanshu glanced at her furtively and started walking away again, up the stairs, towards the classes. He could hear Vishakha walking behind him, and he remained tense, fully expecting another smack. However, what happened next was something he wouldn't have imagined in a million years. There was a slight whimper and Himanshu looked back in surprise.

Vishakha was sitting on the middle step, her head resting on the railing, tears running down her cheeks.

'Hey!' Himanshu ran back to her in alarm. He didn't know how to console any crying girl, much less Vishakha Sahdev. 'I am sorry. Please don't cry—'

The next instant he noticed Vishakha's open water bottle tucked between her legs. The source of the ample fake tears. He swore.

'Oh, damn you!' he yelled, grabbing her by the shoulders and shaking her. He could see her silent laughter, and it sickened him even more. He immediately let go of her and stood up. 'You want to know what happened?'

Vishakha made a mock-serious face and nodded. 'Yes, please, Himanshu Sir. That would be awesome.'

'You lied to me,' Himanshu hissed vehemently. 'You and Rikkhe played me. *You* lied to me! My supposed victory wasn't my own. Then, after two months of friendship, when I told you I was afraid, you lied to me again! All you've done is lie—over and over. You wouldn't have done that had you cared for me one bit—or even respected me.'

Vishakha was silent for a moment. If she didn't respect him before, she certainly did now. 'I am sorry,' she said quietly, 'but I didn't know what Rikkhe was up to. We both agreed, though, that you'd be the best person for the post.'

'*You* decided?' Himanshu said, narrowing his eyes. 'For me? Who gave you the right?'

Vishakha had no answer for that. 'Himanshu, please believe me—'

'You just don't get it,' Himanshu said quietly. 'I cannot believe a single word you say now. You may tell me that you didn't know what Rikkhe's goal was, I cannot believe you. You may tell me that you have my best interests at heart, I cannot believe you. Tell me, then, how I'm supposed to believe that you won't leave my side when I am down and out?'

As Himanshu left her alone on the staircase, Vishakha's mind was blank, her eyes ghost-like. She stared at the little tea stain on her kameez, knowing him to be right.

*

After classes had ended for the day, Ramanujam walked back to his house in the student residential area, fully expecting retribution from his housemates. He'd experienced this a dozen times before, and had no reason to believe it would be any different here; now that he was a topper, a bookworm, the effects of his stunt on the first day would wear off quickly. Unless he gave people another reminder of his unpredictability, he was looking at constant bullying in school—and at home.

'So, where's the party then, bro?' Sid asked Ramanujam surreptitiously, walking beside him. Sid 'Charsi' Malhotra, Ramanujam's classmate and housemate, was always on the lookout for a reason to party. If the more informed students were to be believed, he was the biggest user and supplier of intoxicants at Woodsville. His speech was usually slurred, his body almost malnourished and his gait distinctly swaggering. Despite this, he had never been caught, nor suspected by the administration.

'If I start giving parties every time I top in an exam,' Ramanujam said sarcastically, 'my guardian, the director, is going to have to sell Woodsville.'

Sid laughed; despite their age difference, he and Ramanujam had bonded quite well over the last month. Sid fancied himself to be something of a connoisseur when it came to reading characters, and Ramanujam made for an excellent subject. In return, Sid, through his drunken and drugged soirées with the hip and happening of Woodsville's student body, was an excellent source of information for Ramanujam.

As they passed the amphitheatre, Sid gave him an inquisitive glance.

'You look a little tense today,' he remarked. Ramanujam, who was something of a mystery for the entire school, was a complete enigma for Sid still.

Ramanujam shrugged as though he didn't know what Sid was talking about. When they finally reached their villa, Ramanujam took a deep breath, squared his shoulders, put on an arrogant grin and entered.

He had barely crossed the living room and thrown his bag in his room, before his other two housemates appeared in the doorway.

'So this pansy topped, eh?' said Keshav casually. Only Ramanujam's practised ears could catch the hint of bitterness in his voice.

'Yeah,' Tushar quipped, 'I remember he told us he watched movies all day.'

Ramanujam steeled himself. His housemates had just realized that he was a scrawny little nerd, and they were pissed off for being scared of him for the past one month. Ramanujam, on the other hand, had spent that time baiting them constantly.

He smirked. 'Well, you little puppies shouldn't have believed me then, should you?'

Keshav balked. Ramanujam's bravado threw them. What was about to happen had to happen at some point, and Ramanujam saw no sense in delaying things. So he taunted them further.

'You see,' he continued sagely, 'I prefer to keep the people around me in the dark, so that you don't share my strategies with someone not as big a moron as yourself—'

'Grab the bastard!' Keshav snarled, and both he and Tushar jumped towards Ramanujam.

Ramanujam, who was on the other side of his bed, let the two of them flounder on the bed as they tried to reach for him. He simply walked over to the mirror behind him, and smashed his face right into the glass.

He heard gasps even as he turned around and gingerly took the pieces of glass out of his face. With practice, he'd learnt not to injure his eyes.

'You shouldn't have done that, fellas,' Ramanujam murmured to his shocked audience.

'Done what?' Tushar croaked. 'What the hell did *you* do?'

There was a clatter of footsteps and Sid came running in. 'What happened?'

Ramanujam contorted his face in pain and fear. 'I am sorry I topped! Please tell them not to hurt me any more!' He started bawling at the top of his voice. Tears ran down his face freely.

As Sid took a step forward, Tushar and Keshav took a step back.

'What the fuck did we do?' Tushar said. 'He bashed his face into the glass himself.'

Keshav must've realized how stupid Tushar's words had sounded, so he put up his hands in a conciliatory gesture.

'Listen,' said Keshav, his voice sounding reasonable in his fear. 'Let's forget this happened and let's not bother each other any more.'

Ramanujam immediately stopped crying and shrugged. 'Okay.'

Keshav looked disarmed at the sudden change of tone and unconvinced of Ramanujam's forgiveness.

'We can take you to the infirmary,' he said politely.

Ramanujam pointed at his face. 'You want people to ask how this happened?'

'No!' Keshav and Tushar said simultaneously. Sid, smarter than both of them, laughed silently as he understood what had happened.

'The next time you think you can hurt me,' Ramanujam said to them, gingerly removing a shard from his cheek, 'just remember I am better at it. Now get the fuck out of my room.'

As Keshav and Tushar left the room like whipped puppies, Sid gave Ramanujam an appreciative nod and left as well. Ramanujam locked the door, went into the bathroom and withdrew a box of disinfectant from the closet. He always kept it handy.

After fifteen minutes of cleansing and wincing, with one fist clenched between his teeth, Ramanujam looked at himself in the bathroom mirror. His scarred, pale reflection stared back at him. As usual, he'd refused to be housed with kids his own age. And seventeen-year-old bullies needed a severe demonstration of what he was capable of.

They weren't the only ones, Ramanujam knew. Others like them waited for him at school, seething with envy and annoyance . . . but his face couldn't handle any more smashing into mirrors.

These scars would set right in with the ones his erstwhile adoptive parents had given him, and the ones he'd given himself in order to get away from them. Without fail, each of the eight families that he had been with had treated him like a lottery ticket. Other kids at the orphanage had waited in vain to be adopted, but once Ramanujam's talents had become apparent, he'd never had a problem finding a family to welcome him with open arms. And it didn't take him long to wish he had never been adopted.

Ramanujam had to act, but first he needed information. For that, he needed to see a therapist.

*

Athar was already weary with the day's work and about to pack up, when Ramanujam had contacted him and asked for a session immediately. Athar, who knew of Ramanujam's troubled and abusive childhood, had been too intrigued to refuse.

'May I know about the scars?' Athar asked the funny little creature sitting across from him.

Ramanujam, who'd been looking around the office with some interest, stopped to meet Athar's gaze.

'Oh, the scars, the scars,' he cried out dramatically. 'What shall I tell you about the scars? There are some on my face, but they don't hurt as much as the ones within.'

Athar couldn't be sure whether he was play-acting, so he went along.

'Are you referring to your parents?'

If Ramanujam had been acting before, he certainly wasn't acting now. He looked up sharply and snapped scathingly, 'What parents?'

Athar held his tongue. His job was to listen. He changed tack.

'That's a pretty unusual name you have.'

'Better than being called Chhotu all the time,' Ramanujam muttered, shifting uncomfortably in his seat. 'You mind if I walk around?'

'By all means,' Athar said, looking closely at him. 'Chhotu?'

Ramanujam was fidgeting as he circled the office. 'I was always smaller than the others.' His voice was sardonic.

'Then how did you get—?'

'I named myself, all right,' Ramanujam said shortly. 'Once I knew what I was.'

He had reached the bathroom door. Suddenly, without warning, he opened the door and went inside, bawling, 'Wasn't like I had any parents to do that!'

Alarmed, concerned, Athar followed him inside. The bathroom seemed empty. And then, out of the corner of his eye, he saw a figure move laterally. He turned around to see the door swing shut with a loud bang.

For a moment, Athar wasn't sure what had happened.

'Don't worry, Doc,' Ramanujam called out cheerfully, 'it'll take only a little while. I'll let you out before I leave. It's just that there are some really interesting things in these files of yours.'

'Don't do it, Ram,' Athar called out, trying hard not to panic. 'Those students are no less troubled than you. You cannot profit from their problems.'

'On the contrary, Doctor, I think I can.'

Athar cursed himself. It was late, and no one would hear his shouts for help, and his cell phone lay on his table.

After what seemed like two lifetimes, there was a resounding, triumphant 'aha!' and Athar's heart turned to ice. There was a click and the bathroom door opened. Ramanujam stood outside, grinning.

'You've been naughty, Doctor,' Ramanujam pointed at him with a file clutched in his hand. Athar saw the name on the file and closed his eyes. Himanshu Pathak.

'Give me the file, Ramanujam.' Athar held out his hand.

Ramanujam casually threw the file on Athar's desk.

'I have an eidetic memory, Doctor, I can reproduce everything I have read in here verbatim,' Ramanujam said, tapping his forehead. 'It's already in here.'

'You'll be expelled for this,' Athar said sharply, walking forward and surveying the damage. With growing dread, he saw the psych. files of Rikkhe, Dev, Aniket and Vishakha lying open on his desk along with Himanshu's.

Ramanujam smiled. 'Oh, let's not kid each other. You are not going to report this, not if you want to keep your job.' He pointed at Himanshu's file. 'Like I said, you have been very naughty.'

Athar experienced a constriction in his chest.

Ramanujam started to leave. 'You know,' he stopped and said thoughtfully, 'I was never a big fan of therapy, but I dare say you have changed my mind.'

*

After facing sixty deliveries at more than 130 kmph, with seven lbws and nine body hits, Dev was exhausted and red-faced. It wasn't even five in the morning yet.

'Take ten, Dev!' his coach roared. He had bowled those sixty deliveries. It took a lot out of the forty-five-year-old retired international cricketer to maintain the pace, but he made the effort for his star student, who wasn't proving to be much of a star right now.

'Take ten, Dev,' he barked again. 'Wash your face, clear your mind! It'll take much more than this if you want to wear the blue! And even more to keep it on!'

Dev grunted and walked away from the nets towards the benches. *Clear your mind*. It was easy for the coach to say; he'd been kicked out of the Indian team in the middle of his career due to non-performance. Life was easy for a loser. It was easy for a loser to clear his mind. For someone like Dev, though? Not so much.

The truth was, Dev was waiting for a phone call. And it was a call he simply couldn't put out of his mind. So he sat on the bench and waited. As the adrenaline from practising with the dangerous leather ball faded gradually, he suddenly felt overcome with drowsiness. His eyes were almost shut when the phone rang.

'Good evening, Mom,' he said lightly. It *was* evening in the States.

'Uh, yes, Deb. How're you?' she said in that thick American accent that Dev had come to identify his childhood with and, in turn, loathe. Without waiting for an answer, she continued, 'You have to come back home, son.'

'As my grandfather has already conveyed to you, I'm sure, I have no interest in coming back.'

'What's keeping you there?' she asked sharply. He could almost see her frowning. 'From what I hear, you've lost your election.'

'And you want my help to win yours?' Dev scoffed.

He knew his mother was scowling now. 'Two months. That's all I'm asking.'

'In my final year at Woodsville?' Dev said incredulously. 'That's not how things work here.'

'Ask your grandfather to use that renowned *clout* of his. He's friends with your headmaster, is he not?'

'And you'd do well to remember that influence,' Dev snapped, 'in case you get any ideas about forcing me to come out there.'

There was a long silence on the other end. 'Adviser to the home minister *and* the defence minister, oh my,' Mrs Ranjini Bhushan remarked wryly. 'How do you reckon you'll be able to resist when *he* forces you to fight for his country?'

'Oh, I'll fight for *my* country all right,' Dev said with contained fury, looking at the cricket pitch. 'Doesn't have to be in the air force.'

'You have the old fool's patriotism.'

'At least I don't have my father's cowardice,' Dev said. 'I'll face grandfather when the time comes, instead of running away.'

'You're right,' his mother sighed, 'you're not your father. You're much worse. You take after that vile old fox.'

'I won't leave this country for you. And I won't leave cricket for him. That's a promise.'

'That's a fool's hope.'

Dev opened his mouth to retort but his mother cut him off. There was a tone of finality in her voice.

'You train now, son. Remember, though, there'll come a day when you'll realize that running away from that man is the only way any Bhushan can hope to live the life they want. Train hard, but remember that it'll never be more than a hobby.'

She hung up. Dev stared hard at his phone for a few seconds. Then he got up and made his way back to the nets. His whole body was shaking. He hated his mother, but he did have something in common with his parents. None of them had any idea how to stand up to Brij Kishore Bhushan.

He took his place at the wicket, and his coach bowled. Dev swung his bat as hard as he could, but missed—yet again.

'Concentrate, Dev!' his coach yelled at him from the other side of the net. 'You are a batsman, not a damn baboon.'

Dev's face reddened. Covered in sweat and dirt at five in the morning, he had finally had enough. He threw the bat on the ground, breaking it in two.

'To hell with this!' he snarled, leaving his coach and the people around him stunned. Walking towards the pavilion, he could hear the coach calling after him, but he didn't turn back. He didn't care. Everything he cared about had been snatched away from him in a matter of months: being head scholar, commanding fear and respect, his natural ability to charm women. And if he wasn't going to have a future in cricket, what was the point of practising?

Suddenly, he didn't know what he was doing in India any more. He wasn't sure if it was loyalty that made him stay on, or pure stubbornness. All he knew was that he couldn't leave in disgrace.

He reached the dressing room and vehemently started emptying his locker. A knock on the door made him turn. He blanched. Ramanujam stood in the doorway, his face a mask of calm. It gave Dev pleasure to see scars all over his face; somebody had already got to the rascal, then.

Dev stepped forward instinctively.

'I know that you probably want to tie me up and shut me in your locker,' Ramanujam said. Dev stopped, disarmed, because that was exactly what he wanted to do. 'But you'd better listen to what I have to say.'

Dev paused and then got back to emptying his locker; he had to make room for Ramanujam, after all. 'I have no interest in what you have to say, scum, so you better save your breath. You're going to need it.'

Ramanujam held up his hands innocently. 'I was new here, man. That guy Himanshu told me to slap you. He said it was some sort of a ragging ritual.'

'What?'

'Right hand to God, or whichever dude you believe in,' Ramanujam replied solemnly.

Dev was still unconvinced. 'You didn't look like someone who was forced to do it.'

'Well, I do love a little violence,' Ramanujam admitted, 'but mindless violence? Oh no.'

Dev shook his head. It didn't matter if Ramanujam was telling the truth or not. It wasn't going to change the reality of his situation.

'They didn't betray you, Dev,' Ramanujam remarked quietly. 'The school, the students, they never betrayed you.'

That feeling of being cheated, of losing the election, which Dev had nursed for weeks, resurfaced. 'What?'

'The election was rigged,' Ramanujam said, 'and I can help you get the people responsible. Woodsville needs its star student.'

Despite himself, Dev found himself believing Ramanujam. The place he'd given so much to wouldn't treat him like this. 'What do you want?' he croaked.

Ramanujam grinned mischievously. 'Call me a saint or whatever, but I am here to give you your life back.'

*

'You sure about this?' Vivek asked uncertainly, trying to keep up with Himanshu's pace.

Himanshu shook his head, his teeth clenched.

'Then why don't you just let it go?'

'It's been two weeks, buddy. I have been constantly badgering the administration about following up on Rina's complaint, but they seem simply unwilling to do anything.'

'You've had this post for just a month and a half, and you're ready to stir up an agitation?' Vivek was echoing Himanshu's own doubts.

'I told you I am *not* ready, but this is the first time the administration has refused a request of mine. I have to make sure it doesn't become a habit.'

'But you don't even know what might happen here!' Vivek pointed an ominous finger at the door Himanshu had stopped in front of. The sign on the door read 'Student

Council Office'. 'What if the house captains don't comply? You won't have *any* real say in school policy after that.'

Himanshu stopped to ponder. It was the first time he'd called the council for a meeting. He knew that technically he *could* call a student strike by himself, but he wanted to do everything by the book. Hence the meeting. Besides, on the other side of that door were the four house captains, some of whom held substantial sway over the students. The only problem was that Himanshu didn't hold any sway over *them*.

Himanshu took a deep breath. 'Here goes.' He went in, leaving Vivek outside.

The room was surprisingly small and quite well lit. Himanshu felt guilty as soon as he stepped in, feeling somewhat responsible for not paying more attention to his 'office'. Unkempt, dusty shelves pressed against the marble walls, filled with stacks of the new Woodsville constitution. In the centre was an equally dusty circular table, which had five chairs around it. And in front of each chair, on the table, stood a brand-new metal plate, indicating their posts.

Azad, Lakshmibai, Sardar and Bismil: the four houses of Woodsville, named after the fiercest freedom fighters. And behind each name sat its house captain—Aniket Jain, Radhika Goel, Dev Bhushan and Yash Malik, in that order.

Dev Bhushan got up and extended a hand towards Himanshu who avoided his eyes. Dev was smiling warmly at Himanshu, which only freaked him out further.

'Himanshu, never really got to congratulate you,' Dev said, shaking his hand, 'but we'll have plenty of time for that now.' He gestured at the table. 'And anyway, being house captain doesn't seem so bad either.' He laughed. 'I'm just glad there were no elections for it.'

'Yeah . . . um . . . hey, everybody,' Himanshu said nervously, telling himself that all these procedures were new to the house captains as well.

Himanshu nodded to himself, then took the fifth chair, behind the metal plate that read 'Head Scholar'.

'I take it you've all read the constitution?' he asked tentatively, as Dev took his seat behind 'Sardar'.

Radhika nodded diligently, while Yash gave a careless shrug. Aniket and Dev made affirmative gestures.

'Well, it's pretty simple, actually,' Himanshu continued. 'The constitution says that a strike can be called with the unanimous consent of all members of the student council. So here we are.'

Radhika looked dubious. She was a model student, disciplined and conscientious; a strike went against her very nature. 'A strike? What about?'

Himanshu dived right into the story. 'A couple of weeks back, Rina Singh, a student of class ten, approached me and complained about an instance of cheating—by the unit topper, Lalit Nagpaul, who used his cell phone to look up an answer. She had a number of students to back her claim.' Himanshu paused, gauging their reaction. 'Now, this is a serious allegation and I doubt someone would make it all up.'

Yash snorted. 'Lalit Nagpaul, I know that wimp. His daddy pistol-whips him every time he comes second.' He grinned gleefully. 'Last year he came third. I can only imagine what punishment he got.'

Aniket frowned, and Himanshu felt pity for the boy.

'But why a strike?' Radhika asked doggedly.

'My repeated attempts at getting the admin or the controller of examination to take action have yielded nothing,' Himanshu said bluntly. 'They are intent on acting as though it didn't happen. I guess they are afraid of this becoming public.'

Aniket nodded. He knew how Walia abhorred scandals.

Now Yash Malik looked uncomfortable; he was, after all, Walia's pet. 'But what exactly would a strike accomplish? Even if the administration agrees to investigate the incident, they can simply deny this incident ever took place.'

Himanshu nodded. 'That is why we are not calling a strike for an investigation.'

'What for, then?' Aniket asked, eyebrows raised.

'We won't actually call a strike at all.'

Radhika frowned. 'Why are we here then?'

'We are here because I want your support before I threaten Admin Kumari with a strike if she doesn't ban cell phones inside the campus.'

The reaction, as Himanshu had predicted, was incredulity.

'I'm not even going to go into the loopholes in your plan,' Yash said slowly, 'but why on earth do you think the students would support having their life force snatched from them?'

Himanshu considered it. 'Actually, I was counting on you, Dev. You're the only person here whom the students really listen to. And if we can't convince the students, we simply bluff the admin.'

Dev seemed to ponder over the statement, but no one really knew what to say. Himanshu could tell that they thought him crazy.

'Listen,' he said insistently, 'I've been asking around, and the incident with Lalit was not the only one. It has become common practice among the younger students. *We* might not have seen it, but trust me, it is becoming increasingly prevalent.'

'And you plan to enforce the ban in the student residential area too?' Aniket asked sharply.

'Yes,' Himanshu said with gritted teeth, 'it must be all over. We cannot have a daily checking of the students; the phones must be got rid of in one go. Also, isn't there a landline in every student house?'

Aniket frowned. 'Yeah, and it's in the living room. Why don't you try talking on the phone while everyone in the house can listen to you?'

Dev smacked the table. 'This is going nowhere. I think Himanshu is right in principle, but we should discuss the feasibility of the action again, once the council talks to Admin Kumari about this.'

Himanshu was taken aback. He hadn't expected Dev to be so reasonable.

'I'll schedule a meeting for tomorrow evening,' he said gratefully. 'I hope it won't come to a strike.'

Himanshu cringed as he got up. It was Dev, not him, who had taken control. If this was the way future discussions were going to go in the council, then he was useless as the head scholar.

He nodded at everyone and left.

Once the door clicked shut behind Himanshu, Dev continued, quite calmly, 'I fear for the student body with him in charge,' he said, pointing towards the door. 'A strike, really? He is reckless and arrogant, and will soon corrode all the influence this council wields.'

Aniket and Radhika seemed confused, while Yash watched intently.

Dev grimaced. 'This is a bit premature, as we need the director present for such a decision, but I call for a vote— and remember, the constitution says that this vote must be unanimous.'

He stood up and put a hand over his heart. 'All those in favour of sacking Himanshu Pathak from the post of head scholar, please raise your hands.'

*

Aniket stayed in the library longer than usual that night. The events of the afternoon had left him shaken, more so because of the part he had played in them. After Himanshu had left, Aniket's own actions had surprised even him.

The Woodsville library was open 24/7, and Aniket spent an inordinate amount of time there. The atmosphere, for him, was deeply calming. Until it was disturbed by the most unwelcome apparition.

'Mr Jain,' said Ramanujam ominously. Aniket looked up and instinctively put a protective hand over his accountancy notes. Ramanujam smirked.

'May I join you?' he asked politely. Aniket had half a mind to refuse, but then Ramanujam leaned in and said in an undertone, 'I never had the courage to say this to you before, but you are, like, my idol. There's so much I'd like to learn from you.'

Aniket blinked. 'Yeah? Sit down, sit down,' he said airily.

Ramanujam sat down gratefully. He and Aniket stared at each other.

'You must be pissed at Himanshu Pathak, no?' Ramanujam said abruptly after a few moments of silence.

Aniket was taken aback. 'Where did that come from?'

'Well,' he leaned in again, 'he became head scholar, when clearly *you* deserved it.'

Aniket beamed at him. *Finally someone with brains.* 'I know, right?'

Ramanujam smirked. 'And then there was that incident atop the water tank right after they announced the result . . .'

Aniket squirmed but was defiant. 'That wasn't related; I just sometimes like to let my hair down and party. But yeah, Pathak shouldn't have won.'

Ramanujam smiled. 'Then why did you vote against removing him from the post today at the council meeting?'

Aniket opened his mouth, but could think of nothing to say; he stuttered incoherent questions instead.

'How—how did you—?'

Ramanujam waved that aside. 'Beside the point. What I want to know is why you did it.'

Aniket scowled and stood up, simultaneously gathering up his books. Ramanujam jumped up and grabbed Aniket's hand with an unyielding grip.

'I apologize, Mr Jain,' he said with a grimace. 'I sometimes deal with such dunces that I forget not everyone reveals their cards without asking for something in exchange. Please sit.'

Aniket stopped and sat down again. Ramanujam, however, remained standing, looking down at him, calculating.

'If I had to take a guess,' Ramanujam said slowly, 'it would be that you're afraid. You are afraid that if you remove Pathak, someone *else* might outshine you.'

Aniket pursed his lips, stunned at Ramanujam's astuteness. What he did not know was that Ramanujam now knew everything Aniket had ever told Athar, and everything Athar had deduced about him, jotted down neatly in his file.

'First Dev, then Himanshu—now me?' Ramanujam said in an understanding, reassuring tone. 'The possibility that someone new might become head scholar must be frightening, I get it.'

Aniket shook his head, trying to clear it. How was Ramanujam saying exactly what Aniket was thinking?

'I'll make you a deal,' Ramanujam continued, jovially slapping Aniket on the shoulder. 'You go with whatever Dev Bhushan wants in the student council, and I promise not to beat you in an exam ever again.'

Aniket was lost for words.

'You think about it, and take a decision tomorrow during the council's meeting with the admin. I'll know about it.'

Ramanujam left Aniket alone in the library, carefully closing the door shut behind him. Right outside, waiting, stood Dev.

'How did it—?' Dev began tensely, but Ramanujam cut him short.

'Now you listen to me,' he hissed at Dev. 'Aniket Jain will cooperate with you, but removing Pathak from the post of head scholar is *only* a threat. Don't even think about pulling a stunt like you did today at the council meeting.'

Dev frowned. 'But why try and get him into the student residential area when there can be a unanimous vote to oust him?'

'Because I need him here at Woodsville,' he replied quietly. 'And because I don't intend to just dethrone him, I intend to decapitate him.'

Dev didn't really like the way this angel of death talked about hurting people, but he let it slide. He had too much at stake.

Ramanujam sensed his scepticism and took a step closer to him. Despite the difference in their sizes, Dev steeled himself.

'Now I promised you Pathak's position, but remember this—you'll only get it *my* way. Deviate from my instructions, and you're on your own.'

'How do I know you won't try to grab the position yourself?'

'Rikkhe Rajput didn't, and thus neither will I.'

'And what exactly *is* your way?' Dev asked, his lips pursed.

'Well,' Ramanujam said mysteriously, 'let's just say that when I am through with Pathak, Rajput will think twice before setting up a puppet king.'

*

Administrator Jaya Kumari, with a hawk-like face and an eagle-like grasp, was not generally liked; she herself had no illusions about that fact, although she did occasionally allow herself to forget it. It was days like today that she had to reinforce public perception.

'So, ma'am,' said the pimple-faced boy, 'I hope you won't call my parents. My mother has a weak heart, see, and she wouldn't be able to bear it if I got suspended.'

He surreptitiously pushed the carefully counted ten 1000-rupee notes on to the finely polished table.

Kumari smiled sympathetically. 'I understand.' She picked up the phone and dialled. 'Mrs Anuradha Mahajan?' The kid panicked and frantically pointed at the money lying on the table. Kumari smiled at him. The calm smile only increased his state of panic. He hurriedly added more notes to the pile, as if it wasn't already big enough. Kumari paid it no attention.

'This is Jaya Kumari from Woodsville International. I would like to speak to you regarding your son.'

The kid, arrogant and self-assured a minute ago, was now on his knees, begging, his hands folded.

'Yes. Your son was found inebriated in class, trying to distribute liquor to classmates.'

The boy made a whimpering sound. Kumari spared him a glance. These youngsters never stopped surprising her. She was amazed that her allegations were actually true.

'When brought to my office, he tried to bribe his way out of punishment. Some—' she looked at the pile of notes in front of her, 'twenty or thirty thousand rupees are now lying on my table.'

The boy was close to fainting.

'As a result, we have no option but to expel him.'

He looked as though he'd been given a death sentence. Kumari had learnt over the years that although all kids were terrified of what their parents could take away from them, rich kids simply had a lot more to lose.

Kumari hung up and looked at the boy. Not for a second did she think he was worried about his mother's weak heart. Just his own.

'Get up. You are a Villean. Have some pride.' Kumari's voice was cold.

The kid did so, his knees shaking.

Jaya looked at him squarely. 'Now pull a stunt like that in my school again, and I will *actually* call your mother.'

He looked at her in shock; his gaze carried both relief and revulsion.

'Leave now. And take this money.'

Kumari sometimes had to be cruel to get through to these students. She didn't usually lose sleep over it, though; students might occasionally respect a woman they didn't fear, but they would never be controlled by her. Kumari, as the administrator, needed control.

Still, she had two children of her own. And she felt a rare pang of guilt as the boy trudged out, jolted. She picked up the phone and pressed the intercom button.

'Send them in.'

Kumari took a deep breath and closed her eyes. She had to handle this delicately, which wasn't her style. But she knew Himanshu Pathak's complaint was genuine, and if the student council backed him, they could be a nuisance. Nuisances were what Walia had hired her to take care of.

In came Dev Bhushan, a wide smile on his face, followed by Himanshu Pathak, Aniket Jain, Radhika Goel and Yash Malik. Yash nodded at Kumari as he entered.

Kumari didn't get up from her chair, nor did she ask them to sit.

'Be quick, Mr Pathak,' she said icily. 'I have other things to do.'

Himanshu, who had been looking a little wary now, straightened up and looked Kumari squarely in the eye.

'Apparently. Anyway, the student council wants action taken on the matter of Lalit Nagpaul of class ten. He cheated. We have people who will corroborate Rina Singh's allegations. All of them are waiting outside, if you want to hear from them.'

Kumari raised an eyebrow. *Articulate, precise and direct.* Her experienced eye saw in him a budding lawyer.

'I heard about it. The girl should have complained then and there. Why did she hide it until the boy trounced her in the tests?'

Himanshu frowned as the others looked at him in anticipation.

'The girl's actions do not absolve the boy,' he said sharply. 'If you are unable to take a decision, the student council will. I am afraid that this was not an isolated incident. Other such cases have gone unreported; the management was just too complacent and ignorant to do anything about it.' People seldom looked Kumari in the eye while criticizing her, but Himanshu never once blinked. 'After you have dealt with Lalit Nagpaul, the student council will propose a ban on cell phones inside the campus.'

Kumari had to admire his guts. Touching cell phones was something even she couldn't contemplate, although she herself had wanted to ban them for quite some time now. Half the complaints that came to her were somehow tied up with the use of cell phones.

'If I may,' Dev interjected, having been silent so far. Kumari turned her attention away from Himanshu and noticed that the house captains were looking uncertain. 'I happen to disagree with Himanshu on that last point. The student council, barring Himanshu, is not in favour of this idea. And if you don't go along with it, he plans to call a student strike.'

Himanshu turned around, stunned, but Dev continued.

'Someone who isn't living inside the campus shouldn't even be contemplating such a drastic policy change. The only condition on which I'll support Himanshu is if he agrees to take up residence here at Woodsville.'

Kumari could see from Himanshu's face that he was thinking hard. Finally, he spoke up.

'That's not possible,' Himanshu said in a defeated voice. It was evident from his tone that he hadn't wanted to say what he just had.

'Then it is clear that this decision didn't mean much to you.'

'It did, and I didn't take it hastily.'

'Then shift.'

He couldn't leave his mother alone in that house. 'I simply cannot.'

Dev sighed exaggeratedly. 'You leave me no choice, then. The council feels that he isn't fit for the duties accorded to him. The decision, I feel,' he stole a glance at Aniket, 'will be unanimous.'

Kumari's mind was racing. The guilty faces of the house captains told her that they were complicit in this move. She tried to think of how this would affect Woodsville—to have the head scholar evicted after less than a few months of his tenure. What precedent would it set for the future?

Himanshu's fast breathing was very conspicuous in the silence.

'*Is* the decision unanimous?' Kumari asked seriously.

'We can take a vote before going to Walia Sir,' Dev said unabashedly.

Kumari looked at the lot expectantly.

'I'm with Dev,' Yash said immediately. Kumari smirked inwardly; it was no secret that Walia had been shocked by the election verdict. Yash was doing what he thought would please the director.

Radhika nodded reluctantly. 'I'm sorry, Himanshu,' she said weakly, 'but calling a strike for such a thing is too extreme. If that's the way you're going to react to issues, it'll become an annoyance for everyone.'

Surprisingly, Himanshu had regained his composure by now. 'Deciding to kick me out without even giving me a chance to explain is also extreme, Radhika.' Himanshu looked coldly at the house captains. 'If this is the way you are going to react to issues within the council, you are no good to the students.'

Radhika had the grace to look a mite ashamed of herself.

'Aniket?' Kumari asked pointedly.

Aniket hadn't looked up once since he'd entered. Now he did, his eyes determined. He nodded.

Kumari didn't know it, but she and Himanshu both dreaded what would come next more than what had already taken place. This scene would have to play out again, and this time in front of the director.

*

The Pathak estate, including the mansion, was uncommonly quiet that night. Himanshu, who had been sent home while his fate was decided by the house captains and Director Walia, sat beside the well-lit pool, silent and speculative.

'Why did you say no to their condition, dammit?' Vivek brought him out of his reverie. 'Is it better to stay at home and be nothing or stay on campus and be the most celebrated student of the country?'

'I can't leave my mom,' Himanshu said for the umpteenth time. 'Not with him.'

Vivek's strangled sound of irritation echoed Himanshu's own helplessness.

'Why doesn't she simply leave your father, then?' Vivek asked hopefully.

Her reputation. Her status. Her children. Himanshu shook his head vigorously and his spectacles came forward, towards the tip of his nose.

'Where is he anyway?' Vivek prodded him.

Himanshu shrugged. 'At some convention in Berlin . . . with a woman he met in Paris.'

Vivek raised an impressed eyebrow and Himanshu chuckled. At times like this he didn't know whether he detested his father or admired him. Shreyas Pathak was everything Geeta Pathak wanted her son to be—ambitious, successful, charming . . . and ruthless.

The roar of an old Chevrolet shattered the silence. Himanshu and Vivek got up and headed towards the house. Through the glass walls of the drawing room, Himanshu saw Director Walia get out of the car.

'You'd better disappear, Vivek,' Himanshu warned him. 'Walia isn't going to be too pleased with me. It won't do you any good to be seen with me.'

Vivek nodded and turned on his heel and vanished into the night, while Himanshu walked through the house to the driveway.

'Good evening, sir,' Himanshu said, approaching him. Walia looked ruffled and very much unlike his usual cheery self.

'Good evening, boy,' Walia said roughly. 'Although, I must say, you didn't make it a very good afternoon for me.'

Himanshu tried to look apologetic as he touched the director's feet and walked him in.

'Are you here to talk to my mother?' Himanshu asked.

Walia gave Himanshu a furtive glace. The boy didn't look anxious to learn the outcome of today's fiasco. Himanshu Pathak perplexed Walia, even with Athar giving him weekly reports of their sessions.

'I don't think it will do any good to talk to you, will it?'

Himanshu stopped walking. 'I won't back down from the issue, sir.'

Walia opened his mouth, then closed it. 'The issue? The issue is whether you'll be the first Villean to get *kicked* out from the post of head scholar. You know the house captains voted for your dismissal?'

Himanshu nodded. 'I also know that you wouldn't be here talking to me were I not still the head scholar of your school . . . Nanaji.'

Himanshu heard his mother's car pull up outside. She came rushing in, beaming at Walia. 'Dad!' Her eyes were moist as she hugged him. 'It's been so long. I hope I didn't make you wait.'

Himanshu smiled. At least some good had come of Walia's visit.

Walia clumsily patted her head and led her to the drawing-room sofa. Himanshu sat before them.

'No, I just got here. So, um, how's work?' Walia asked gingerly.

Himanshu frowned as all traces of emotion were wiped clean from his mother's face and she sat up straight.

'The quarterly reports are in and we are doing much better than we were a year ago. The profit margin is good but the market share is still low. We are working around the clock, contemplating a number of acquisitions and tie-ups. But the retailers are proving unforgiving for a manufacturer like us. We need a reputation that isn't merely built on word of mouth alone. We need a viable, long-term media partner. What would you suggest?'

Walia had been listening with rapt attention, whereas Himanshu hadn't caught a word. He was lost in thought. His mother was a wreck—an efficient, successful wreck, but a wreck nonetheless. Left to his grandfather's machinations, Himanshu was headed the same route.

'I have someone in mind,' Walia said. 'These guys are experienced media professionals, but lack the funds. Once you meet them, I dare say you'll want to expand into the media sector yourself. I'll have my assistant forward the references to you.' He paused. 'I am really happy to see you doing so well. I wish I could say the same about your son.'

Geeta, who had smiled artificially at the compliment, was so engrossed in her performance that it took her a few moments to stop smiling.

'What do you mean?'

Himanshu took deep breaths.

'He almost had his title taken away from him today.'

'Title? What title?' Geeta was genuinely confused and even forgot her own troubles for a moment.

Walia stared at his daughter and then looked incredulously at Himanshu. 'You never even told your mother?' He turned to the bewildered woman. 'He was elected Woodsville's head scholar in April.'

Geeta Pathak's face displayed a second of blank shock before she rounded on Himanshu.

'What is this?'

Himanshu, practised at calming his mother, raised a soothing hand. 'It was nothing to be proud of. I wanted to wait until I had actually accomplished something. Anyway, it's probably not going to happen now.'

Himanshu was dreading the thought of going to school the next day, disgraced.

Geeta opened her mouth, all set to admonish him, but Walia cut in.

'I never understood this boy of yours, Geeta,' he said placatingly, 'and I suggest you stop trying as well. Let's focus on the issue at hand.'

Himanshu wholly agreed. 'First of all, why did you say I *almost* lost my title?'

'Because you did not lose it.'

Himanshu was in no mood for games. 'How is that possible? I rejected Dev's offer to stay in the hostel. Case closed.'

'Yeah,' said Walia, slowly and thoughtfully, 'for some reason he seemed really stuck on that point . . . didn't relent even when I wrote his expulsion letter.'

Himanshu stood up with a start. 'You expelled him?' he exclaimed.

'Don't be silly,' Walia said patronizingly. 'Dev Bhushan will be an icon some day. And when that day comes, he has to be known as a Woodsville alumnus.'

'If he didn't budge, how come I'm still——?'

'The others were more cooperative,' Walia said, sounding satisfied. 'They want you to come to the hostel to prove your resolve, but not so desperately as to forsake their posts.'

Himanshu walked away from his grandfather. He looked out through the glass wall at the pool outside, wondering. Was his grandfather actually doing something that wasn't self-serving?

'You threatened them?' he asked quietly, straightening his spectacles. His vision blurred for a moment.

'No, I simply stated a fact—their captaincy was dependent on how cooperative they would be with the head scholar,' Walia said calmly.

'Oh, Dad!' Geeta exclaimed gratefully, the tears back in her eyes.

Himanshu couldn't help but feel a little happy in spite of the guilt. For once, Walia had treated him as his grandson, and not some shameful anomaly.

'Don't think I did it for you,' Walia said sharply, bursting his bubble. 'In fact, I'm in full agreement with Dev—you are not fit for the post, or the responsibilities.'

'But, Dad—' Geeta began reproachfully. Himanshu turned back and raised a hand to silence her.

'Please, continue,' Himanshu said silkily. 'Why did you help me out, then?'

'Because of your mother,' Walia said soberly. 'She already has a lot to handle right now, and I didn't want to add your troubles to the list. But remember, Geeta and I are not always going to be able to fight your battles for you. Learn to take care of your own business.'

'You did Geeta Pathak a favour then, no?' Himanshu asked coldly.

'You could say that.'

Himanshu smirked bitterly, his hands clenched tightly into fists. 'What do you see when you look at her, sir?' He pointed towards his mother.

Walia frowned. 'What do you mean?'

Himanshu walked towards him angrily. 'When you look at her, do you see your daughter, or do you see the CFO of a multinational who *happens* to be the mother of one of your students?'

Walia was silent. Himanshu's mother shot him a look, both warning and pleading at once, but Himanshu ignored her.

'I think it is the latter, sir. Because you don't do *favours* for your children.'

Walia stood up.

'Yes, leave,' Himanshu said, standing face-to-face with the director, 'and tell the house captains that I will move to the campus tomorrow, *before* I ban the phones.' He smiled at Walia. 'And I promise *you*, I will not leave until I am in complete control of my council.'

Walia seemed somewhat amused and pleasantly surprised at this outburst. 'Well, I wish you luck.' He nodded at Geeta and made for the door.

'And remember, Director,' Himanshu called out, 'now that I have succumbed to the council's wishes, my mother owes you no favour . . . neither do I.'

One thing time had proved was that the only place worse for his mother to be in than her husband's house, was in her father's debt.

*

The sun hadn't yet set on Woodsville, but the August afternoon was tinged with a greyish hue, owing to the late monsoon. It looked like it was about to rain, perhaps congruous with the arrival of the evening. The student residential area was littered with teenagers in their front yards, just back from school, who hadn't even bothered to keep their bags inside. The lovely cool air after an abnormally severe summer was something that the youngsters, despite inexperience, knew not to miss.

The light banter all over that had accentuated the liveliness in the air came to an abrupt still as something suddenly felt amiss in the scene . . .

Rikkhe Rajput walked down the street, his gaze focused and his shoulders squared, neither offering greetings, nor responding to any that came his way. On any other day, Rikkhe taking a stroll in such weather would have made the scene exude more grandeur, but presently it just seemed to disturb the decorum of things.

It wasn't because of his unbuttoned blue Jodhpuri jacket, his kurta, fluttering behind him as he walked briskly, or even his new earring. What seemed out of place were his eyes—purposeful, enraged and cold. And the fact that Vishakha Sahdev walked beside him, equally purposeful, didn't help diminish the attention they were getting.

Soon they were at the far end of a long line of houses. They turned left on to one of the few empty yards, walked up to the door and knocked.

It took a full minute and another knock before someone answered.

'Coming, coming—' said Himanshu, as he opened the door, and stopped short when he saw Rikkhe and Vishakha.

'I'm afraid, Himanshu,' Rikkhe began, although Himanshu's eyes were fixed on Vishakha, 'that I have to confess something.'

Himanshu looked coolly at Rikkhe. 'I bet you do.'

Rikkhe hesitated. 'It would be prudent to conduct this conversation inside. There are some who'll sleep better if not informed of our meeting.'

'Forgive my manners,' said Himanshu sardonically, 'and do come inside. I was almost done unpacking.'

Rikkhe ventured in smartly, while Vishakha was more hesitant.

'You don't need to confess,' Himanshu said bluntly, once they were ensconced in the safety and privacy of his new room. 'I know about the election.'

'*That* confession, Himanshu, I must admit, is meaningless, as you already know of my involvement in your victory. There is another, though, which will serve our immediate course of action better.'

'And what might that be?'

Rikkhe contemplated. 'There are some people I have upset with my actions in the past few months.' Himanshu snorted. 'And in order to undo those actions, they'll be targeting you. I have a feeling this forced move to the campus,' Rikkhe said pointedly, 'was just the beginning.'

Himanshu narrowed his eyes. 'How omniscient are you, my lord?'

Rikkhe was unperturbed. 'A friend told me about the council meeting.' At the blank look on Himanshu's face, he added, 'Radhika Goel, one of the guilty house captains.'

Himanshu grunted. 'And who might these "people" be?'

Vishakha answered, pacing between the unpacked suitcases on the floor. '*These people*,' she spat out contemptuously, 'are the ones that feel that being the best is a fucking team sport.' She added in anger, 'Ramanujam, Aniket and Dev.'

Despite himself, Himanshu felt a chill down his spine. 'And they are all working against me?'

Rikkhe put a hand on Himanshu's shoulder, which the latter felt too stunned to shrug off. 'From the looks of it, Ramanujam has seen to it that their interests align.' Rikkhe's voice grew stronger. 'I am here to propose,' he pointed, one by one, at the three of them, 'that since our interests already align, we should put them to use.' He smiled. 'After all, what's a team sport with only one team in the fray?'

THE PRINCE'S PLAY

'**W**HY DON'T YOU LISTEN?' Athar yelled.

Himanshu stared. 'I'm sorry, sir, but you need to calm down.'

Athar did, but with great difficulty. Himanshu raised a judging eyebrow. Admittedly, it had been some time since Himanshu had last attended a session with him, but that was no reason to bottle up all the counsel Athar had to offer.

It was evening, and exactly one day had passed since—after much deliberation—Himanshu had accepted Rikkhe's proposition.

'We have been over this, sir,' Himanshu said testily. 'I told Rikkhe that I wanted to have as little to do with Vishakha as humanly possible and that he'd have to be the go-between. Allying with her is in my interest. It has nothing to do with my feelings for her. Purely business.'

'But it can be so much more than that!' Athar countered earnestly.

Himanshu shook his head. 'It can't be. Sometimes I cannot get her out of my mind, you know.' He struggled to find the words. 'But sometimes she—she repulses me.'

Athar didn't know what to say to that.

'And besides, Vivek also agrees that—'

'Oh, SCREW VIVEK!'

Himanshu stood up and glared at Athar. 'That is my friend you are talking about.'

Athar seemed exasperated. 'A friend who's dragging you down, Himanshu . . . He has no future, nor does anyone who stays with him.'

Himanshu wondered what could possibly have affected Athar so greatly as to make him this harsh. He just seemed out of control today, insistent on imposing upon Himanshu whatever *he* felt right. Something was wrong and Himanshu had a feeling that Athar wanted to tell him what it was.

Athar put up his hands. 'You told me that Vishakha Sahdev, a girl you have been pining over for years, finally gives a damn about you, and you are seeking out advice from *Vivek*?'

Himanshu frowned.

'Vivek is the one who has held you back all these years,' Athar said vehemently, standing up, 'and Vishakha is the one who can take you forward.'

Himanshu turned to leave. He had had enough.

'Please be careful of Ramanujam, Himanshu,' Athar's voice changed so completely that Himanshu paused. He was pleading. 'He'll use your weaknesses against you.'

The doctor for mad people has gone mad, was all Himanshu could think. He spared him one confused glance before

163

he left. He was surprised to see Athar sink to his chair, exhausted and helpless.

*

'I am not glad that it turned out the way it did, either,' Radhika Goel hissed to Charu as Himanshu Pathak crossed them in the cricket stands. 'I did not want him to move to the hostel, I just wanted to belay that mad little idea of his.'

Within a week, the news had reached the ears of the sharpest of Villeans and the dumbest of Woozies—the head scholar had been whipped by the student council to leave his mansion and come live among them as a commoner. The reactions had been mixed; while some blamed the council for weakening the students' position with unnecessary dispute, others just enjoyed watching the drama being played out.

The house captains, including Radhika, were getting a lot of flak for it. Himanshu made his way to the very back, trying to avoid the many stares he was attracting. He had decided, as head scholar, to be part of all events. Moreover, it was due to his doggedness over the past couple of months that today's event had come to fruition.

Even with the attention he was getting, and despite it being the inaugural match of the first inter-house cricket tournament, it was Vishakha Sahdev who was stealing the show. In designer trousers and a frilly black top with a white shrug, she looked extremely elegant. Her hair fell in waves, her face looked radiant as the kohl accentuated her lively, animated eyes. Her movements were exquisitely delicate. Although Walia wasn't present, the huge screens were on, and the camera focused exclusively on Vishakha, even as Dev Bhushan led the Sardar House team on to the ground.

It was odd that Vishakha was getting such attention, but she seemed to be taking it in her stride. Himanshu tried not to look at that smiling, gloating, mesmerizing face on screen, resisting the temptation to use his post to acquire the footage of today's proceedings.

To most others, it seemed like Lisa Chauhan finally had a rival. Lisa, looking as flawless as ever, gazed appraisingly at the screen. Always fond of pretty things, the image before her earned an appreciative nod.

Such was the furore that the teams walking on the ground—Dev's Sardar and Aniket's Azad—also glanced intermittently at the screen that had ignored them completely. Aniket felt particularly fidgety. Not having made it to the school team, this was his debut match playing as the Azad House opener.

Vishakha reached into her glass-studded handbag, drew her phone and dialled. And although her face looked jovial as she spoke, Himanshu, though sitting more than fifty paces from her, could tell from her eyes that the person on the other end was being told off.

Her lips curved in an artificial smile. 'I didn't go to the length of borrowing my roomie's clothes just so you could cut them out of the frame, you idiot!' she hissed into the phone.

Shikhar Lohia, handling the two groups of professional cameramen his father had sent for the day, immediately bellowed instructions to them through the microphone. He had waited a long time to get another date with Vishakha, and he wasn't going to let a couple of bad camera angles mess it up.

The next instant, a much more stately view of Vishakha Sahdev swum across the stadium. She smiled widely.

Aniket Jain was visibly agitated. He gazed up at the screen in anger. He'd been preparing for this day for a while now, having taken time off from studying, something he felt he could afford to do, owing to his pact with Ramanujam. And here she was, stealing all the limelight. It was bad enough that Aniket hadn't been picked as the captain of his team.

He watched in trepidation as Azad House won the toss. Prashant, Aniket's captain, calmly chose to bat.

'You're up, stud,' Ashwin said from his left.

'Yeah, looks like it.' Aniket's mouth was dry. He had fought hard to become the opener of his team, the same position Dev played for his.

Ten minutes later, Aniket descended to the pitch in full gear. After two hours, as he left the ground at tea break, he was shaking with humiliation and anger. Of the forty balls he'd been bowled, he had made just two runs.

He looked at the screen, incredulous. It *still* had Vishakha; he had got less coverage as the primary batsman! They were making him a joke.

As he walked towards the boundary, he realized Vishakha was standing at the entrance to the pavilion, talking cheerily to Dev. Aniket quickened his pace; he knew the amount of screen time she'd got was no coincidence.

She was up to something and Aniket was the only person bold enough to confront her.

'A really good show there, Dev—' she was saying, shaking hands with him.

'What the hell do you think you are doing?' Aniket snarled at her, breaking away from his batting partner. A couple of players from Sardar also stopped to look, though from a safe distance.

Vishakha broke her gaze from Dev. 'What do you mean?'

'The fucking cameras! They just don't seem to be leaving you, and it's distracting as hell! What have you promised the cameramen in return, huh?'

To his extreme shock, Vishakha, instead of the usual snide remark or challenging smirk, put both her hands on her face and started crying. Everyone but Dev and Aniket recoiled; Dev stayed put out of confusion, and Aniket out of shock.

However, the shock of her crying didn't match the dreadful realization that hit him the next instant—the screen now showed him on one side, a neutral Dev in the middle and the crying Vishakha on the other.

'Vishakha?' Dev said tentatively.

With a wail, Vishakha flung herself on Dev's shoulder and wept harder. It was incredible how she had managed to produce such a copious amount of tears so quickly.

Dev patted her head awkwardly, acutely aware that all eyes were on him.

'Stop this charade,' Aniket hissed fearfully. 'Please.'

Vishakha reacted as though stung by a giant wasp. She jumped backwards and took cover behind Dev, hysterically pointing her index finger—and the nail art on it—at Aniket, the giant wasp.

It took Dev Bhushan, who was used to the scrutiny of his peers, a mere instant to take stock of the situation and gauge his position. A girl crying on his left, and her aggressor on his right; what was the school champion to do except swat the wasp?

Dev puffed out his chest, and while shielding Vishakha with one arm, used his other to roughly shove Aniket to the ground. Aniket was expecting neither such a reaction nor such strength. As soon as Dev's hefty arm hit his chest, he struggled to find his footing. In his uncertainty, he swung around, and his bat hit Dev right on his calves. Both he and Dev hit the ground at the same time.

As teammates and some of the staff rushed in to prevent a full-fledged fight, Himanshu looked sadly at Vishakha's face on the screen. He doubted whether anyone else could notice it, but through the fake tears, her eyes clearly told him that she had got exactly what she'd wanted.

*

Ramanujam grinned. 'So he's finally fighting back.' He leaned back leisurely on the stairs of the stone amphitheatre, looking up at the moonlit sky. The structure divided the student residences from the teachers', and at midnight, it was completely isolated, although Ramanujam was expecting company.

'Who's fighting?' asked Sid 'Charsi' Malhotra.

'Rajput, who else?'

'But Shikhar—the guy who was handling the camera crews—told me that it was on Vishakha's instructions that he'd focused only on her.' Sid snorted, his voice slurred because of the alcohol he had distributed and consumed in exchange for this information. 'She promised him a date, though after seeing what happened to Bhushan and Jain today, I am not sure he's so keen on it.'

'Nah . . .' Ramanujam said thoughtfully. 'The person who planned this knew exactly where and how to hit my guys. That person knew how they'd react, and what the upshot of it would be.'

'It still could've been Vishakha,' Sid said, offering a cigarette to Ramanujam, who carelessly declined. 'You're new here; you don't know half the stories floating about her. There's a rumour she once outsmarted bloody *Walia* himself.'

Ramanujam got up, annoyed that his housemate couldn't see what was so clear to him.

'The intended target today was not Dev; that was just a lucky accident—well, lucky for us. The one set up to take the fall today was Aniket Jain. And the one who set him up had to know that Aniket was working for me. And the only one who could've made such a connection is Rikkhe Rajput.' Ramanujam walked up and down the steps. 'I guess that girl Radhika told him how Aniket had so abruptly changed his position to match Dev's . . .'

'I don't know, man,' Sid said uncertainly, 'Rikkhe doesn't really seem the scheming type.'

Ramanujam snorted. For a long time he laughed mirthlessly, celebrating the irony of Sid's statement.

'That no one knows his reality,' Ramanujam said, containing himself, 'is the finest of his schemes.'

Suddenly there was the sound of footsteps, coming from opposite directions. While Aniket Jain appeared in front of them, emerging from the hostel grounds, Dev walked in from the side facing the main school building. Both of them stopped on the topmost step as they laid eyes on each other.

'In one corner,' Ramanujam shouted, startling everyone, 'is our current heavyweight champion, the Blob of Brawn, Dev Bhushan! And here comes the challenger, the Skinny Studious Speck, Aniket Jain! Come on into the middle of the ring, gents, and let the bout begin.'

Aniket seemed a little apprehensive of getting within striking distance of Dev.

'Why did you call me here?' he asked suspiciously.

'Well,' Ramanujam said in mock-graveness, 'I called you—both of you—to ask you something. What do you think happened today?'

Aniket glared at Dev. 'What happened?' he shrieked. 'Someone tried to be the knight in shining armour to a damsel who wasn't in distress—'

Dev narrowed his eyes. 'And someone got really close to getting their head bashed in with their own bat!'

Ramanujam cut in. 'In short, both of you have no idea what happened.' He paused while Sid chuckled. 'You both got played, you dimwits!'

Aniket was quicker to comprehend than Dev. 'Vishakha,' he breathed in realization. 'She *wanted* me to get upset with her so that Dev would come to her aid.'

'To what end?' Dev said, confused.

'To the end that you'd never agree with each other when Himanshu Pathak calls for a vote in the student council.'

It took a few moments for that to sink in.

'Vishakha!' Aniket exclaimed.

'Rikkhe,' Ramanujam corrected him. '*He* is the one I threatened and he is the one who bears the guilt of putting Himanshu Pathak on the throne. Naturally, he wants to protect him.'

'What are you talking about?' Dev said sharply.

Sid, in his stupor, gave another amused chuckle.

'Oh, I'm sorry,' Ramanujam said, 'I forgot you guys are a little slow. It was the chief election commissioner who supervised the counting of the votes . . . Are you guys really dumb enough to believe Himanshu Pathak won on his own merit?' His tone grew sarcastic. 'I mean, I know he's so popular and all, but still.'

No one spoke for a full minute, during which Aniket sat down and Dev punched a stone pillar repeatedly without flinching. As intended, they'd both forgotten how much they detested each other.

'We got lucky today . . .' Ramanujam muttered placatingly. 'First, even though his aim was to humiliate Aniket, he inadvertently made sure you went down on the ground, too, Dev. I think that the grievances being even, you might be able to work together? Or with me, at least?'

Aniket and Dev didn't look at each other, but gave curt nods.

'Good. Second, they revealed their hand—go for Pathak, and you'll have Rajput and Vishakha to deal with.'

He fell silent at the apprehensive faces of his comrades; they hadn't thought twice before joining forces against Himanshu, but the other two were formidable adversaries. 'That's why we are not going to focus on Himanshu right now. Let the ban on cell phones pass; let them think they've turned Aniket against us.'

'Right you are, my friend,' Sid cried out absent-mindedly between hiccups. 'Leave them to eat each other's tails!'

'We are not going after Himanshu?' Dev said harshly.

'Not right away.'

Aniket frowned. He knew what Ramanujam was hinting at, but he couldn't actually believe it. 'Who, then?' he asked, dreading the answer.

Ramanujam gave a lopsided grin. 'We are going after Rikkhe Rajput.'

*

It was raining in the old part of town. The monsoons, late to arrive, had advanced well into September, and almost felt more intense as a result. The meteorological department had predicted heavy rains for the coming days, but there still seemed to be some hope that the rains would actually continue.

The streets of Old Delhi were paved with mud and muck. Barely wide enough for a car, the magical streets were still somehow able to accommodate not only moving cars, but parked cars, rickshaws, bikes, scooters and, of course, the sludge. In the midst of those superhumans who created the chaos and navigated around it, a contrasting figure walked unhurriedly, lost in thought.

He seemed uncaring of the fact that his impeccably white trousers were getting dirty, or that his designer kurta was getting wet, or that the rain, mingling with the waste on the tin roofs and lintels, was corroding his lustrous hair.

Rikkhe trudged along, unaware of his immediate surroundings, which, given his immediate surroundings, was quite a foolish thing to do.

'Aah!' A sharp jolt on his elbow brought Rikkhe back to the present, while the bike that had hit him swerved and tried to zoom away. But Karamveer, who'd been following Rikkhe, had already stopped the biker a little way off.

Rikkhe kept moving, sinking back into his thoughts, his lips pursed in anger. He ought to have guessed something like this would happen . . . Two weeks had passed since that match between Sardar and Azad. Aniket had turned against Dev, who, in turn, had lost control of the council; and Himanshu had passed the ban on cell phones.

It shouldn't have surprised him when Dev lashed out. On this perfect Sunday morning, there had been another message at Rikkhe's doorstep.

Dear Vishakha is there to protect Himanshu, but who will protect the girl smitten by Rikkhe Rajput?

Rikkhe felt vulnerable, and it was a feeling he despised. He was now headed towards Paranthe Wali Gali to de-stress; the chaos cleared his mind.

He enjoyed the water—unmindful of its quality—falling on his head as he walked towards a relatively new addition to the parantha shops, labelled 'Jahalgarh Wale Paranthe'.

'Namaskar, Rikkhe babu,' the middle-aged shop owner said, jumping up from his chair. From the looks of the many scraps of paper surrounding him, it seemed he had been practising some self-designed way of maintaining accounts.

Rikkhe nodded curtly and forced a smile. 'Shyamji.'

Shyam immediately motioned Rikkhe towards the cramped wooden benches. The one luxury Rikkhe accepted was an entire, one-and-a-half-seater bench all to himself.

Shyam didn't require Rikkhe to place his order; he had his favourite gobi parantha in front of him in less than five minutes.

'Thank you, Shyamji.'

Shyam stuck his tongue between his teeth and grabbed his ears as though apologizing for this sacrilege.

'Thank you? No, no, it is all yours only, babu.' He gestured at his flourishing, albeit small, eatery.

Rikkhe smiled and Shyam retreated to the corner, keeping an eye out for anything Rikkhe might need. It had been a year since he'd helped Shyam, a migrant miner from Jahalgarh, set up this place. Although, technically, he and Shyam were partners in the venture, Shyam acted like he was Rikkhe's employee.

Rikkhe was savouring his first bite of the parantha when a familiar, unwelcome voice rang out in the small shop.

'Look who it is, Lisa! The man himself.' Dev Bhushan was smiling icily as he led Lisa Chauhan in by the hand.

In the absence of immediate comprehension, Rikkhe kept himself from reacting.

'Rikkhe,' Lisa murmured, sounding pleasantly surprised. It didn't seem like she had known where she was headed, as her clothes, fit for the ramp, were most certainly designed for swankier places than this. To Rikkhe, she looked guilty and almost apologetic.

'Lisa!' He rose up, graciously offering her his seat. Shyam instantly had someone place another bench on the other side of the table. 'Dev, a pleasure seeing you here,' he said drily.

Dev cocked his head to the side and smirked. Slowly and deliberately, he lowered himself on to the bench to sit by Lisa's side. As the bench wasn't big enough to accommodate two people, Dev threw his arm around Lisa, moving in closer.

Rikkhe was unable to control the sharp pang of rage and helplessness from showing on his face. Lisa interpreted his expression as jealousy, and consciously tried to move away from Dev, now perched precariously on the edge.

'Congratulations, by the way, Dev,' Rikkhe said. 'A well-deserved victory for Sardar House.' He raised a glass of lassi that had just been served. 'To a good start to inter-house cricketing.'

Dev raised a glass and reciprocated. 'Yeah, with the cell phones being banned and all, I think everyone needed something to cheer for.'

Rikkhe just had to take one look at Dev's face to know that Aniket had never left Team Ramanujam. They had let Himanshu have his small victory to hand him a bigger defeat. And Ramanujam had misled Rikkhe into thinking that the worst was over, buying himself more time.

Lisa still looked a little nervous. 'What a coincidence, meeting you here, Rikkhe,' she said.

'I have been asking her out for months,' Dev said conspiratorially. 'She finally said yes.' He gave her shoulder a little squeeze.

'Anyway,' Lisa said, sounding uncomfortable, 'you are all wet, Rikkhe. Didn't you have an umbrella?'

'I like the rain,' Rikkhe said matter-of-factly. He looked at Dev. And though his demeanour remained friendly, there could be no mistaking the threatening chill emanating from him. 'It makes me feel like there is someone greater than me.'

The absence of a sneer on Dev's face made it clear that he'd been sufficiently threatened. Lisa, on the other hand, gave a squeal of delight.

'Oh! That's so philosophical,' she said, and after a pause, added, 'I love the rain, too.'

Rikkhe smiled at her, realizing that he was actually quite fond of her and her adorable little quirks. He would be very upset if someone hurt her.

'Well, Dev,' Rikkhe said quietly, 'I wonder who suggested this place to you.'

There was a twinkle in Dev's eyes. 'The gali is quite famous, really.'

'It is,' agreed Rikkhe, 'but for the older, more central eateries. This one opened just last year.'

'Indeed?' Dev said, challengingly.

'Yes. I invested in it.'

Lisa's eyes were round, making her look like a freshly revived Sleeping Beauty.

Rikkhe got up. 'I am sorry but I have to leave. You guys enjoy your meal; and please don't bother paying. Shyamji does not accept money from friends of mine.'

Dev and Lisa both looked equally disappointed—but for very different reasons. Although Rikkhe didn't want to leave Lisa alone with Dev, he knew he couldn't protect her all the time. The only protection he could provide her was by pretending that she meant nothing to him.

Lisa got up too, and it was almost a little comical; Rikkhe could tell that she was trying to copy his courteousness, but in the cramped space all she managed to do was place herself diagonally over the table in an unintentional bow.

'There's that school dance coming up, you know . . .' she said hopefully.

'And I am sure you two will enjoy yourselves,' Rikkhe replied genially. 'The star couple, so to speak.'

Lisa seemed hurt, but Rikkhe couldn't risk giving her a second glance. He couldn't let Dev know he cared.

'I am asking you to go with me,' Lisa said bluntly to his back.

Rikkhe didn't let the relief flooding him show. He faced her slowly, as though wondering how to respond. Quite honestly, he could not say no, if he wanted Dev to think he was neutral with regard to Lisa. Moreover, he found he didn't *want* to say no.

'Well, we won't make too bad a pair ourselves, will we?' he said airily. Dev remained impassive. He wasn't all brawn; he understood the social manoeuvres of Woodsville's elite better than most.

Lisa brightened up so much that her impossibly beautiful face seemed twice as hypnotic.

'I practise a little with Nandini after school, so I will pick you up from your house at seven,' Rikkhe said before he left. He had never felt so glad or relieved. In fact he was quite excited as he had never been on a date.

He spotted Karamveer and Shyam talking outside the eatery. Being childhood friends, it was Karamveer who had brought Shyam to Rikkhe. The old guard jumped on seeing Rikkhe.

'It is all right, kaako, you can walk with me,' Rikkhe said wearily. 'No need to hide.'

'Leaving so early?' Shyam asked with concern. 'Did you not like the food?'

'It was delicious as usual, Shyamji, I just have to be somewhere.'

As Karamveer walked by his side, Rikkhe was silent and deep in thought.

'By the way, kaako, please send a heater for the restaurant,' he said, breaking his chain of thought. 'There is almost no shelter from the wind; Shyamji could use one for the winter.'

Karamveer nodded.

'I also have a job more suited for you,' Rikkhe said grimly.

Karamveer was silent, listening intently through the blaring horns and the shouts and the hissing of frying food. At times, Rikkhe had Karamveer run errands befitting his traditional role of someone who'd risk everything for loyalty.

'I need you to ascertain how Ramanujam and Dev knew I visit this place on Sundays.' Rikkhe's tone grew more ominous. 'And I suggest you start with Dr Athar's office.'

The student counsellor was the only person Rikkhe had told about Jahalgarh Wale Paranthe.

*

Himanshu had still not got used to not leaving the campus after school. While he waited at the entrance of the Woodsville campus, it was with some degree of self-control that he kept himself from searching the road for his driver and his car.

One by one, and many by many, the non-resident students exited the campus, most of them managing to spare a glance or two for Himanshu, standing in his loose T-shirt and with the scarlet–silver head-scholar badge pinned to his chest. All the looks he got were befitting someone who had got their precious little cell phones banned.

'You actually think this is a smart thing to do?' Vivek whispered in his ear. 'He's really the only partner you have, seeing as you won't speak to Vishakha.'

Himanshu grunted. Vivek didn't understand. It was *because* he couldn't talk to Vishakha that he had to do this.

They spotted Rikkhe Rajput exit through the campus gate, walking his usual understated walk.

'You sure you want to spoil his mood?' Vivek asked doubtfully. 'I heard Lisa's going to the school dance with him . . .' He grunted something incomprehensible. 'Lucky bugger.'

Himanshu took a deep breath. 'Time to see if he really is the sort of person I want as a friend.' He still hadn't forgiven Rikkhe for rigging the election without his consent.

As Himanshu approached him—Vivek stayed behind—Rikkhe quickened his pace. He gave an almost imperceptible nod to Himanshu, which said, *follow me*. Himanshu didn't much like this cloak-and-dagger game, but he walked a few steps behind Rikkhe to his Rolls, where Rikkhe's creepy guard stood sentinel. Once they were concealed behind the tinted windows, Rikkhe smiled.

'I apologize for this,' Rikkhe said, 'but as I said, the fewer people who know about our interactions, the—'

'Don't worry about it,' Himanshu said brusquely.

Rikkhe bowed his head and raised his eyes in scrutiny. 'You have something to say?'

Himanshu cleared his throat. 'The inter-house match—' he said. 'If you and Vishakha pull a stunt like that ever again, I am done with you.'

If there was any confusion in Rikkhe's mind, he hid it well. He tilted his head slightly, still thinking. His earring glinted dangerously. 'You wish you'd been consulted before that happened?'

'I wish it had never happened at all,' Himanshu retorted.

Rikkhe's eyes were cold, but Himanshu stood his ground under the penetrating, commanding gaze.

'You can't put Vishakha in such a dangerous situation again,' he clarified. 'She was messing with Dev Bhushan and Aniket Jain, for God's sake!'

Rikkhe shook his head incredulously. 'Have you spoken to Vishakha about this?'

'I am not going to,' Himanshu said harshly. 'As I said before, you are to be the buffer between us. Just make sure you don't make another move like that—'

'Tell you what. This . . . *move*, as you say, has presented me with a bit of a problem. In return for your help with that, I promise you'll have a satisfying answer.'

'What problem?'

'That incident has allowed Ramanujam to guess the key players standing against him. He has been able to reconcile Aniket and Dev, and lull us all into quite an incapacitating complacency.'

'But the ban—?'

'They *let* you pass it. I fear Ramanujam's planning something far graver.'

Himanshu exhaled. 'What do I have to do?'

'You are enrolled in the after-school Vedic maths class, right?'

'Yeah,' Himanshu said, confused. 'I have one in fifteen minutes.'

'Then you'll work with me. If you want the truth, you'll have to help me tell it to someone else as well. Aniket Jain has been mistaken about me for too long.'

Himanshu started to say something, but Rikkhe cut him short.

'And I am sorry that I have to ask you this,' he said, 'but we will need two cell phones.'

Himanshu's eyes widened in amazement. 'You're joking, right? Banned, remember? By me!'

'Well, the confiscated cell phones in the head scholar's office might help . . .'

Himanshu groaned.

'They are indispensable to our endeavour.' Rikkhe had a rare, mischievous glint in his eyes. 'And Himanshu,' he said matter-of-factly, 'our plans might also entail fooling Vishakha Sahdev.'

*

Aniket was one of the few class-twelve students in the Vedic maths class, and one of the fewer still to be promoted to the advanced level. There were barely a dozen of them in the room, but the intensity of competition was exponentially higher than in a regular class. Everyone here belonged to the small group of people who were as serious about their futures as they were uncaring of public opinion. They were the rebels among the already rebellious breed of adolescents.

Aniket was enjoying a rare happy moment. He could feel himself inching ahead of his classmates. Despite his agreement with Ramanujam, he was leaving no stone unturned to gain an edge. Aniket could easily deal with the moral ambiguity of his actions, just as he was dealing with the guilt of his pact with Ramanujam, but it was all proving to be extremely distracting in his up-till-then focused, target-driven life.

He stole a furtive glance at Himanshu, who had his head bent over his register as usual. Aniket, on Ramanujam's directions, had been walking a fine line between animosity and opportunism with the head scholar.

In front of Himanshu sat Vishakha. Aniket still smouldered at the very sight of her. It didn't help that she was now getting more attention than she ever had. Her dolled-up avatar at the match had made her scary persona fade somewhat. It had left behind a mysterious, complicated image that seemed as timeless and impregnable as religious dogma.

'Sorry to disturb your class, sir, but I need Vishakha for a moment.'

Aniket didn't need to look back. He knew the voice only too well.

Their professor, one of the world's best Vedic maths experts, didn't hesitate. He even felt it necessary to make small talk with Rikkhe, a mere student.

'Of course, Rikkhe,' he said politely, 'just be sure to give her back to us soon. Anything important?'

From the corner of his eyes, Aniket saw Rikkhe give a curt nod, which neither admitted nor denied anything. 'Routine stuff, sir.'

The professor nodded gravely. 'Sure, sure, carry on.'

Vishakha looked a little annoyed, and Aniket knew precisely why. She hadn't been asked if *she'd* wanted to go. But follow Rikkhe she did, for no one defied him openly; Rikkhe didn't ever give anyone reason to.

She didn't come back by the end of class; it was seven in the evening. As people filed out of the room, a peon came running towards them, looking urgently at the faces of all those present.

'Aha!' he said finally. 'Himanshu Pathak, you are, no?' He was talking to Aniket.

Aniket frowned. It irritated him that someone inside the Woodsville campus did not know who he was. He made to snap at the man.

'Rikkhe bhaiya sent you this,' the peon handed him a note, and Aniket recognized Rikkhe's prim handwriting.

He checked himself from the nick of time. 'Yes,' he smiled, 'I am.'

He stole a look at Himanshu, who was being chatted up by a couple of girls in the class. Then he looked at the note.

Meet us in the auditorium. R.

Aniket's heart started to race. Of course, students didn't have mobiles now, hence the need for a note. And Rikkhe had just taken Vishakha with him. Weren't they the two people Ramanujam had said were helping Himanshu? And now Aniket had the chance to find out what they all got up to at their little gatherings.

He walked as fast as he dared, so as not to attract unwanted attention. By the time he was at the reception, however, he had broken into a run. With his long, spindly legs, he jumped up the stairs three at a time on the now switched-off escalator.

As usual, he avoided the general entrance as well as the ones to the balconies, and headed towards the green room. Without thinking, he slammed the door open, and the bang echoed in the thankfully empty room. Startled by his own carelessness, he proceeded more cautiously.

As he approached the wings on the right side of the stage, he heard them. He slowed his breathing and, under cover of the red velvet curtains, inched forward. Rikkhe and Vishakha seemed to be arguing.

'I don't know why he isn't here yet, but I can speak on his behalf. Himanshu feels he should've been informed of your ploy against Aniket,' Rikkhe was saying insistently, 'and frankly, I agree.'

Vishakha seemed angry. 'He's not interested in talking to me, and he's made that clear plenty of times. What was I supposed to do, send him a telegram?'

Aniket raised an eyebrow. They were fighting among themselves? He was perplexed; according to Ramanujam, the entire incident had been orchestrated by Rikkhe.

Rikkhe's voice was steely. 'All right. Then would you mind explaining why you didn't confide in me? As far as I remember, *we* were on talking terms.'

Aniket suppressed an astonished gasp. Rikkhe wasn't involved, after all. Ramanujam had been mistaken.

Vishakha seemed to be learning all the nuances of behaving like a diva. She flipped her hair to the side with a supremely uncaring expression on her face, raising a finger to silence Rikkhe.

'First of all, I don't work for you—' Vishakha began.

'No, you don't,' Rikkhe admitted. 'We agreed to work together. For Himanshu's sake. Then why did you not work *with* us?'

Vishakha, up till then, seemed to have been struggling to find a way out of the conversation without giving Rikkhe an answer. But his last statement had apparently incensed her.

Her eyes narrowed and her voice matched Rikkhe's coldness. 'The keyword there, Rikkhe, isn't "together", but "work". We were supposed to *work* together. And you were doing nothing!'

'What should I have been doing?'

'Anything!' Vishakha said shrilly. 'Those pricks, Aniket and Dev, had made Himanshu shift to the campus and were still blocking all of his policy changes. Both of us were in this for Himanshu, weren't we? What was the point if we weren't going to help him?'

Rikkhe was silent and thoughtful. So was Aniket. It wasn't like Vishakha to 'help' someone. She was almost as apathetic as Aniket was, and just slightly more cunning.

'And so you thought turning Aniket and Dev against each other would give Himanshu his control over the council back?'

'It did, didn't it?' Vishakha said defiantly. 'Himanshu got the ban passed.'

Rikkhe sighed. 'I am afraid not.'

'What do you mean?' Vishakha was no longer combative. She sounded worried.

'Ramanujam saw through it. They have just been buying time.'

'Buying time for what?'

'I don't know,' Rikkhe admitted, 'but definitely something graver than blocking a ban.'

Vishakha was silent. She had probably just realized how bad she'd made things for Himanshu.

'What happened at the match was unnecessary,' Rikkhe continued gently. 'Not only did it fail to achieve anything, it also alerted Ramanujam to our involvement. Ramanujam threatened to hurt Himanshu to my face. When I reply, it will not be to his back.'

Vishakha's throat seemed to be constricted.

'A true strike at your enemy,' Rikkhe said, as though recalling someone else's words, 'ends the war.' He added quietly, 'And that happens only when the enemy's revealed every last one of his cards.'

'I'm just worried for him.' She lowered her head. 'Please, you tell him to be careful . . . I doubt he wants to hear my voice.'

She made to walk off the stage, and Aniket barely had time to conceal himself. Fortunately, she was shielding her face as she crossed him.

Aniket counted to thirty, furtively glimpsed at the motionless Rikkhe, and hurried out the back. He didn't see Vishakha anywhere on his way out.

As soon as Aniket had left, a mobile vibrated in Rikkhe's pocket. He relaxed his posture and took it out.

'Has he left?' Rikkhe spoke quietly.

From his vantage point in the upper balcony of the auditorium, Himanshu could clearly see the stage as well as one of the wings. 'Yes, Aniket's gone.'

'You heard and saw everything?' Rikkhe said calmly.

Himanshu's voice was quivering with emotion. 'Yes.'

'You have your answer?'

'Yes.'

'Are you satisfied?'

'I am confused.' Himanshu hung up and found his eyes were wet. Now what?

Rikkhe held his position for another minute and, from the corner of his eye, saw Himanshu get up and exit the balcony.

'You can come out now,' he said, turning.

Vishakha emerged from the folds of a curtain in the wing opposite the one Aniket had hidden in.

'Was it okay?' she asked.

Rikkhe nodded. 'I just hope Aniket keeps whatever he's heard here today to himself and doesn't share it with his new friends.'

'Thanks for giving me the chance to . . .' her voice tapered off.

'Himanshu needed to hear it,' Rikkhe said simply, 'one way or another.'

'I wasn't acting, really, you know . . .' Vishakha said abruptly. Rikkhe wasn't surprised to see her eyes blazing.

'I know.'

DEMONS

'You know what's weird?' Sid mumbled, half asleep, from Ramanujam's bed.

'Other than the fact that you think I'd take anything you have to say seriously, considering the state you are in?' Ramanujam said, seated at the study table, barely looking up. He was working on a way to halve the time taken to solve a certain type of statistical problem.

'It's about Athar's office,' Sid sang temptingly. 'You know, the place you had me poking about.'

Ramanujam's ears perked up. 'What about it?'

'You know how much he calls me there . . . on account of me being an *alleged* addict and all,' Sid said, with a slurring slowness Ramanujam didn't really have the patience for.

'You are worried he experiments on you, like with Pathak?' Ramanujam snapped.

Sid sat up straight in his bed, alarmed. 'You think so?'

'No, dammit,' Ramanujam said. 'Will you get on with what you wanted to tell me?'

'Oh, yeah,' Sid exclaimed, as though he had forgotten about that. He paused. 'You know how you wanted me to check if Athar had those pills in his office?'

'I wanted you to *get* those pills from his office. But of course, you are a junkie, and I couldn't possibly trust you to do it, now, could I?'

Sid shrugged sheepishly. 'Yeah, whatever. Guess whom I saw snooping around outside the window today?'

Ramanujam didn't say anything, afraid he might break his housemate's flighty concentration.

Sid had an expression akin to Santa Claus's plastered on his face. 'Guess who?'

'WHO?'

Sid frowned. 'Come to think of it, I don't really know his name.'

Ramanujam stood up involuntarily. To be surrounded by idiots was something he'd never been able to come to terms with, but to actually be forced to rely on one? He felt like breaking something.

'It's that funny-looking guy that stalks Rikkhe all the time.'

He's quick, was the first thought that came to Ramanujam's mind. Rikkhe had deduced there was a leak from Athar's office. He didn't know the nature of it, though, and that's what he'd sent his guard to find out.

'Athar will break,' Ramanujam said to himself, his teeth gritted. The slightest nudge or the sight of a friendly face would make Athar reveal everything, incriminating himself and screwing up Ramanujam's plans in the process. People with a conscience so rarely saw reason.

The school dance was scheduled for tomorrow. Rikkhe was going to be there with Lisa, and Dev was going to use her to distract Rikkhe. There was no use doing that now, though. Rikkhe was just one step away from spoiling everything Ramanujam had been working on since reading Himanshu Pathak's file at the counsellor's office. Ramanujam had managed to keep Rikkhe distracted for a while now, but Dev and Lisa wouldn't hold his attention much longer.

And tomorrow, Rikkhe and Athar would come face-to-face. There was no way Ramanujam could allow that to happen, no matter what it took. For he was sure that if Rikkhe went to the dance, he'd confront Athar, *and* he was sure of what would happen next. *Athar will break.*

*

The day of the dance saw everyone in a flurry. There was more awkwardness, ecstasy, envy and nervousness than the campus had witnessed in a long time. Whatever the state of their love lives, almost everyone seemed to be in agreement with the sentiment that Himanshu Pathak was 'the man'. The head scholar was credited with organizing this last stress buster before the half-yearlies, which, by Woodsville's standards, would be exponentially harsher than the boards.

Some people opposed to Himanshu spread a rumour that he was doing all this to create and maintain a sway over the student body, and, in turn, the student council. It seemed plausible. But then, there was also a rumour that

Rikkhe Rajput was finally going out with Lisa Chauhan. So nobody really knew what to believe any more.

A few hours before the event was about to start, the entire campus looked abandoned. Everyone was busy getting dolled or duded up. The polo ground was quieter than usual. No one was there to see Rikkhe Rajput gallop across the field on his favourite horse.

Only Karamveer, who watched him regularly, could make out that there was something amiss today. Instead of the fierce look of concentration, or the occasional blissful spells Rikkhe had while riding Nandini, he was almost absent-minded today. He smiled when Lisa came to watch him from the stands. He waved at her and she waved back. Neither made a move towards the other.

Rikkhe swept a hand over Nandini's mane and continued with his practice. Another twenty minutes or so later, he steered her into the stable for her bath.

'You see that girl?' Rikkhe spoke softly to Nandini as he brushed her, pointing towards Lisa, who hadn't got ready for the dance yet either. 'She is going to the dance with me.'

Nandini neighed agreeably.

Rikkhe nodded. 'I like her too, Nandini, but she doesn't really know me.' He paused. 'Maybe that's why I like her.'

He peered out towards the stands and saw that they were empty. His chest felt hollow, until his eyes found her walking across the ground towards him. She was beaming and had the same admiring look in her eyes he so craved these days.

Suddenly Rikkhe felt sick and lowered his head, speaking more quietly now. 'See, Nandini? That's what I'm talking about.' He shook his head. 'She thinks I'm something special. Someone noble. A real prince.'

Nandini rested her head against Rikkhe's hand, as though to assure him that he was, indeed, a prince.

He patted her sadly. 'A real prince doesn't do the kind of things I have done. All Lisa will find when she gets to know me is a person bound to his king's ideals, incapable of dissent. What's more, I don't really want to disagree with my father, Nandini. I do yearn for supremacy.'

Nandini's face was inquisitive, if such a thing can be discerned on a horse's face.

'You know when I feel truly alive, Nandini?' he said slowly. 'When you help me annihilate someone on the field.' He turned away from her. 'Maybe that's why I like *you* so much.'

Karamveer appeared at the stable's entrance.

'I am satisfied,' he said quietly. 'Doctor Athar isn't helping that boy.'

'You sure?' Rikkhe inquired, an eyebrow raised.

'Yes, Rajkumar,' Karamveer said, conferring on him the title of Prince in affection. 'I have been keeping an eye on Dr Athar since you asked me to, and I can confidently say that he's had no contact with Ramanujam.'

Karamveer's tone told Rikkhe there was more. 'But?'

'Dr Athar seems stressed. More so than his worst patients.'

Ramanujam had got to him somehow, then. Rikkhe sighed. As far as he knew, Athar was a decent man. What could Ramanujam possibly have on him that ensured his silence?

'Guess the doctor's a patient now,' Rikkhe stated matter-of-factly. 'I'll be seeing him at the dance, no?'

'Yes, Rajkumar, Director Walia wants him there . . .' He paused. '"To mend broken hearts and counsel lost love", as it said in his letter.'

Rikkhe smiled.

Karamveer looked outside. 'Ms Lisa is here to see you.'

'Show her in, kaako,' said Rikkhe, again calm, confident. 'And regarding the potential partners in the construction industry my father asked me to do some research on, the dossier is in my study; please have it sent home and say I'll be expecting him next week.'

'Ranaji won't be coming this month,' Karamveer said with a straight face. 'Things are keeping him busy back home.'

'The entire month?' Rikkhe asked, and Karamveer nodded.

Rikkhe grunted, frowning. He was instantly suspicious; the rana's visits to Delhi were imperative to their business's survival. What could be more important than that?

'Whatever he's planning, watch my back, kaako. I have enough on my plate here. I don't want to be blindsided.'

Karamveer nodded, and then hesitated. 'This girl . . .' he said quietly, looking towards the approaching Lisa.

'What about her?' Rikkhe asked.

'You think, um, she would be accepted back home?'

'Accepted as what?' Rikkhe inquired icily. He knew what Karamveer was insinuating; Rikkhe's stay here in

Delhi was to help him find his bearings before he went back home, a man. There was no scope for romance in this phase of a Rajputana prince's journey.

Karamveer faltered under Rikkhe's piercing gaze. 'Nothing . . . I will show her in.'

Rikkhe sighed as Karamveer proceeded to bring Lisa in. Rikkhe had always liked Lisa, but he knew there was no point taking it further to an inevitable dead end. He'd known it each time someone had flirted with him.

But Dev's threat to harm Lisa had made Rikkhe realize just how much he liked this girl who was smitten by him, who admired him and thought him to be a good person.

'I am not disturbing you, am I?' Lisa's nervous voice interrupted his thoughts.

Rikkhe drew himself up to his full height and smiled. 'Not at all. I was just finishing up with Nandini.'

'She's magnificent,' Lisa said, slowly stepping closer.

'One of a kind,' Rikkhe said lightly.

Nandini neighed softly and pressed her head against Lisa, who yelped with laughter and surprise.

'Oh, my!' She ran a jumpy hand over Nandini's face.

Rikkhe smiled. Nandini had always been a better judge of character than he; the first time *he'd* met Lisa, he'd been judgemental and cautious.

Lisa came closer to him, her darting eyes avoiding his. 'I was just wondering what to wear for the dance . . .'

Rikkhe had to suppress a smile. 'I doubt you'd need to think about it.'

She reached out and rested her hand on Rikkhe's polo shirt. 'No, I mean, you're always wearing those traditional dresses of yours.' She'd moved closer. A heady fragrance infused the air between them. 'I could wear something to complement that, if you want . . .'

Rikkhe's breathing became shallow and his pulse quickened. He blinked, and regained control of his senses. He prised her hand away from his shirt very gently. It took great force of will for him to do so.

'That won't be necessary,' he said, averting his eyes, aware of the hurt he knew he had to cause her. He *had* to, though, for he was dangerously close to losing control of himself. 'I won't be able to make it to the ball with you.'

Lisa stopped short, her hand still in his. 'What?'

It was then that Rikkhe decided to be selfish. He could have told her that he had better things to do—it would've made her loathe him and made getting over him easier. He couldn't, however, bear the thought of her thinking any less of him. So he told her the cruel truth.

'I am bound by tradition, Lisa,' he said quietly. 'I have a duty towards my family and my subjects—' Rikkhe checked himself. 'I mean, my people. They are relying on me to come back an able leader, or at least an apt businessman.'

'But what has that got to do with us?' Lisa said.

Rikkhe took a deep breath. 'You might think we are alike,' he said, 'but we are from very different worlds, Lisa.' Rikkhe willed her to understand and accept something he struggled with every day. He wanted to warn her . . . and himself. 'The royalty thing fades after a while, and all that's left are obligations; it's not about the things you can do, but about the things you *can't*. And one thing I can't do is be with you.'

Lisa couldn't speak.

Rikkhe continued, 'Marital alliances have always been decided and blessed by the rana and rani, keeping in mind the best interest of the family and their people.' Rikkhe cleared his throat. 'With royalty, it's families, and not the individuals, that are considered as being joined in marriage. And as such, choosing the family is a business decision, nothing else.'

'We don't have to marry or anything,' Lisa said in a small voice. She was dumbfounded at the thought that Rikkhe, someone she'd feared didn't think much of her, had already thought that far ahead.

Rikkhe sighed. Lisa might be a fashionista, and the most popular girl in school, but she was so simple. She had no inkling of the pain it would cause them both if they ended their trysts later rather than right now.

'I am sorry about the dance, Lisa,' Rikkhe said stoically. 'I was really looking forward to it.'

*

Dev was mortified. A dance, and the school champion had no date?

'You are messing with my star status, you know that?' he said tersely, walking beside the little demon.

Ramanujam looked him over. 'There are important things I need you doing today as opposed to impressing a bunch of nonentities.'

Dev didn't really appreciate being an errand boy to a thirteen-year-old, but by now he knew better than to cross him; Ramanujam worked very hard to make things unpleasant for his enemies. The dance was to start in another hour, and Rikkhe Rajput had just left in his Rolls, probably heading back home to get dressed.

'I wasted so much time on Lisa. I never had a chance,' Dev said.

'Tonight isn't about getting you a damn dance partner!'

'What's it about, then?' Dev was irritated. Not being able to go to the dance because of a plan he wasn't privy to was more than he could tolerate.

In the distance, Ramanujam saw the stables of Woodsville shrouded in darkness. The light of a single lamp glowed within. He narrowed his eyes. 'Tonight is about stopping Rikkhe Rajput from going to the dance and meeting Dr Athar. By all means necessary.'

*

The palatial bungalow in Chanakyapuri was usually quiet, unless the owners threw a mixer, inviting neighbouring diplomats, businessmen or politicians. It was twice as big as the residence of the state's chief minister, but the stillness divulged its foregone glory.

Since the day he was born, Karamveer, the last guard of a fading power, had had his life bound to an ancient institution that he had watched end, a tradition that barely managed to cling on to the present, and a family that he was and wasn't a part of.

Rikkhe had been his respite from the constant uncertainty he felt about the future and the confusion from the lingering echoes of the past . . . Karamveer saw Rikkhe's grandfather in him.

So unfortunate, Karamveer thought, *that he couldn't really get to know the man.* Rana Bhanu had died in his decrepit castle. Rikkhe, tears on his face, had seen him take his last breath. An infant at the time, he hadn't known the man, nor understood his pain. The tears on his face had been Karamveer's.

Karamveer clenched his fists, cursing himself, feeling the sombreness of the bungalow engulfing his young master. *Do you think she would be accepted . . . back home?* He should have said what Rana Bhanu would have, but the voluntary servitude had got the better of him. Karamveer's words had only echoed Rana Dhananjay's diktat.

I am not going back tonight, Rikkhe had told him on reaching home, right before he'd locked himself in the refuge of his room.

Karamveer had failed Rana Bhanu. He had let Rana Dhananjay guide the boy, and now Rikkhe was torn between who he was and who he was taught to be.

Karamveer closed his eyes. *Enough,* he told himself, over and over. *Enough.*

He opened his eyes and walked into the bungalow. He barged into Rikkhe's room without knocking.

Rikkhe was sitting on the floor, photographs a hundred years old lying neatly in grids in front of him. His hand was on the picture that had immortalized the moment of Rana Dhananjay's coronation. It had been taken two days before the uncomprehending Rikkhe would see his ailing grandfather die.

Rikkhe looked up as Karamveer entered, his face impassive. 'Yes, kaako?'

Karamveer didn't blink. 'There's something I think you should know—it's about your father.'

Rikkhe nodded once, asking him to go on.

'Jahalgarh is having—'

Karamveer was cut short by the shrill ring of the landline in Rikkhe's room.

Rikkhe got up tepidly and held the receiver to his ear. He feared it might be Lisa.

'Yes?'

Karamveer watched as Rikkhe's face clouded over with shock, fear, anger, and finally, panic.

'Don't do anything except for keeping her pain-free till I send a doctor. I'm coming.'

'What is it?' Karamveer said, alarmed.

'Tell Dr Pandey to reach Woodsville immediately,' Rikkhe said, his voice shaking.

Karamveer's heart sank. Dr Pandey was their veterinarian.

Rikkhe began running, trampling the photographs with his bare feet as he said the words, 'Nandini's hurt.'

*

The congregation room in the main school building had been decorated to perfection. Circular tables, some reserved for the faculty, had been set to afford those seated a decent view of the elevated dance floor. A few of the more eager Woozies were already hovering near the platform, but nobody wanted to be the first one on the floor.

The organizing committee was buzzing about, preparing for the arrival of Director Walia and his guests, with Vishakha barking orders at them. Since the day she had got a sports channel to cover the inter-school tournament, Walia had made her the de facto head of the committee, although she only took up projects that benefitted her somehow. And the school dance certainly did: Himanshu was as involved in it as her committee.

Vishakha shot a glance at the hall entrance, where Himanshu stood welcoming everyone who arrived, playing the perfect host. He was wearing a tailored suit, accompanied by a bow tie. And for once, his spectacles weren't lopsided.

In the few days since he'd heard all that Vishakha had said in the auditorium, he'd thawed somewhat. He still avoided unnecessary interactions with her, but his previous indifference was gone.

Himanshu caught her staring at him, and she hastily looked away.

'Get the name plates out of here,' she snapped at Shikhar, her face red from her little encounter with Himanshu. 'This is supposed to be a party, not a conference. The director can sit anywhere he wants.'

There was a little tap on her shoulder. 'They're not dancing, Vizac,' a quiet voice whispered. She turned to see Himanshu standing behind her with a grim expression on his face.

'What?' she said, taken aback by how close he was. No one ever invaded her space like that.

'This is supposed to be a party, right?' he asked, gesturing at the room. 'No one's dancing.'

Vishakha looked around. Sure enough, no one looked keen on being the first on the floor.

'You want me to *make* someone dance?' Vishakha said, already looking around for the perfect chumps.

'I don't think that'll make such a good impression,' Himanshu interjected, mildly amused. 'How about *we* dance?'

'Don't worry, I'll get these spineless morons to take—' she stopped short, just realizing what Himanshu had said. 'What?'

'Yeah. For the party, right?' Himanshu still looked dead serious.

Vishakha stood speechless for some time. That is, until Himanshu grinned sneakily, his spectacles becoming lopsided, as usual. Vishakha smiled, happy for the first time in months.

Despite his suaveness, Himanshu's hands were unsteady as he held Vishakha. But the minute they took the stage, the apprehension was gone. Vishakha was leading, and he trusted her fully. He was in safe hands.

Himanshu chuckled as he saw Vivek raise his eyebrows, impressed, from amid the now keenly watching crowd. Things were finally going to be all right. He had Vishakha, he had the student body shifting in his favour, and he had Rikkhe Rajput watching his back. What could go wrong?

*

While most people had headed off to the dance, there were still some who remained and were now outside the school stables, for there was no mistaking the gravity of the situation. The faces of those present were sombre, sad and slightly afraid. For it had become clear that Rikkhe Rajput's favourite horse wasn't just hurt. She'd *been* hurt.

The poor boy. Everyone from the night-time security to Admin Kumari agreed on one thing—the attack was unprovoked and malicious, and couldn't have happened to a nicer person.

Rikkhe's Rolls-Royce hadn't stopped at Woodsville's entrance. A terse statement from Karamveer, and the gate had been opened without hesitation. The car had barely stopped near the polo ground, when Rikkhe shot out, running with the surety of an athlete and the drive of a predator.

He arrived on the scene to see Dr Pandey fussing over Nandini who lay in the mud, breathing fast, wincing every now and then, a bandage covering her left forelimb. Francis, the horse trainer at Woodsville, lay a comforting hand on her head.

'Rikkhe,' Admin Kumari said importantly, 'on behalf of the school administration—'

Rikkhe walked forward without listening to her, his eyes darting in every direction, taking in each detail of Nandini's enclosure. The stable boys who'd been crowding the place to get a glimpse of Nandini immediately shrunk back under Rikkhe's probing gaze.

The vet had finished with his examination of Nandini, and stood up as soon as the royal was done with his.

'Some blunt instrument was used to break her—' began Dr Pandey.

'Will Nandini be all right?' Rikkhe cut him off.

'She'll recover, yes, although there is a fracture. I wouldn't recommend straining her any more than you absolutely have to.' He took a deep breath. 'Probably no more polo matches for her . . .'

Rikkhe's face was impassive as he gave a curt nod at the doctor's statement.

Meanwhile, Admin Kumari, not one to let go without saying her part, had followed Rikkhe inside.

'As I was saying, Mr Rajput, we'll get to the bottom of this incident. Is there anyone you think might've been involved in this?'

'Involved in what?' Rikkhe asked innocently.

'Well, the, um, injury of your horse . . .' said Admin Kumari slowly. She knew full well that Rikkhe was no fool.

'Oh, this?' Rikkhe pointed to the unconscious horse behind him. 'This was an accident. She slipped and fell. That's the doctor's diagnosis.'

Admin Kumari stared hard at him. She knew that by no means could Rikkhe possibly be missing the obvious. Nor was he a person easily intimidated. Why the feigned naivety?

'You absolve the school of any responsibility in this incident?' she asked sharply.

'I see no reason to absolve anyone of anything—it was an accident,' Rikkhe said simply. 'As for the treatment, that's my responsibility.'

Admin Kumari assessed Rikkhe for another split second, then turned and snapped at the straggling onlookers to get back to their business.

Karamveer was consulting with Dr Pandey. Rikkhe bent down to touch Nandini's face, and she opened her eyes to convey her thanks.

'I have to leave,' Rikkhe said, getting up. 'Please make arrangements with Dr Pandey for Nandini's looking after.'

Karamveer, who had got up to follow Rikkhe, hesitated. 'But—'

Rikkhe held up a hand. 'It's okay, kaako.'

Karamveer was clearly torn between his orders and his need to guard Rikkhe after such a brazen attack.

Rikkhe turned without another word and walked out on to the polo ground, shivering. Away from the crowd, a voice called out from behind him, the direction he'd come from.

'So, your lapdog obeys when you say "stay"?'

Rikkhe stopped. His grandfather's earring seemed to be searing into his skin.

'Ramanujam.'

'Say my name! Say it!' Ramanujam yelled mockingly, and then stopped abruptly. 'Oh wait, you already did.'

Rikkhe remained silent. Ramanujam was bobbing on the balls of his feet, restless.

'Pity about the horse,' Ramanujam said in a not-so-sympatheic voice. 'That Bhushan guy is literally unstoppable when he sets his mind to something.'

Rikkhe's fists had clenched at the mention of Nandini, though he couldn't help but smile lightly at the way Ramanujam had brought up Dev as the patsy.

'Why the act?' Rikkhe said. 'I am sure Dev held the hammer, but it is also true that you handed it to him.'

'Why the act, Rikkhe?' Ramanujam said quietly. 'You are sure the horse was beaten up, but you treated it like an accident. Should I fear a little retribution coming my way?'

'Justice would be more precise.'

'And who are you to determine what justice is?' Ramanujam's voice was challenging.

Rikkhe knew it was a trap, but he didn't care any more. 'I am a king.'

'Like hell you are . . .' Ramanujam said triumphantly. 'I always knew there was something off about you, Rikkhe. You aren't the goody two shoes everyone thinks you are. You kept out of the race, not because you don't seek power . . . you just think it's already yours.'

Ramanujam had worked himself up into a fit of incredulity and indignation.

Rikkhe took a step towards him. 'I simply know what's better.'

The answer seemed to incense Ramanujam further. 'Because you're a king?' he shrieked, taking a step forward himself.

'Because I am a fit king.'

'And how do you figure that?' Ramanujam said derisively.

'Because I know what's better.'

Ramanujam seemed to have reached a point past frustration. 'I knew it. You are a fraud; a very well-concealed fraud, but a fraud nonetheless. All the fools here think Rikkhe is all rainbows and sunshine, but I—*I* discovered you.'

'Yes, you did.' Rikkhe's tone implied that it might not be so good for Ramanujam that he had.

'And now, since you are a king, you mean to deliver swift justice for the horse?'

'Well . . . justice requires a punishment commensurate with the crime. Yours won't be.'

'Whatever it is,' Ramanujam said with relish, 'it *won't* be swift. After all, you have things closer to home to tend to.'

In response to Rikkhe's uncomprehending look, Ramanujam threw a newspaper at him. Rikkhe caught it and saw his father's face in black and white.

By the time he was through with the report from Jahalgarh, a lonely district in a corner of Rajasthan, he knew what Karamveer had wanted to tell him back at the house.

He heard someone exhale deeply, and turned to see his guard standing by him, his head lowered in shame.

Jahalgarh is having elections. And your father, against everything he stood for, everything he made you *stand for, is contesting. You were a fool to deny who you are on the orders of a man who knows not who he is. A fool to deny yourself the one truly real thing that happened to you . . .*

Rikkhe didn't need to ask Karamveer if it was true, if his father had really betrayed him. The resignation on the face of the weary old guard told him everything.

Rikkhe's eyes lost their steely impassivity and revealed that fury of the old kings that Karamveer had so often heard about.

He walked past the leering boy. Ramanujam would be dealt with, but he was right—Rikkhe had things closer to home to tend to.

'Get the car, kaako,' he said imperiously. 'We leave for Jahalgarh immediately.'

*

'He's gone.' Ramanujam wasn't smug; he was merely repeating what he'd said before.

'You're sure?' Dev asked.

Ramanujam's face showed how insulting a question that was. Dev didn't notice, however. He was already attracting quite a lot of attention in the crowded congregation room. Dev Bhushan talking to Ramanujam? What a scandal!

Suddenly unfettered, Dev bemusedly watched Himanshu and Vishakha do a slow dance. Those not preoccupied with dancing or with Dev were focused on the couple.

'That guy amazes me,' he admitted, looking at Himanshu. 'I didn't think *any*one had it in them to get Vizac. Not even me!'

Ramanujam chuckled. 'The need for love makes fools of the best of us.' He meant every word.

Dev turned to Ramanujam and spoke calmly, firmly. 'Remember this, Ramanujam. The next time you make me do anything like what we did today, it'll be *your* legs I'll break, not a horse's.'

Ramanujam didn't look at Dev. 'You did what was required. You'll do it again if I ask, because you gave me your word. And I doubt you break your promises easily.'

Dev took a deep breath and a deliberate step towards him. 'I am losing everything I had, Ramanujam. Pretty damn fast. You don't want to push me into becoming unpredictable.' Even as he said it, Dev knew that he was going to be with Ramanujam till the very end. For him, loyalty wasn't a matter of choice but of principle. And somehow, Ramanujam knew that.

'Unpredictable, my ass!' Ramanujam laughed. 'I accompanied you to the stables only because I knew you wouldn't risk doing it alone. You are the most cautious guy I know, Dev, and that's your weakness.'

Dev stormed off as Ramanujam shifted his gaze from Vishakha to Himanshu. With Rikkhe out of the picture, Ramanujam would be able to do what needed to be done, what he'd been planning for a long time. If all went well, Vivek, Himanshu's reliable crutch, would be dead by tomorrow.

*

The ancient haveli, home to Jahalgarh's royalty for aeons, was covered with posters; posters which renounced the royal lineage that the haveli was a product of, and, in the same breath, said that Rana Dhananjay was the best bet for his constituency.

Anubhav. Experience. The word was plastered all over the walls of the house Rikkhe was born in. The experience of ruling—experience his father never had, experience Rikkhe could never have. It was due to the lack of that experience that Dhananjay hated democracy, and the obsession with that experience was why he had now embraced it.

The desert gave fangs to Jahalgarh's air in the night. Despite its bite, though, Rikkhe stood rock-still at the door to his parents' bedroom. The crackling from the fireplace and a steady howl from the wind were the only sounds the darkness carried. Rikkhe stayed motionless for another moment, and then walked in, the sound of his footsteps amplified in the heavy silence.

'Who is it?' His father sounded groggy. 'Rikkhe?'

The rani jerked awake. She rubbed her eyes to get a clearer picture of her son, but Rikkhe could tell that she hardly recognized him. How could she? He was a mere boy when he'd been taken away on his father's orders. Besides, everyone in the room knew that she had always craved a daughter. She was anything but close to her son.

'I learnt something that made me think I should look in on you guys . . .' Rikkhe's voice was soft as he dropped the newspaper on the bed, between his parents.

The rana took a long, hard look at his own photograph in the paper, and then his brow creased into a frown.

'You don't understand . . .' he said.

'Make me.'

'Let's talk in my office,' he said, getting up, casting a disdainful look at his wife.

'Let's talk here.'

The rana stopped short. 'These are complicated matters, Rikkhe, you can't just look at the distortions reported in the papers.'

'Distortions which say you went against everything you stood for?'

'I stand for this family!' the rana snarled. 'I stand for the Rajputs! I stand for our right to rule!'

'I thought you were already a king . . . I thought democracy unmade us?'

'And it'll be our making!'

'And what of those who were supposed to follow in your footsteps? When were you going to reveal this change of heart to them?'

'I didn't think it was necessary for you to know—'

'A *cheat* hides his tricks, a patriot admits them proudly! Your own father said that, in case you forgot.'

Rikkhe's open contempt sharpened the fangs of the night. Rana Dhananjay, despite being a son of the desert, had always found it difficult to bear with its extreme moods. Rikkhe's voice proved too much for him. Involuntarily, he inched towards the fireplace.

His wife was sitting upright on the bed, torn between happiness and desolation. Their son stood between them, rigid as a rock, formidable as an executioner and final as a judge.

'Forget about this,' Rikkhe said, picking up and throwing the newspaper past his father, into the fire. 'I'll take *your* word for it. Who are you?' Rikkhe asked his father's back.

Dhananjay inched closer to the fire. His eyes were fixed on his inked face, burning in the fire he had lit.

'I have, in action, done all you ever wanted me to do. Now, after all these years, I wish to know—who are you?'

'I am your father.' Dhananjay's reply was weak, lacking in conviction.

Rikkhe was unforgiving. Unrelenting. 'Before that . . . *beyond* that?'

Dhananjay didn't answer. He was deep in thought. After all these years, however, his son had run out of patience.

'Who are you? What are you?' Rikkhe's voice was earnest. 'A king? A politician? A liar? A hypocrite? A coward?'

'Rikkhe!' his mother beseeched on his father's behalf.

Fury gave back Dhananjay his speech, and he rounded on the young man. 'How dare you talk to your king like that?'

'So you are a *king*, then?' Rikkhe pressed. 'Be sure, father, because whatever you are, I'll be an extension of that. So what am I to be today? A prince? Or a fool?'

'I did what was good for this family.'

Rikkhe nodded. 'Very well, father. Then by your example shall I act—my actions should be good for the family.'

Dhananjay frowned. 'What are you implying?'

'That this principle will direct me henceforth, as it directs my king.'

Dhananjay looked wary.

'I will return to Woodsville now. I need to set some things in order. When that is done, I'll come back to my mother.' He turned to her coolly. 'Maybe I'll bring back the daughter you always wanted.'

The rani averted her gaze to hide her tears. It was true that she'd wanted a daughter. She'd cried inconsolably at his birth, and he knew that.

It wasn't abhorrence for her son that made her act indifferent towards him. It had been cruelly hard for her to have him snatched away, but she hadn't wanted to make it as hard for Rikkhe to not have a mother. So she had kept him at a distance. Seeing him today, she yearned for her son more than ever; he seemed to have grown into the kind of person she would be proud of. The only reason she had wished for a daughter was because she would've stayed with her mother a little longer.

Rikkhe sympathized with his mother and the life she'd led, but he didn't know her well enough to understand her—yet. Maybe he would, some day, given time . . .

He cleared his choked throat and addressed his father. 'For the sake of the people of Jahalgarh, I remind you today that what you *think* you have was left by my grandfather in a trust fund for *me*. Henceforth, you will not touch those resources for the purposes of this election, unless you have to buy fuel to make it to the poll booth.'

If the rana looked scandalized now, it was nothing compared to what was in store for him.

'My trust fund will support a new candidate, someone who also happens to be the trustee of my estate. Meet your new opponent.'

For the first time in his life, Karamveer entered the presence of the king with his head unbowed.

'And I do this,' Rikkhe said slowly, 'for the good of my family.'

'You will end this family!' Dhananjay took a step forward, looking frenzied. In that moment, Rikkhe saw how powerless he was.

The rana of Jahalgarh was the rana only because of unquestioned tradition, and because of his family; only because his *son* believed him to be one. And when the prince stopped believing, the rana was lesser than a shrunken shell of who he thought he was.

Rikkhe shook his head in pity. 'A king's family is his people.'

Dhananjay's voice was stuck in his throat. No one knew, and no one ever would, but those were the last words his father had said to him.

*

Athar hadn't had a good night's sleep since the day Ramanujam had gone through his files. And on the morning after the school dance, he was particularly tired and disoriented. All through the event, he had kept an eye on Himanshu, who had been among the last to leave. The only solace Athar had was that Vishakha had kept the boy company; maybe Himanshu would overcome his weakness, after all, before something bad happened.

It took Athar three tries before he could open the lock to his own office.

'Good morning, Doctor.'

Athar jumped and swerved left to see Rikkhe Rajput seated on the sofa. His eyes were red, like he hadn't got much sleep either.

'You gave me a start—'

'What did you do, Doctor?' Rikkhe asked.

Athar gulped. He had been waiting for someone to ask him that question. Still, he couldn't believe it when the wait was over.

'What are you talking about?'

'Dev Bhushan knew about my Sunday excursions to Old Delhi, something I'd told only you about. How?' Rikkhe was sharp, prodding.

Athar closed his eyes for a moment. 'The files I keep on the patients, Ramanujam got his hands on them.'

Rikkhe's worst fears were confirmed. 'Who all?'

'You, Vishakha, Dev, Aniket . . . and Himanshu.'

'And you didn't feel it necessary to report him?'

Athar walked to his file cabinet and withdrew Himanshu Pathak's file. Without meeting Rikkhe's eyes, he handed the file to him.

Rikkhe continued to stare at Athar for just a second more, and then looked at the psychiatric evaluation report that Athar had pinned over the first page.

Five minutes later, Rikkhe was running through the main school building, panicked, searching for Himanshu Pathak. Everything was suddenly clear to Rikkhe—why Ramanujam had wanted Himanshu in the campus, why he hadn't bothered to undermine Himanshu once he was *in* the campus, why he'd kept Rikkhe distracted with Lisa and Nandini, and why he'd wanted Rikkhe absent last night. The meticulous cruelty of what Ramanujam was trying to accomplish shocked him. Ramanujam was a sociopath. And it might already be too late for Himanshu Pathak.

*

Himanshu's footsteps felt heavy as he walked over the marble floor of the reception, slightly later than usual, right into the half-sleepy, half-excited swarm of students. He'd had a wonderful morning, owing to the even more wonderful night that had preceded it. His hard work was finally paying off. He was no longer the head scholar of Woodsville in name alone; he truly was the head scholar.

He had also finally plucked up the courage to talk to Vishakha. He had no doubt that she was still a cunning little savage, but after what he had heard in the auditorium, he knew that she'd be *his* cunning little savage.

Even so, he was aware of feeling more dispirited than he had in ages. His feet felt heavy.

Dispirited and calm, he remembered thinking. That was yesterday. *Dispirited and restless*, he revised his opinion.

His ears were hearing less than usual. He noted it and put it away for future use.

Himanshu pulled on his shirt collar. His expensive shirt; he had started dressing better. He gave his head a brief shake, trying to stay on track. Why had he pulled on his collar?

He suddenly realized that he was sweating. It couldn't be the weather . . . it must be anxiety. The possibility jolted him so hard that the anxiety he didn't know existed a moment ago increased tenfold.

His breathing became fast. Correction: his breathing was already fast; his breathing got faster. His mind registered the fact, and his anxiety increased.

Stop. Think. Himanshu did as the voice said. The voice in his head. His hands were trembling now. *Why?*

Too much happiness. His answer sounded ridiculous even to him. It was true, though, he realized. His vision was blurry now. Or rather, the people in it were.

He'd had too many good things happen to him these past few days. He'd bettered himself in ways he hadn't thought possible. He was no longer invisible and he was no longer afraid of not being invisible.

He was afraid now.

Too much happiness. Not enough space in him.

Share it with someone! Let it out! The suggestion, oddly enough, made perfect sense to him. The name that instinctively came to mind was Vivek.

Himanshu put his hand in his pocket for his cell phone. They had been banned, though, hadn't they? He found it in his pocket. Rikkhe had insisted he carry one at all times. Keep it hidden, he'd said. Don't want the head scholar seen flouting the rules, he'd said.

And here Himanshu was, in full view, pressing the buttons of his phone, dialling Vivek's number. People must be looking. He put the phone to his ear.

The service for this number was unavailable. What did that mean? Himanshu looked at the phone, expecting an answer.

Suddenly, the phone vibrated in his hand. Himanshu kept staring at it, realizing some time later that this might be the phone answering.

There was a message. Good. Just one line. Better. A question. Wasn't the phone supposed to answer instead?

`can't find dear Vivek, can you?`

It was from an unknown number. Himanshu was confused. Why would his phone send him a message from another phone number?

No, it was someone else. The sender of the message had asked a question, whereas his phone was still expected to answer one.

Can't find dear Vivek, can you?

Of course he couldn't find Vivek. The service for his number was unavailable. Why was he searching for Vivek? Oh, right, too much happiness and not enough space. He wanted to tell him about the dance. He hadn't told Vivek about what had happened last night with Vishakha. He hadn't seen him after the dance. He hadn't even heard him enter the house all night—

Himanshu jerked forward towards the marble floor as realization hit him again—like a moving truck. Rather, a Blueline bus; it took away everything. His ears were hearing normal again, he noted. His hands weren't shaking, people who were looking at him weren't all blurry, and he wasn't sweating so much.

The fear hadn't gone away, though. It had clawed its way into his heart.

All he could see was the marble floor.

'VIVEK!' he screamed. The people standing closest to him, hovering over him in apparent concern, jumped.

Himanshu got up and looked around the reception. Everyone was standing still, even the usually unreceptive receptionist. Everyone was facing him. That made it easier for him to quickly determine that Vivek wasn't there.

He threw his books and cell phone on the floor and started running to where the crowd was thickest.

'VIVEK!' he yelled again.

Everyone on the escalator looked at him. *Not here.*

Himanshu ran past them.

'VIVEK!'

Not there.

'VIVEK!'

No one.

Most of the crowd was behind him now. They were coming up behind him, teachers and students alike. Many were shocked into silence. Many were yelling at Himanshu to calm down.

'They killed him!' Himanshu rounded on them, tears rolling down his face. 'VIVEK!'

He ran forward again, only just noticing that he was headed towards the auditorium. The weekly assembly.

'Has anyone seen him?' he cried. 'VIVEK! I am sorry! I am so sorry!'

He spotted Director Walia coming up towards him, a frown on his usually cheery face. A wave of relief coursed through him. For the first time ever, he was glad that Walia was his grandfather.

'Why aren't you all heading towards the assembly?' Walia demanded of the people around him. 'And who in the name of God is screaming in the hallway?'

Walia got the answer to both his questions when Himanshu reached him and shouted again. 'VIVEK! They took him. You have to help me.'

'What on earth are you talking about, boy?' Walia said in bewilderment.

'VIVEK! He—'

'WHO is Vivek?' Walia said loudly.

Himanshu threw Walia a look of disgust. Of course, why would the director bother with a nobody?

'He's one of your students, dammit. And he's been missing since last night!'

There were gasps all around.

Walia frowned. 'Jayaji, get to the bottom of this,' he addressed Admin Kumari, 'although I suspect it's nothing more than a misunderstanding. The rest of you, off to the assembly.'

Nobody moved except Walia, who turned to leave.

'STOP!' Himanshu yelled, and Walia obliged.

Kumari approached the frantic Himanshu.

'This Vivek,' she said, 'which class is he in?'

'Mine! Twelfth! Commerce!'

There were murmurs in the crowd. Himanshu heard some of his classmates mutter, 'Who is he talking about?'

At the back of the crowd someone else was shouting, sounding as panicked as Himanshu.

'Himanshu, stop!' Rikkhe yelled, making his way to the front.

In the deathly quiet, Himanshu heard a dull roar emerge from the auditorium ahead. It was rising steadily to a din that echoed in the hallway. Rikkhe had to shout into Himanshu's ear to be heard.

'I know where Vivek is. I'll take you to him. Come with me.'

Himanshu didn't listen. Everyone was looking at him. Fascinated, fearful.

'Who is he talking about?' again, the murmurs.

'Himanshu, believe me.' Rikkhe was almost pleading.

Himanshu turned towards the assembly and moved forward, leaving Rikkhe, leaving them all, and going past Walia. It felt like he was sleepwalking. Soon, he broke into a run, with everyone following him.

The auditorium. It was pandemonium.

Somebody had pasted hundreds of flyers all over the walls, strewn them across the floor and on the chairs. Half the school was already there, and every single student was going through the leaflets.

It was just two paragraphs. The same two paragraphs repeated on every freaking flyer in the auditorium.

As all those who'd followed him instantly picked up the flyers lying on the ground, Himanshu walked over to the nearest wall and began to read.

The subject presented a peculiar case of schizophrenic disorder. Lack of a comfortable social circle, enormous peer pressure in academics and difficult conditions at home are the probable causes of this. The subject has created a persona that serves to mitigate the risk from these factors by providing mental support.

It is still not clear to me if this persona also acts as a point of release at times when the subject has too much information or an emotional overload. Treatment is to be experimental: I have desisted from giving the subject antipsychotics, as the sudden loss of his mental crutch might be catastrophic. To prevent the use of antipsychotics, it is also imperative that neither the subject nor his family be alerted to the schizophrenia.

Additions: Recently the subject has encountered seriously transformative circumstances, including proximity to a girl he's previously shown much interest in. I believe this girl has induced enough positive changes in the subject to act as a substitute for the imaginary persona.

Note: The subject calls this creation 'Vivek'.

In one calm, horrific moment, Himanshu was acutely aware of the truth. He was aware of every person's gaze upon his face. His quest to be invisible finally made sense to him; maybe it was something he'd always known—that when people really saw him, they'd be sickened. Why wouldn't they be? *He* was.

Himanshu took a deep breath and tried to steady himself. The effort this took was monumental and proved too much for him. His mind gave out. In another moment, he collapsed. The last sight his mind registered was dozens of eyes peering down at him, finally seeing the head scholar of Woodsville Scholars International.

WAR

'There's not going to be a criminal investigation.' Director Walia was curt but his tone indicated a sort of finality.

'So the ones who were involved in today's . . . stunt will go scot-free?' There was no mistaking the disapproval in Admin Kumari's voice.

Vishakha didn't listen to them. She was transfixed, looking at Himanshu lying on a bed in the infirmary, unconscious and sedated. She wished they would go argue someplace else.

'I am surprised,' an unfamiliar voice remarked, as its owner went through Himanshu's medical chart. 'Despite the reckless decision that Dr Athar made—of not using medicine to help with his condition—it was actually the antipsychotics that did the most damage. His vitals were surprisingly weak an hour back. The drugs might've been bought from the black market, or maybe the dosage was wrong.'

'What antipsychotics, Dr Garg?' Walia asked sharply.

Dr Garg frowned. 'I am no psychiatrist, but it's clear, isn't it? The boy, Vishal or whoever it was, couldn't really die, as he didn't exist. He was only present in Himanshu's mind. And the only way he could have vanished so quickly, the only way Himanshu could have become aware of this reality so abruptly, is if he'd consumed antipsychotic drugs.'

'So he always knew the boy wasn't real?' Admin Kumari asked.

'Going by his reaction to that boy's disappearance this morning, it doesn't seem so.'

'Then why would he take antipsychotics?' Kumari said, frowning.

'I don't reckon he would, not knowingly.'

There was a momentary silence, and Vishakha couldn't unhear the doctor's words. She turned away from Himanshu and looked at the doctor, impassive.

'You are saying someone drugged him without his knowledge?' Vishakha's voice was toneless.

The man nodded. 'Over several days, as a matter of fact.'

Silence again, as Vishakha turned back to Himanshu.

'Well, excuse me,' the doctor said, clearing his throat, 'but I'd better update Mrs Pathak that her son is fine . . . physically, at least.'

'You still think the police doesn't need to be involved?' Admin Kumari asked Walia.

Walia sighed and motioned her away from Himanshu and Vishakha. As Vishakha heard their agitated whispers, she dispassionately wondered how Walia had managed to get Himanshu's family to not file criminal charges against the student counsellor. She felt like she could kill Athar right then, but at the same time, she knew him enough to know that whatever he did, he must've thought it was in his patient's best interest.

Suffocated, Vishakha made her way out of the infirmary, going nowhere in particular, thinking nothing in particular. There remained the matter of those who'd drugged Himanshu. The thought came and exited her mind in the same instant. What would happen now with school politics? That thought, too, exited after a fleeting moment.

She couldn't stop picturing Himanshu lying there on the infirmary bed alone. She had left. She had to. She knew why she had to. She pushed that thought out of her mind as well.

After a moment of blankness, she involuntarily pictured her mother lying on her bed in that decrepit little room. Try as she might, *that* image didn't let go of her. It was a powerful magnet; for years, Vishakha had kept it at a distance, and now that she'd let it get close to her, its hold on her was unbreakable.

As if on cue, her phone vibrated in her pocket. She took it out and saw seven missed calls from her father. She'd just received a message, also from her father.

Come home as soon as you can.

She tried calling him back, but his phone was continuously engaged.

Some time later, Vishakha found herself in an autorickshaw, outside her house. She had no idea why she was there, but she got out and paid her fare. Climbing up the stairs to her house, she noticed a lot of the neighbours just standing outside, whispering.

The door to her house was ajar, and she went in. More people in the living room, all watching her like she would explode any moment. She headed to the bedroom and saw her mother lying on her bed, as usual, asleep. Her father sat beside her, holding her hand.

Vishakha took a step into the room and her world changed. Her father's face was ashen, his eyes wide with shock, tears running down his stubble. Her mother wasn't wearing her oxygen mask, nor was she breathing on her own. He clasped her hand so tight that he may have broken a bone or two—which would have mattered had she been alive.

In death, he wouldn't let go. In life, Vishakha hadn't held on.

*

'So what have you decided?' Radhika asked, the evening after the incident.

To not push it any further, Rikkhe thought. 'I won't push it.'

Radhika frowned. 'Admin Kumari was against glossing over the entire affair, too, you know,' she prodded him as they exited the admin office.

They could see the other house captains a little further ahead, all walking away, deep in thought. Aniket Jain, Dev Bhushan and Yash Malik.

'Yeah,' Rikkhe said drily, 'she doesn't really hide her displeasure too well.'

'So? Shouldn't there be an investigation into who managed to break into the auditorium and set the stage for the ruckus?'

If only that was the extent of it . . .

'Any investigation into this will be ugly, shocking and a huge scandal. I think it's best that we leave it alone.'

Radhika looked sceptical but didn't pursue the matter any further. She trusted Rikkhe, and she knew that if there was a dignified way out of any situation, Rikkhe would know it.

What she *didn't* know was that the Rajput was in a dilemma. Walia was intent on quashing the entire incident, terming it a 'common student mischief'. This meant that no one would even try to find out what had really happened in the auditorium, something Ramanujam had probably counted on. The thing that made Rikkhe hold his tongue, however, was that any official probe into the matter would mean permanently besmirching Dr Athar's name. By tying Athar's fate to his own, Ramanujam had ensured Rikkhe's silence.

'I still can't believe Himanshu Pathak was schizophrenic,' Radhika muttered. 'Will he be all right?'

Rikkhe didn't know. 'Director Walia has arranged for the best care in the infirmary.' He didn't add that Walia had probably done so to avoid the many questions that would come up were Himanshu to be treated anywhere else.

'I heard Vishakha has been in the infirmary since morning,' Radhika whispered, sounding scandalized. 'Seems like they were really into each other, huh?'

This time Rikkhe knew the answer but didn't say anything. Vishakha had headed straight back to Woodsville after cremating her mother the night before, and had been sitting next to Himanshu since then. Maybe she thought she was helping him, but the truth was that there were two patients in Woodsville's infirmary at the moment who needed counselling, neither of them of any use to Rikkhe. With Karamveer gone as well, he now had to fight the elections without any assistance, against Ramanujam, Dev and Aniket.

*

It had only been a day since Himanshu's breakdown and people were already referring to him as the 'high head scholar'.

Aniket Jain had skipped school for the first time in his life. His legs were steady, but his mind was agitated as he walked through the deserted student residential area.

The one thing that kept him from getting violently sick was the possibility that it wasn't as bad as he thought. That Ramanujam hadn't somehow found out that Himanshu was sick. That he hadn't used Aniket and Dev to get Himanshu to move to the campus so that it'd be easier to gradually drug him. That once Himanshu was here, he had procured antipsychotics to 'cure' him of his delusions. That he hadn't surreptitiously been feeding Himanshu those medicines so that one day, suddenly, when his imaginary friend vanished, it'd push Himanshu over the edge, trapped within a whirling vortex of his own making.

Aniket stopped and looked at the house to his right. He took a deep breath and walked through the yard towards the front door.

The only person who could answer all his questions was Himanshu Pathak's cook.

*

Dev's eyes followed Walia as he paced, or rather hobbled, in front of the bay windows of his office. He seemed to be in high spirits.

'So, Dev, have you given some thought to being the head scholar?'

Dev had expected this. He was not, to say the least, too pleased with the old back-stabber's suggestion.

'I *was* the head scholar, sir,' he said icily, 'and then you removed me.'

'Ah, but that's not entirely true, is it?' Walia said, pointing a mischievous finger at him. 'I authorized elections is all, effectively turning that inconsequential title—which you'll nevertheless have on your résumé—into something of vital importance in student politics. It was simply time that Woodsville affected debates on student issues at the national level. That was possible only with an election backed by the prestigious—if I say so myself—student community of Woodsville.'

Dev narrowed his eyes. 'Didn't turn out so well, did it?'

Walia suddenly looked irritated. 'The title can do only so much,' he said, waving his hand dismissively. 'Finally it's up to the person who holds it.'

'Yeah,' said Dev, 'Pathak sure made a mess of things . . .' He was thinking hard. What was Walia trying to tell him?

'A mistake not to be made again,' Walia said quietly. 'I need someone deserving to sway the votes and control the power that accompanies them. If you are elected, and subsequently backed by the offspring of the most influential people in the country, you can use the post of head scholar to its full potential. I am talking about separate press releases by Woodsville and its student lobby, television interviews, dedicated columns in the leading dailies.'

And you have the contacts to ensure all that happens. Dev was still unconvinced.

'So my exile is over?'

'You were never in exile, boy,' Walia said simply. 'You misread me . . .'

Dev frowned. There was no use pretending. He had already used his sessions with Athar to communicate his true intentions to Walia. 'You expect me to believe that your okaying elections had nothing to do with the disagreement between me and my grandfather?'

Walia smiled. 'Your grandfather was, and still is, an extremely influential figure in the power circles of this city. But I fear that you've misjudged the hold his friendship has on decisions that affect my school.'

Dev breathed slowly. 'So it wasn't all about making me leave cricket and focus on joining the air force?'

Walia laughed lightly. 'I appreciate your frankness, boy. In answer to your question, no, it wasn't. Why would I want one of my best to forgo something he's the best at?'

'Why didn't you let me know?' Dev asked, aghast. 'You knew what I was struggling with. I was explicit in my talks with Dr Athar.'

'I assure you, Dev, that Athar would not let himself be more than a one-way communication device. I heard what you were saying, but Athar wouldn't be my voice to my students. It wasn't until it was too late that I figured that out.' He glanced towards his desk; a freshly signed resignation letter from his student counsellor fluttered under the paperweight. 'Another little mistake I made. Not to be repeated again, of course.'

Walia didn't mention the frenzy of phone calls that had consumed his days since the incident. Politicians, diplomats, bureaucrats, all calling him to learn more about the rogue psychiatrist their children had told them about. Walia had attended to every call himself, assured every parent that action was being taken, and finally forced Athar to sign the resignation letter his office had prepared. He would never again find a job that mattered.

'And what did you want to say to me that Athar didn't want me to know?' Dev asked, curious.

'Just that your family's foolish if they want you to join the army or go back to America. The land of opportunity is where you are standing now.'

'You want me to continue in cricket?'

'Not the way you've been performing, though,' Walia said jokingly. 'I hear nothing but bad news from our coach these days.'

Dev chuckled involuntarily, suddenly feeling light-headed. 'What about being the head scholar?'

'Mr Pathak is, as you know, indisposed, and will not be able to carry out his duties as the head scholar. There'll be a re-election.'

Dev scowled. 'I don't put much stock in them.'

'Do not worry. This time I have ensured you'll not be denied your prize, provided you can get the requisite votes.'

'I am not so sure, Headmaster . . .' Dev began hesitantly.

'Rikkhe is not on the election committee,' Walia said pointedly.

Dev stared at him. Walia knew?

'That was another mistake on my part,' Walia said thoughtfully. 'I thought I had the measure of Rikkhe. Turned out I was wrong; that young man is bold. Taught me something important, though.' He looked Dev in the eye. 'Votes aren't just a number that are going to suffice in these elections. The head scholar will need the actual voters behind him to be able to realize the potential of his position.'

Dev nodded and got up. 'So I needn't worry about Rajput?'

'I never said that,' Walia said, walking to his desk. 'I just got a letter of candidature. Rikkhe Rajput has entered the fray.'

Dev stopped short, stunned. He recovered quickly, though. 'May the best man win.'

'Indeed. And one more thing, Dev,' Walia said, looking at him from his desk. 'Let Ramanujam know not to repeat anything like the stunt he pulled with Himanshu. I don't care if he is my ward now, the school cannot afford another crisis like this.'

The clouds parted in the sky and sunlight streamed in through the windows, turning Walia's figure into a silhouette. Dev was seeing him in a very different light, literally as well as figuratively.

'Tell him he can plan what he wants. I just don't want any noise. A pin-drop silence, so to speak.'

*

Lisa Chauhan hadn't been her usual outgoing self ever since Rikkhe had cancelled their date. What was worse, his horse had got hurt the same night, making it impossible for her to be mad at him.

She was rarely angry with Rikkhe. Usually she just felt bad for him. How completely lonely a person had to be to ignore someone so eager to give them happiness . . .

And now there were rumours floating about that Rikkhe was running for head scholar. Lisa threw her newest dress on the floor.

She was pissed. Rikkhe hadn't had the time to explain anything to her but was free enough to fill out a stupid candidature form?

'That's such a beautiful dress,' Shikha, her housemate, sitting on Lisa's bed, said ruefully, pointedly staring at the discarded dress. She had got ready for their excursion to the campus shopping mall, which, in the evening, was also flooded with regular, non-Woodsville shoppers. Not that either of them intended to do any shopping. Lisa was to introduce Shikha to Woodsville's up-and-coming athlete, Brian Ludlum.

Lisa looked down at the floor. 'Take it. It'll look nice with those turquoise earrings of yours.'

'Really?' Shikha exclaimed delightedly. She felt a little guilty for making Lisa set her up on a date so soon after she'd had her own heart broken. She got up to pick up the dress, when Lisa noticed the red gown in her cupboard. She'd bought it for the dance.

'Although,' she said slowly, 'I think this will go better with the black heels.' Lisa thrust the red gown into Shikha's hands. 'Keep it.'

Shikha's eyes widened in astonishment. Now she felt even worse about the way Rikkhe had broken things off with Lisa. Her sole comfort lay in the fact that Lisa's friends had made sure that news of Rikkhe's rudeness was spread far and wide. As Lisa was mostly adored, it wouldn't do him any favours if it was true that he was running for head scholar.

'Gee, thanks, Liz.'

Lisa nodded absent-mindedly and looked at her closet once more, suddenly tired.

'I don't think I can come with you today.'

Shikha, having just accepted two extravagant gifts, felt obliged to cajole her friend into going, but Lisa introduced a deal-changer.

'Keep the gown as a sorry for bailing on you tonight,' Lisa said, 'but I honestly don't think you'll need any help, looking the way you do.'

Shikha beamed at her gratefully. 'Wish me luck.'

'Knock him out.' Lisa smiled. *At least normal boys responded to beauty.*

Lisa got back to her wardrobe and pulled out the oldest, the most ill-fitting and worn-out of her clothes—a blue top and a pair of white shorts. They were her sister's; from a time when her family didn't have much. A time when Lisa Chauhan didn't own a single brand-new article of clothing, make-up or jewellery. When all she had were her sister's old clothes.

She wore them almost every night before bed, and no one ever saw her in them. She curled up in her bed and instantly stopped thinking about Rikkhe.

*

On the other side of the street, watching from his window in the semi-darkness, Ramanujam vaguely registered the light going off in Lisa Chauhan's room.

'So Rajput has definitely registered, then?' asked Ramanujam.

'Yash Malik's not the well-behaved fart of a diligent student he pretends to be,' Sid said airily. 'But he speaks the truth when given enough incentive.'

Ramanujam nodded. 'Dev was telling the truth, then.'

'You knew?' Sid sounded a little irritated. 'An awful lot of trouble I went to for a useless thing.'

'On the contrary,' Ramanujam said consolingly, 'you just confirmed for me that despite his outward hostility, Dev's still with us. I must thank you for it.'

Sid nodded pompously. 'It's no trouble.'

Ramanujam went and sat down beside Sid on the floor. He knew why Sid 'Charsi' Malhotra was helping him. He was one of the few mediocre students here, and was in Woodsville only on the basis of the donations and favours his family could do for the school. Sid knew his limitations, and so did Ramanujam. Nothing could motivate Sid more than to simply matter in Woodsville, and being Ramanujam's right-hand man gave him that.

Sid was also the only person he'd met here who didn't feel emasculated taking orders from a thirteen-year-old. He suspected that even Rikkhe thought of him as a kid.

'Will you be contesting as well?' Sid asked him excitedly.

Ramanujam thought about it. His reputation wasn't something he'd ever tried to preserve; he'd never needed anyone. People had been using unfavourable adjectives to describe him for a while now, and referred to him with unflattering proper nouns, of which Ramanujam's favourite was 'Napoleon'. It was highly unlikely that he could secure enough votes to beat Dev or Rikkhe . . . unless he did something outrageous. But that was the problem, wasn't it? Walia had conveyed, through Dev, that there was to be no big splash in his neat little pond.

'I don't think so,' Ramanujam said. He was settling in nicely at Woodsville, and he didn't want all the hassle that came with being the head scholar. 'Taking him head-on won't be nearly as much fun as beating Rajput at his own game. I'll prop up a puppet.'

'Dev? A puppet?' Sid seemed sceptical.

'Oh, you'd be amazed at how many strings that guy has.'

'You think he'll win?'

'He has a following, and funnily enough, he's a more genuine fellow than our prince . . .' Ramanujam said thoughtfully. 'All he needs is a nudge. Holding Rajput back will be a problem, though.'

'He's all alone now,' Sid said, smirking. 'Himanshu's in the infirmary, Vishakha's got a dead mother, his old guard seems to have abandoned him, and people are saying Lisa's pissed that he stood her up.'

Ramanujam smiled. 'Yeah, that worked out quite well. That girl,' he gestured to Lisa's house with a jerk of his head, 'was besotted with him. And he let her go.' Ramanujam shook his head in disbelief.

'And that horse!' Sid said, just remembering. 'He lost the horse too.'

'Imagine my surprise when I found out that Dev and I had broken that rare creature's leg after Rajput had already cancelled his date. Such a waste! But yes, Rajput's completely on his own now.'

Ramanujam was satisfied. Rikkhe stood for nothing, which he had proved by shunning his earlier belief and choosing to run for election. He was as crooked as Ramanujam and almost as Machiavellian. What right did he have to the love of everybody who knew or didn't know him?

It wasn't like Ramanujam was envious of the adulation Rikkhe got. After eight sets of parents, the people who were *supposed* to care about you, Ramanujam knew he was unlovable. He didn't consider himself unlucky for being an orphan. He considered himself unlucky for being *him*.

It just wasn't fair that Rikkhe had everything in spite of being exactly like him. It just wasn't balanced. And it was balance Ramanujam craved above all else.

People thought of him as chaotic, but all Ramanujam wanted was to restore order. That's why he'd slapped the power-crazy Dev the first day at school, why he'd demolished an undeserving Himanshu, why he'd trapped Aniket in his own web of self-aggrandizing bullshit and why he'd put a discarded talent like Sid to such great use. And it was precisely why, instead of helping Dev better his image, Ramanujam was going to destroy Rikkhe's.

'I'll expose him,' he muttered, more to himself than Sid. 'I'll show everyone what he is. I'll bring him down to my level . . .'

*

As Ramanujam prepared for his blissful slumber, there was more trouble brewing in the bowels of the campus. The game wasn't over yet.

Dusk had given way to an unusually still night. The infirmary was a dungeon of short breaths and uneasy sleep. As a dull murmur in the distance broke through the stillness, someone's breathing changed rhythm; he was no longer slave to sleep.

The first sight that greeted Himanshu on opening his eyes made him gasp in shock. Vishakha was curled up on the edge of the bed next to him, her face turned towards him. Only, it wasn't the Vishakha he knew; the appearance she was always so conscious about keeping up had abandoned her, giving way to something vulnerable. Her clothes were the same as the ones Himanshu remembered from his dreams over the last few days, but shabbier, dirtier. Vishakha's face looked worn, brittle; dried tears clung to her lashes. Her hair looked like it hadn't seen a comb in weeks and it seemed as though she had made it her mission to take up as little space as she possibly could on the adjacent empty bed.

Himanshu got up from his bed, still staring at Vishakha in horror. Somehow he knew she needed to sleep more than she needed the comfort of his recovery. He let her be.

The murmur outside had grown louder. It was coming from the general direction of the playground. Himanshu moved towards it. The murmur was moving too. Towards the student residences. He followed it outside.

A throng of people was following Rikkhe Rajput, who walked in silence beside his magnificent equine. The horse was limping. She walked without guidance, though, lending such an eerie, mythic feel to the scene that no one tried to approach them. They just followed at a distance. And a little further back, Himanshu followed them.

As they passed through the student residences, the crowd grew larger. People came running out of their houses to gaze at the erstwhile prince of a forgotten kingdom.

Himanshu could tell Rikkhe had stopped in front of one of the houses, for the crowd had stopped as well. By the time Himanshu caught up to them, there was a commotion in someone's front yard.

What had been low murmuring till just a while ago had now risen to a loud chant. 'Rikkhe! Rikkhe! Rikkhe!'

And then he saw him. Standing by his horse, looking his most stately, was Rikkhe, locked in a tight embrace with the most beautiful girl Himanshu had ever seen. The hug was so fierce, and Lisa's tears and laughter so moving, that Himanshu felt himself inching back towards the infirmary, towards Vishakha.

Lisa's nightclothes seemed peculiar; no one could have imagined seeing her so underdressed. But she still looked beautiful. When she let Rikkhe go, she nodded vigorously, tears streaming down her face, unrestrained. 'Of course I forgive you.'

Rikkhe cleared his throat. His voice was clear, loud and calm. 'There are only two instances a Rajput is brought to his knees—when defeated by his enemy, which you most assuredly are not . . .'

Lisa struggled to wrap her head around what he was trying to say, while everyone, including Himanshu, watched with bated breath. 'And the other?'

Then the students saw something they'd never thought possible in their dreams. Rikkhe, the quintessential well-mannered gentleman, clumsily lowered himself on the muddy ground, quite literally on his knees.

'Is you.' He closed his eyes. 'I surrender.'

Before the entire school, most of the maintenance staff and half the faculty, Lisa knelt down in front of her prince, in her old shorts and plain top, and kissed him.

The spell cast upon the viewers was broken by this less awe-inspiring scene, and there were whistles, cheers and louder chants of 'Rikkhe! Rikkhe!'

Rikkhe broke the kiss. Nobody but Lisa could have guessed it was his first.

He got up and ran an affectionate hand over his horse.

'It is a custom to bring a gift,' he said, 'and here's mine to you. Nandini.'

Lisa's mouth opened in surprise. 'But I don't . . . I don't know how to . . .'

'She'll teach you to ride,' Rikkhe said, lowering his voice. 'And I hope you'll teach her how to run again.'

Lisa couldn't speak, but beamed at him. Everyone knew how much Rikkhe Rajput's horse meant to him.

Rikkhe smiled and turned to the crowd, as though noticing them for the first time. He spoke up, and there was silence once more.

'Responsibility. Commitment. Loyalty,' Rikkhe called out into the night. 'These are no ordinary words. I propose to you, as I have just proposed to Lisa, to accept me. I vow to make the students of Woodsville the biggest consensus-builders for the school-going population of the country. I'll be responsible if we fail. And more than that,' he glanced at Lisa and Nandini meaningfully, 'I'll be loyal to all of you, no matter what we face.

'Accept me, if you will!' Rikkhe spoke imperiously, his voice never once rising to a shout, yet ringing in the air. 'As the new head scholar of Woodsville Scholars International.'

A moment of silence, and then mayhem. If Rikkhe's peers were cheering before, they were positively jumping up and down with glee now.

No one noticed Himanshu leave, satisfied that his old job was in safe hands. Neither did anyone notice the figure lurking at the window across the street.

Ramanujam's insides twisted and turned with each passing moment. In one fell swoop, all his hard work to break Rikkhe had come undone. The prince's teary-eyed audience was clearly won over. Ramanujam hadn't been able to stop Rikkhe through those he was close to, and he now understood why. In spite of himself, he'd still believed that deep down, Rikkhe was actually virtuous.

As he saw Rikkhe use Lisa's goodwill to climb the power ladder of Woodsville, Ramanujam knew he was dealing with a monster as depraved as himself.

'I'll bring you to your knees, too, Rajput,' he breathed. 'If it's the last thing I do, I'll bring you to your knees . . .'

Almost as if he'd heard him, Rikkhe looked straight at the silhouette by the window, smiling, as if to say, *We'll see.*

*

The aftermath of Rikkhe's grand declaration saw a flurry of activity among the potential candidates, the student body and the administration.

There were whispers in the corridors that although Walia had wanted the election conducted as soon as possible, the faculty, as well as Admin Kumari, were up in arms about this idea. It was then decided that the election would take place after the half-yearly exams, so as to enable the students to give their studies undivided attention. But instead, the students were now distracted by the incessant campaigning.

Within a couple of days of Rikkhe's announcement, Dev led their cricket team to a much-awaited and long-due win against another premier institution, the Delhi Public School. In the post-match ceremony, which was being broadcasted live on the campus radio, he announced his candidature with all the glamour and flourish that was expected of him. Despite this, Rikkhe remained the favourite.

Almost immediately, Aniket Jain entered the fray as well, although without making a spectacle of himself, as he'd done the first time around. His chances had been slim then, now they were slimmer still.

Spurred by Himanshu's unexpected win just months back, Radhika Goel, Yash Malik and a few other model students also submitted their names for the post, although, subconsciously, none of them really expected to win. It was just a way to get noticed by the eminent members of the faculty and, if they got really lucky, by the director.

Among these unlikely aspirants was one who attracted a fair bit of attention—Ramanujam, the child prodigy. He'd already outperformed everyone in the unit tests, earning him a lot of appreciation from a delighted faculty. His eccentricity had already become legendary at Woodsville, although most attributed it to his genius. All anyone really knew about him was that he was an orphan; a fact that was easy to sympathize with, but not enough to get him votes.

One thing had become clear immediately—everyone was competing with Rikkhe Rajput. Flyers (much like the ones that had rocked the school a few weeks back, Admin Kumari noted) were scattered all over campus, posters went up, all condemning the silver-spooned royalty. Makeshift booths were erected by candidates in the most frequented areas around the school. The once beautiful campus of Woodsville seemed like a diffused shadow of its past.

All the campaigning, however, seemed to have been copied from second-rate movies, and held no real relevance for the Villean voters. For instance, the 'silver-spoon' barb was futile, as a majority of the students came from extremely well-off families. It was almost as if the advocates of the negative campaigning just wanted Rikkhe to react, which, of course, he didn't.

Prime among these campaigners was Ramanujam himself. He harped on and on about how Rikkhe was a fraud, how he was just using Lisa to enhance the aura of mystique that surrounded him, and how he had been unfair to the candidates in the previous election. This, other than being absurd, was quite ineffective in besmirching Rikkhe's name. All that it accomplished, besides making Ramanujam immensely unlikeable, was to put his animosity towards Rikkhe in the limelight.

Walia had put no restrictions on the nature and expense of the promotions, and on the eve of the half-yearlies, Yash Malik could be seen distributing a list of 'expected' questions in the student residences.

Aniket, who had neither the means nor the necessary people skills to gather votes, spent most of his evenings sitting on the steps of the amphitheatre with his books.

The evening before the first exam, Aniket sat studying in the amphitheatre, trying to focus desperately while getting frequently distracted by the animated conversations Yash Malik was striking up with all his studious voters, discussing their syllabi and allaying their fears. Somehow, he seemed to know what everyone was worried about. Aniket grunted, disgusted.

'He's gonna lose, you know.' Aniket agreed with the words, but that didn't make the familiar voice any less unwelcome.

'I know.' Aniket tried to stay cool as Ramanujam sat beside him.

'He's still gonna get more votes than you, though.'

Even though Ramanujam's comment infuriated him, he refrained from reacting. In his last year at Woodsville, Aniket had been learning not to take things for granted. 'He seems to be putting in a lot of effort.'

'*You* seem to be putting in a lot of effort as well,' Ramanujam remarked, nodding at the R.D. Sharma lying on Aniket's lap.

Aniket shrugged, getting back to his tome.

'I am still gonna get more marks than you,' Ramanujam chanted.

Now Aniket was pissed off. 'What do you want?'

'The question, Sir Aniket,' Ramanujam said coolly, 'is, what is it that *you* want? Do you want to top in the half-yearlies or do you want to lose to me like you did in the unit tests?'

Aniket felt a chill ripple through him, a mix of anger, violence and irrational fear.

'You're with us, or you're against us,' Ramanujam continued. 'And if you're with us, then focus on bringing Rikkhe down.'

'So that you or Dev can win?'

'Not me.' Ramanujam put up his hands innocently. 'I have no illusions; I have no chance of becoming head scholar. I pray, sir, that you harbour no illusions about winning yourself.'

'You want *my* help to put Dev back on top?'

'There can be no cheating this time,' Ramanujam said simply. 'The voting's gonna be electronic. And what's more, it'll take place right after a debate between all the candidates. You can't possibly hope to win.'

'You seem pretty certain of what I can and can't do.'

'Yeah, I do. You can't beat Dev at getting votes. You can't beat Rikkhe at a debate. You can't beat me at academics. What you *can* do is back me up at certain points in the debate, so as to torpedo Rikkhe's entire campaign.'

'Now who's being unrealistic?' Aniket snorted.

'Oh, he's ahead right now all right, but he isn't invulnerable. There are still some skeletons in his closet that'll be damaging enough to sway the voters against him.'

'What kind of skeletons?' Aniket wasn't sure he wanted to know.

'Oh, I think it would make for an interesting story if we were to reveal how Himanshu Pathak came to be the head scholar. How the election commissioner, Rikkhe Rajput, misused his powers—'

'Why will they believe us?'

'—and how you helped him.'

Aniket stared at Ramanujam. He wasn't shocked at what Ramanujam was asking of him. He was shocked because he fully expected Aniket to go along with it. And Ramanujam usually got what he wanted.

'You're joking? Why would I implicate myself in something like this? Something I didn't even do?'

'Respect,' Ramanujam shot back confidently. 'That's what you're after. I figured it out through Athar's file on you.' He waved aside Aniket's scandalized expression. 'Now ask yourself, will losing to Rikkhe in the election, and to me in the exams, do any good to the respect people already don't have for you?'

Aniket was silent.

'Or—picture this—you bring down the Rajput in an act of bravado. And on the same day get the half-yearly result that says that you beat the prodigious Ramanujam . . .'

Despite himself, Aniket found himself imagining it. Hell, he could almost taste it.

'You don't have to be the villain to discredit Rikkhe. I'll fight with him on stage. I'll be the villain. You just have to lend credence to what I accuse him of.'

'Why would anyone believe what I say?' Aniket said tensely.

Ramanujam smiled. 'They don't need to; the accusation just needs to be scandalous enough. Someone as prideful as Aniket Jain confessing to his guilt on stage? That'll give them enough reason to doubt Rikkhe for a few hours, by which time the votes will have been cast. Rikkhe'll lose, and by nightfall you'll hear that you topped in the exams. I'll let you win.'

This blatant insinuation of charity made Aniket catch himself from committing rashly.

'You think you can beat me at will?' His voice had a hint of danger.

'You think I can't?' Ramanujam challenged.

Aniket was disarmed by his surety.

'Interesting thing you're working on.' Ramanujam pointed at a differential problem their Fields Medal winning mathematics professor had given to Aniket. The man had said it was one of the most complex questions he'd come across. Aniket had been working on it for the better part of the last six months.

Ramanujam took his pen and wrote something on Aniket's hand.

'Show this to whoever gave you this assignment.' Ramanujam nodded at Aniket's balled fist. 'Chances are they haven't found the answer themselves.'

Aniket couldn't breathe as he stared at his hand.

Ramanujam got up and started walking down the steps, calling over his shoulder. 'Make sure you yell "Eureka! Eureka!" when you find them.'

*

Instead of the usual air of idleness, the day after the half-yearlies was filled with the hustle and bustle of activity. Instead of the results, all anyone could talk about was the debate that would precede the ballot. Even the two students who'd written their papers in the infirmary weren't oblivious to the anticipation. Himanshu Pathak was, by now, the resident patient of Woodsville. Vishakha still thought of herself as his carer, and he had continued letting her think that. Till today.

'You aren't participating in the election at all?' he asked her quietly. He'd let her study next to him in peace for the last few days, but the time for procrastination was over.

Vishakha, seated on a chair next to him, shook her head unconcernedly, concentrating on the gazette she was reading.

'Rikkhe can't face them alone,' Himanshu said urgently. 'He'll need someone in his corner.'

'He got us into this mess,' she said without looking up, 'he can get himself out.'

'How's your father?' Himanshu asked her abruptly.

She shrugged. 'He knew it was going to happen. I knew too. We were prepared.' She looked better now, but her voice sounded unnaturally calm.

Himanshu sighed. How would she know how her father was? She hadn't left Himanshu's side since her mother's last rites.

'Don't you think you should go home?' he suggested.

'No, I am staying here,' she said resolutely. 'With you.'

Himanshu was silent for some time. His brush with absolute insanity seemed to have given him surprising clarity. He knew what it was that kept Vishakha glued to her chair. And he'd be damned if she retreated into herself, like he had.

'I am not your mother, Vizac,' he said pointedly.

She stared at him. 'What does that mean?'

'That you can't use me to assuage your guilt. You'll only add to it by not being with your father right now.'

'I am not feeling guilty about anything,' Vishakha said mechanically.

Himanshu smiled sadly. 'Then why are you here?'

Vishakha glared at him. 'I care about you, in case you didn't realize.'

'The Vishakha I know would be out there, trying to help get the people responsible for this,' Himanshu gestured at himself. He had lost a lot of weight and colour in the past few weeks. 'Or she'd be next to her father, although that's less likely. What she certainly wouldn't be doing is being in here . . . hiding.'

Vishakha leapt up as though he'd snapped at her. She gathered the stuff she'd accumulated on the bed next to Himanshu's, stuffed it into her bag and started walking towards the door, never once meeting his eyes.

Gingerly, with his eyes on her, Himanshu got out of bed. He'd been there too long. Now that he realized that Rikkhe was all alone, he couldn't rest. If Vishakha wouldn't help him, Himanshu would.

First, though, he had to push her over the edge. That, he had learnt, was the only way to truly survive. He called after her, the words painful to utter.

'The Vishakha I knew wasn't a coward!'

He could only guess how painful they were to hear.

THE ORPHAN'S LAST PLAY

The first week of December brought with it the inevitable chill Delhi's populace had come to expect and brace themselves for. Woodsville, situated smack in the middle of the Central Reserve Forest, felt it harder than anyplace else.

In addition to the unforgiving weather, there was the equally harsh debate. A last-minute opportunity to gather support, it had been optional for the candidates. Most of them had chosen to sit it out, with only Rikkhe, Ramanujam, Aniket, Dev and Yash Malik participating. Dev's inclusion was a surprise, as he had done more than enough campaigning on the cricket ground, where he'd captained his house to a well-earned victory.

Ramanujam woke up on the day of the election with a sense of happiness. He wasn't going to win, but at least Rikkhe was going to lose.

Sid was still sleeping when Ramanujam sat down at the table to write. By the time he'd finished, he could see people up and about in their yards. He felt detached, even more than usual.

He put the paper in his pocket, separate from the cards which held his talking points on the debate. If he failed to destroy Rikkhe's reputation in the debate today, he had an insurance in his shirt pocket.

*

The auditorium was jam-packed. The morning was dedicated to the debate, the afternoon to casting the ballots and the evening to the results—of the election as well as the half-yearlies. Both were starting to look like pretty unpredictable affairs, with so many contenders for the position of the academic topper and the head scholar. The auditorium still had some vestiges of the stubborn glue-stuck pamphlets that had proclaimed Himanshu's insanity, but nobody really paid attention to them. It was human nature to forget. The Villeans already had.

Reverberating, repeated thuds brought a hush over the auditorium.

'Welcome,' Walia spoke from the stage, resting his walking stick by his side. 'Today you decide on your representative at Woodsville and in the outside world for the remainder of this academic year. The somewhat unfortunate incident a few weeks back notwithstanding,' glances went to the faint tape marks on some walls, 'it is with renewed vigour and optimism that we conduct this debate today.'

There was clapping. Polite, with a tinge of impatience. The audience wanted the contenders at each other's throats, something the negative campaigning had assured them would happen.

'To ensure the utmost transparency,' Walia continued, stressing each word, 'the votes will be cast and counted digitally in real time. For casting the votes please head to the makeshift tent in the main grounds, and you can observe the live electronic count in the reception hall of the main school building.' He clapped his hands. 'Let us begin the debate!'

One by one, the candidates took their place at the specially erected podiums on the stage. The debate format was completely free-form, just as the rest of the campaign had been. There were no rules at all.

Most eyes were on Rikkhe, who stood uncharacteristically inert. His head down, he looked oddly expectant.

Yash Malik started to speak fervently. His restlessness over the past few days was the perfect example of how events were influencing the regular majority. The persistent itch to win had grown stronger with all the hysteria.

'Friends, welcome to—' Yash began.

'—the last day of uncertainty!' Dev cut in briskly. 'Today, you put an end to the circus we've been witnessing over the last few months. Today, you choose someone you know can assume the mantle of head scholar for the rest of the year. The only viable options,' he paused, looking around at the others, 'are Rikkhe and I.'

People in the audience exchanged incredulous stares. In the front row, Walia raised an eyebrow.

Rikkhe, however, looked unsurprised and unmoved by this statement, as did Aniket and Ramanujam, at their respective podiums.

'Indeed,' Dev continued, stealing a glance at Rikkhe, 'I doubt anyone else here can provide the school with the stability it needs or represent the school at prestigious events as well as Rikkhe and I can. I urge you to remember my involvement in inter-school cricketing over the last three years, not to mention debates, quizzes and other extra-curricular drives. And Rikkhe, as we all know, is in a class of his own.'

There was an audible, incredulous clearing of throats from the spectators. Dev wasn't the magnanimous type.

'Yeah, His Highness surely is something, no?' Ramanujam spoke up venomously. 'He's still living in a bygone era, though. When I topped in the unit tests, he felt it necessary to declare "war" on me!' He chuckled, and some students joined him, probably thinking he was joking. 'I mean, come on. A fight? Okay . . . A grudge, I can understand. But war, what the hell?'

Rikkhe didn't speak.

'That's a pretty serious allegation you're making there, my little friend,' Yash Malik said, apparently reinvigorated by the possible decimation of a bigwig.

'No, my big friend,' Ramanujam continued with relish, 'he's felt so threatened by me academically that he's threatened me to get out of the race twice now. Or as he said, he'll "beat me up".'

There were some gasps from the students and glares from the faculty. Rikkhe looked bemused.

'I am telling you, he can do anything for a little bit of power. It'll be a disaster if you give it to him,' Ramanujam's voice was hypnotic, 'because then he'll only want more.'

Like a well-rehearsed act, Dev pretended to look shocked. 'If what you're saying is true, then I'd like to withdraw my earlier support of Rikkhe.'

'Leaving you as the only viable option, right?' Yash was scathing in his attack.

'As opposed to you, Yash?' Dev shot back. 'Certainly.' He faced the audience. 'I have done a lot for this school.' His eyes smouldered, as if to say, *And now you all owe me.* He turned back to Yash. 'Don't get me wrong, you've done a lot for the students, too. Let's just say, you can give Santa Claus a run for his money now.'

There was a hearty laugh from the audience. Yash was stumped. After spreading the word, over the past few weeks, that he was open to giving and receiving bribes, he could not now deny it.

Rikkhe looked up finally. His face was sombre as he addressed the students.

'I am sorry that instead of talking about the issues that concern the student body, the candidates are choosing to make allegations that can't be proved.'

Ramanujam mocked shock. 'Oh my goodness, you're right, my prince, I can't prove anything I said.' Everyone waited. 'So I'll say something I *can* prove. I know the reason Dev lost the first election.'

He'd touched a nerve. Rikkhe knew it. Ramanujam knew it. There had been so much speculation over

Himanshu's miraculous win that the students would believe any explanation Ramanujam offered.

'You were the election commissioner, no?' he asked, pointing a finger at Rikkhe. 'And you couldn't see him,' a jerk of his head towards Dev, 'win. So you cheated on the vote-counting.'

There was a shocked silence.

Rikkhe pointed at the audience. 'They know me.' There was a sustained cheer. 'Do they know you? And what do *you* know, considering all of it happened before you came to this school?'

'There's someone who was there,' Ramanujam said, 'who helped you, who saw everything you did. You've been uncharacteristically quiet, Aniket. Have anything to add?'

All eyes turned to Aniket. For the first time, Rikkhe looked tense.

Aniket didn't speak immediately, his eyes fixed on the podium. But when he looked up, there was resolve in his eyes.

'Yes, I'd like to add something.' Aniket turned to Rikkhe and met his gaze coldly. 'I believe you're the best person for the job. I'd like to officially withdraw from the race.'

There was a stunned silence. Himanshu, who was backstage, waiting to counter Aniket's allegations, stopped breathing. There were no allegations. Aniket Jain had defected to their side. Slowly, discreetly, Rikkhe raised a finger, signalling Himanshu to back down. Himanshu finally understood what that subterfuge in the auditorium all those months ago had been about—Rikkhe had made himself less of an enemy in Aniket's eyes.

'What?' Ramanujam barked.

'You are despicable, you and Dev,' Aniket said passionately. 'You read Himanshu's file from Dr Athar's office. Then Dev forced him to move to campus, where you bribed his cook to discreetly feed antipsychotic drugs to him. Drugs that made his hallucination of a friend vanish without explanation. Drugs that I helped steal for you.'

Aniket was sacrificing himself all right, but instead of taking down Rikkhe with him, he was destroying his own allies. Ramanujam and Dev could do nothing but look.

The spectators erupted in a barrage of noise. Admin Kumari rushed to the stage.

'We'll cut this short. Now,' she said sharply. 'Back to your classes—'

Walia's stick made a resounding thud, which could be heard over all the commotion.

'Off to the main grounds, you mean, Ms Kumari,' he corrected her loudly. 'The voting will take place now.'

*

The contest wasn't even close. Rikkhe was so far ahead that the combined votes of all the other candidates couldn't match his count. Surprisingly, Aniket's name wasn't removed from the ballot. Even more surprising was the fact that he had come in second.

The celebration lasted all day. Rikkhe was the man of the hour, and beside him was Lisa, jumping up and down with happiness. None of the other candidates were anywhere to be seen.

In the evening, news came in that Ramanujam had aced the half-yearlies. Even there, Aniket had stood second.

But nobody was paying attention to the exams any more. Everyone believed that, with Rikkhe, they were now part of something bigger than themselves. The student body would finally matter and the new head scholar would make sure that they were a force to be reckoned with.

The next morning, most people forgot about it all. A topper was found lying in front of the school building. Dead.

*

Two silhouettes stood against the moonlight on the roof of the country's toughest school. A gigantic neon-white banner towered over them. Placed on a raised platform, it illuminated the night sky with the words 'Woodsville Scholars International'. The 200-acre school campus, located in the Central Ridge, almost seemed to be a part of Lutyens's colonial-era design of the Rashtrapati Bhavan, which was visible in the distance. Both structures had the old-school charm of red sandstone on the outside.

'I am going to kill you,' one of the shapes said, shivering with anger, its voice hushed with fear.

There was an involuntary bark of laughter from the other figure. 'You know what the problem with being a topper is? There's always someone waiting in line to beat you.'

A moment later, the two shadows merged in a scuffle. A part trying to wriggle free and the other intent on engulfing the struggling captive.

'Let me go' . . . 'What're you doing?' Two rasps punctuated the short but intense fight. The finale, however, came with a dull thud on the unfeeling concrete below. The shadow had been split once more, right down the middle. One half stood leaning forward at the edge of the roof, seemingly reeling from the shock of the abrupt separation, while the other lay immobile on the ground.

Fifteen-year-old Nabil, who had been dutifully cleaning the banner a few minutes ago, could do nothing but stare on in shock, the neon light behind him outlining a third silhouette that went completely unnoticed.

THE DAY AFTER—PART I
(A DOCTOR'S APPOINTMENT)

On the insistence of his family, Dr Athar had spent the last week at various psychiatric conferences. He had to get another job, and having burnt old bridges in his unceremonious exit from Woodsville, he had to build new ones.

He was up early, dreading having to go to another one of those things, when Walia called.

'Athar, get to the school, now.' Walia sounded harassed.

'I don't think I heard you right,' Athar said, putting the phone closer to his ear.

'Get to Woodsville!' Walia was panting as though he'd been running. 'I need you back on the job.'

Athar heard panic. 'What happened, sir?'

'A student was thrown off the roof!'

Athar stopped short, cold.

'Athar!'

'Who was it?'

'Ramanujam. He was murdered.'

*

Classes had been suspended for the day. There was a discussion between the faculty and the administration, who concluded that the kids should be sent home temporarily. The police strongly opposed the decision. Getting the kids to talk in front of their parents would be far tougher than questioning them at Woodsville.

Which was, by no means, to say that this task was an easy one. Inspector Satyarthi was having a hard time getting through to Walia. He was a good investigator and that's why he'd been put on the job, but all he'd heard since entering Walia's office half an hour ago was how he couldn't do his job.

'You'll not talk to the students,' Walia said to him. 'Our school therapist, Dr Athar, will do the talking. You can observe.' Satyarthi assumed that he was referring to the man sitting quietly on the sofa.

Inspector Satyarthi, who'd had a dozen calls from his seniors since he'd been put on the case, citing procedural nuances and the need for tact, nodded.

'I can see that you still haven't noticed that a kid died,' he remarked coolly, as Walia stared.

'Of course I've noticed!'

'Then stop playing these power games and let me get to the truth.'

Walia closed in on him. 'Our board of trustees includes a former Supreme Court chief justice, my dear *Inspector*.

He'll gladly reassure you if you have any doubts regarding my position on the matter.'

One thing that made the middle-aged Satyarthi good at investigating was his ability to read situations. The fact that he was still just a senior inspector might have been due to his inability to handle those situations.

'You can call him,' he said calmly, 'but I don't think you want to. Because then the judge will call his pals in the South Block. The home ministry will get in touch with the commissioner, who'll let my boss have an earful. My boss knows me. He will let me go on until they suspend me.'

Walia stared. He was starting to understand that the inspector wouldn't be easily controlled.

'So,' Satyarthi continued, 'do you want to involve that many people just to tell me something, or would you rather tell me yourself?'

The man on the sofa cleared his throat and got up.

'Mr Satyarthi,' he said, extending his hand, 'I know these kids better than they do themselves. And you seem to know your job,' he glanced at the flustered Walia, 'pretty well.'

'You're saying I'll need your help to catch the kid who did this?' Satyarthi said challengingly.

Athar said gravely, 'Oh, I think I already know who did it.'

*

Athar's old office was converted into a makeshift interrogation room. Although Satyarthi wouldn't have been able to tell, as he paced around, Athar was sitting in his chair after a long time. He hadn't thought he ever would, again.

'Then what you're saying is that conducting these interviews would be redundant?' Satyarthi asked. Athar seemed competent enough to him, although the unkempt office suggested something other than a meticulous man.

'Yes,' Athar said, sighing, 'I don't think anyone else was involved. These are the top students of the country we're talking about. They have their share of problems, but nobody would do such a thing. Except Ramanujam.'

'You're sure about that?'

'He'd just lost the election, and I don't think he was accustomed to losing. It was suicide.'

Satyarthi put his phone on the table. 'Explain this, then.'

Athar saw it and felt sick. It was Ramanujam, lying face up in a pool of his own blood. His shirt pocket was torn, his left eye was bruised, and there was a distinct cut on his lower lip . . . Unmistakable signs of him having been in a scuffle.

'Okay, it wasn't suicide,' Athar said, putting the phone away. He'd seen too many school fights not to recognize one.

Satyarthi nodded. 'The fatal injuries to the back that resulted from the fall were nowhere near as gentle as the ones on the front. The injuries on his face couldn't have been caused by anything *while* falling, because, as far as I know, nothing broke his fall. The only explanation that remains is that he was pushed off—maybe accidentally—in a fight.'

Athar closed his eyes. He couldn't help but feel a little guilty. He had detested the kid. There was no need to share that with the inspector, though.

'This probably won't help much, but I can tell you that a lot of people disliked that boy.'

Satyarthi shrugged. 'Actually, it does help. It means more people will be willing to say stuff about him. That's what a case like this comes down to. Getting people to talk.'

Satyarthi continued, still pacing. 'But whom do we talk *to*?' he asked. 'I cannot stop students at random. If they let their parents know that the police are talking to them about a murder, I'll be swimming in lawsuits.'

'From what I've gathered since this morning,' Athar said slowly, 'things did get a little heated during the campaigning.'

Satyarthi stopped pacing. 'Go on.'

Athar hesitated.

'Trust me not to make hasty judgements, Doctor, and go on.'

'Rikkhe Rajput, the one who became head scholar yesterday . . .'

'What about him?' Despite his reassurance, his voice sounded sharper.

'Ramanujam's campaign targeted Rikkhe specifically,' Athar said. 'A few of the kids I spoke to at the crime scene this morning said that it felt kind of personal between the two.' Seeing Satyarthi's intrigued face, he added, 'Rikkhe never struck back during the campaign, though. All of them attested to that.'

Athar's heart skipped a beat as he remembered something else one of the younger students had said, while his friends had nodded in agreement. *He threatened to beat him. That's what Ramanujam had said during the debate. That Rikkhe had told him he would beat him. Twice.*

Athar, however, had learnt to take anything that came out of Ramanujam's mouth with a bucket of salt. So he decided to keep quiet. For now.

'So what now?' Athar asked.

'I'll go to the primary crime scene and see if I can't find out whom you *should* talk to.' As Athar looked quizzical, he said, 'The roof, Doctor. I am going to the roof to look for clues.'

*

Walia had had a slew of calls since this whole shebang began. Some were condolences, others anxious remonstrations, while the rest were curious reporters seeking to enter the campus. It was all so chaotic that he didn't know what to expect any time his phone rang; deals were being made, compromises being reached.

He was a little more than intrigued, therefore, when his secretary announced that it was Dev's grandfather on the line for him. As far as he knew, Brij Kishore Bhushan didn't waste words on condolences or complaints.

'Old friend,' he said gravely, as soon as Walia picked up, 'so sorry about your student.'

'Yeah, a tragic accident,' Walia replied animatedly, 'and what a brilliant student he was.'

'Is there something I can do?' Bhushan got straight to the point.

'Like what?'

'The hounds haven't come calling yet?' Bhushan feigned amazement. 'From what the TV channels are saying, other students might've been involved, what with the child being a prodigy and all. The situation you're in, I'd imagine people might try to take advantage.'

Walia had spent a decade wading through bureaucratic mess before he'd managed to build Woodsville. He knew a veiled threat when he heard one.

'What do you mean?'

'The kid was your ward, was he not?' Bhushan asked innocently. It was something Walia had boasted about at a social gathering once. *Educationist slash philanthropist.* 'His guardian will be held responsible for his death.'

Walia knew he was being threatened, but he still didn't know what for.

'People these days will say anything,' Walia agreed.

'Better to have your friends vouching for you in such situations,' Bhushan said.

Walia was being told that he had grown cavalier with his friendships. He'd forgotten that there was a world outside his nice little school. He was being reminded that he was not invincible.

'I understand how unfair it must feel . . .' Bhushan continued soothingly. 'It's such a sacred bond between you and the child you are responsible for. Never feels good when someone comes between you and him, does it?'

Finally it was clear. Brij Kishore Bhushan, the retired general, had learnt in the army to strike the enemy only if he could bring him down. Walia knew this because they had learnt it together. Bhushan hadn't reacted immediately on realizing that Walia was fuelling Dev's ambitions of becoming a cricketer. He had bided his time. Today was different, though. Today, he had smelled blood.

Walia paused for a moment. He weighed his desire to see an alumnus be a star cricketer with how badly he needed this whole mess to be over. He chose the latter.

'I know I can rely on you,' Walia said, sighing, 'the way you can on me.'

He hung up the phone and shook his head, reminding himself that it was just one of those days. Deals would have to be made, compromises would have to be reached.

*

At first, Satyarthi didn't find much on the roof; teenagers didn't leave any damage on the concrete when they fought. He hadn't expected to find anything substantial anyway. He'd just wanted to look at how far down the ground was from up there. How ruthless and unscrupulous a kid would have to be, to throw someone down from that height . . .

As he peered down from the parapet, two things seemed odd to him. One, the parapet was too high for the thirteen-year-old to have been tossed over easily. His assailant would've had to lift him up halfway to be able to push him off the edge.

The second thing he noticed was the Woodsville banner. It stood at a slight angle, and he could see the front. Stark white, unlit during the day, it still gleamed in the winter sun. *Woodsville Scholars International.* There was something amiss, though, visible only to as experienced an eye as Satyarthi's.

The first half of the banner was gleaming, spotless. The other half wasn't as clean. Satyarthi went closer to make sure it wasn't a trick of the light, and found that he was right. Half of the banner was coated with over a day's worth of dust.

He retreated a few steps, away from the edge of the roof, and looked behind the banner. A wooden plank with ropes attached lay neatly concealed behind the grilled support. Something a worker would sit on while cleaning something high up.

Satyarthi rushed back downstairs. He'd found someone for Athar to talk to.

He had found either a suspect or a witness.

*

It was nightfall by the time the story finally started to take shape. The delay, as Satyarthi later learnt, had been due to the reluctance of the administrative head, Ms Kumari, to call on the witness. As it turned out, the worker assigned the precarious job of cleaning the banner every night was a fifteen-year-old. Although not technically illegal, it wouldn't make the school look good.

The kid, Nabil was his name, had been there when it happened. It took some cajoling from the student counsellor to get him to relive the events of the night before. By the end of it, Satyarthi was certain that the boy and his version of events were genuine.

'I am going to kill you,' the attacker had said.

Ramanujam had laughed. 'You know what the problem with being a topper is? There's always someone waiting in line to beat you.'

And that's all Nabil had heard. Hidden behind the banner, he'd seen nothing. He'd heard the scuffle that followed, the fall and the culprit hurrying off the roof.

After they'd sent the scared Nabil off, there was silence in Walia's room. Neither Walia nor Admin Kumari seemed to take the events as lightly as they had done just that morning. Standing near the window, looking down, Athar breathed heavily.

'You were right, then, Inspector,' he said. 'It would seem it was premeditated.'

'What gave it away?' Satyarthi replied sardonically. 'The "I'll kill you"?'

Athar didn't say anything. He knew how frustrated the policeman must feel, being forced to work with his hands tied. Athar had worked that way for years.

'That's it,' Satyarthi hissed, rounding on the director and his administrator, 'the gloves are off. This kid is still out there, and he's dangerous. I don't care what you think any more. Now *you* lot will cooperate with *me*.'

Walia sank into his chair. He was exhausted.

Kumari took a step forward. 'Anything.'

'Isn't it obvious by now?' Satyarthi said. 'Get all your toppers here. All those involved in the election yesterday. Anyone the victim had ever beaten by even the smallest margin. Anyone he'd ever lost to.'

Walia's office door was open; it was late and his personal assistant had left for the day. An unobtrusive figure entered quietly, unnoticed by all but Athar. The counsellor took one look at his former patient and knew that he was there to confess. He closed his eyes, suddenly as tired as Walia.

'There was only one person who ever beat Ramanujam,' the newcomer announced with his trademark calmness, 'and that's me.'

*

Satyarthi hadn't yet asked the boy anything, but as he mentally prepared himself, outside the interrogation room in the police station, he had an inexplicable sense of foreboding. He felt it was, in part, due to how they'd all reacted to the boy's statement, back in Walia's office.

I was on the roof with Ramanujam yesterday, but I didn't kill him.

Walia, Kumari, Athar, all of them had been *relieved*. They'd actually believed him. It was then that Satyarthi had made the decision to take the proceedings out of their control.

He entered the room and bolted the door behind him. He knew, as he'd known since he'd first laid eyes on that boy, that he wasn't without resources. He was from one of those influential families that every policeman knew not to trifle with.

But he hadn't asked for anything. No parents. No phone call. No lawyer. Nothing.

He just sat there in his unbuttoned Jodhpuri jacket, looking expectant.

'So, what's your story, Mr Rajput?'

Rikkhe cleared his throat. 'First, let me apologize to you for not coming forward earlier.'

'Well, killing a competitor surely earns you a day of forgetfulness.' Satyarthi was not playing. He had a sense of people, and he felt Rikkhe wasn't going to give him what he wanted.

'I can understand why you would think that,' Rikkhe said, nodding.

'Let's hear what *you* think happened.'

'Certainly. After the celebrations last night, I headed to the roof for a quiet moment.'

'Where you met the boy?'

'Ramanujam?' Rikkhe looked confused. 'No, he followed me.'

It was Satyarthi's turn to look confused. 'Go on.'

'As I said, Ramanujam must've seen me heading up there, because barely a minute later, he was behind me.'

'*He* attacked *you*?' Satyarthi snorted. 'That's bloody convenient, no?'

'As opposed to me attacking him?' Rikkhe said sharply. 'That's bloody unprovable, no?'

Satyarthi shrugged. 'It would be, if we had no witnesses, but someone saw you two up there. So if your story is true, I'll know. If it isn't, I'll know.'

Rikkhe looked disconcerted for a moment. It was obvious that he knew nothing about Nabil.

'I had no motive,' Rikkhe said.

'You had plenty of motive,' Satyarthi retorted. 'From what I hear, the kid tried to besmirch your good name at the debate yesterday.'

Rikkhe waved it aside. 'That was a cheap trick, nothing more. We'd all got used to it during the campaign.'

'Not used to it enough, though. Threatened to beat him, did we?'

Rikkhe was impassive. 'A cheap trick, by definition, is a lie.'

'So he arrived, angry with you?' Satyarthi prodded. 'And threw himself off the roof?'

'It was an accident.'

'Explain.'

Rikkhe obliged him with his version of the events.

'I am going to kill you,' Ramanujam snarled, defeated.

Rikkhe laughed. 'You know what the problem with being a topper is? There's always someone waiting in line to beat you.'

'And then the *thirteen-year-old* attacked you, a boy twice his size?' Satyarthi tried to inflect his voice with scepticism, but his heart sank. Rikkhe had said the exact words Nabil had told them.

'Ramanujam wasn't exactly a beacon of rationality,' Rikkhe said wryly.

The inspector had nothing to counter that.

'He attacked me, there was a tussle, I pushed him away, he lost his balance and fell. That's what happened.'

Satyarthi was convinced . . . almost.

'Why didn't you tell someone earlier?'

Rikkhe looked uncomfortable. 'To be honest, Inspector, I was inebriated last night. The victory party, you see. I went to the bathroom and got sick—because of the alcohol and what had happened on the roof. I collapsed there, and was in no shape to answer your questions till later this evening, when I headed home, changed and came back.'

Satyarthi still had a smidgen of doubt. It wasn't to do with the story, which fit perfectly. Neither with corroborating accounts, which fit perfectly as well. It was the boy's calmness that irked him. No average school kid could be so calm after watching someone die.

'I am this calm, Inspector,' Rikkhe said, watching him closely, 'because I am not your average school kid.'

THE DAY AFTER—PART II

(THE PATIENTS)

While the doctor, the director and the inspector had been working on the case, Himanshu spent most of that day oblivious to what had happened. It wasn't common practice, even in Woodsville's infirmary, to tell patients about violent murders in the vicinity. And Vishakha hadn't been to see him since he had called her a coward. He knew, though, that she hadn't been home either; Rikkhe had told him that much after the debate yesterday.

Himanshu had recovered physically, but he'd still headed back to the infirmary after Rikkhe's victory. As it turned out, Rikkhe hadn't needed him, after all. He'd won on the strength of Aniket's unexpected support.

Preparing his lies for the stage, however, had taken a lot out of Himanshu emotionally. He and Rikkhe hadn't known what allegations—real or concocted—might be thrown at Rikkhe, so they had readied rebuttals for all eventualities. He was still resting in the evening when he had a visitor. Since Vishakha left, a host of curious and sympathetic people had visited him. Some had even asked for tips during their election campaigns.

'Hey, there.'

Himanshu looked up to see the petite Rina Singh, the girl he'd helped with the cheating case when he was head scholar. She looked concerned.

'Hi,' Himanshu said, hastily sprucing up his appearance. 'How're you doing?'

'Sorry I didn't come by earlier.' She glanced at the bed where Vishakha had, until recently, taken up residence. 'I guess I thought you didn't need any more trouble.'

Himanshu chuckled, for the first time in days.

'I was heading home,' she said hesitantly, 'and I wondered if anybody had told you about what happened.'

'Oh, I know, Rikkhe won.'

Rina gasped. 'So you *don't* know!'

Himanshu sat up straight.

'Someone threw that poor kid off the roof,' she said tearfully, 'the prodigy.'

Himanshu felt struck by an acute lack of oxygen.

'He's dead,' Rina added. After a pause, she wailed, 'Who would do such a thing?'

Death seemed to have changed everyone's opinion of the 'poor boy', because all Himanshu could think was, *Who wouldn't?*

'When will this all be over?' Rina continued in exasperation. 'The elections are getting worse with each round. And it's so distracting for those willing to be distracted that the rest of us, who just want to focus on our work, can't help but be sucked into it all as well.'

Himanshu nodded.

'You know what I loved about Woodsville?' she said with longing. 'There was always this buzz in the air . . .. of academia, of learning something new. Now the students are restless and the faculty unfocused.'

Himanshu was paying attention, because he remembered that feeling as well.

'The buzz is gone, hasn't it?'

She bowed her head.

His grandfather had made a circus of the school, with clowns clowning about and trapeze artists falling off from great heights. 'It will be back,' he promised.

*

Vishakha was in a daze. She had been, since that withering, burnt woman died. Fragments of her life since then now came to her as dreams rather than as memories. She dreamt that she was burning the pyre of a woman who was already burnt. She dreamt that she thought the irony was funny. She dreamt that she was lying beside Himanshu in an infirmary, on a bed much like her mother's at home. She dreamt she wanted to kill Ramanujam.

And now he was dead. A large patch of blood was all that remained of him. How could that small a body have held so much of it?

She was in a daze. She stared at the ground from where they had collected Ramanujam's body.

She was alone there. The staff and the police had cordoned off the approach to the main school building for all students. Even the faculty had to have direct permission from Walia to cross the checkpoint. Vishakha, however, had sneaked in through a back entrance adjoining the Central Reserve Forest.

She wasn't the only one in front of the school building, though.

'What did you do?'

Vishakha trembled. 'I don't know.'

Himanshu approached her from behind—from the same back entrance she'd taken—and took her hand in his. He still had his infirmary gown on.

'It's not your fault,' he said firmly.

She tore her eyes away from the hypnotic bloodstain. 'I wanted him to die.'

'I did too. Still not your fault.'

'It isn't?'

Himanshu smiled. 'I know you better than to think you had anything to do with this.'

For some reason, not apparent to her, Vishakha began to cry. Himanshu held on to her hand as she sobbed uncontrollably. It wasn't that no one had been kind to her. They had, overly so. Himanshu had been kind too, before he'd called her a coward.

'I cannot go home . . . I cannot leave you. I cannot leave anyone else, ever again.'

Himanshu pursed his lips. 'Then I'll do it for you. I won't be staying on campus any more; I'm going home.'

Vishakha didn't say anything. It was almost as if she'd known this was coming. It took more courage and foolishness than either of them could appreciate at the moment, but they let go of each other.

As Vishakha walked away, Himanshu felt anxious for her, but, after a long time, a little hopeful too. He didn't know when he would see her again, and he didn't know who she would become. All he knew was that he would no longer be an excuse for her staying hidden at Woodsville.

It was nightfall by the time he headed into the school building behind him. He didn't know it, but at that very moment, Rikkhe was being taken for questioning by the police, with the director in tow. The building was empty.

Himanshu would wait. He had never formally resigned as head scholar. There was one last matter that he needed to take care of.

A meeting with his dear grandpa was long overdue.

*

The first thing Rikkhe had done the fateful morning Ramanujam's body was found was switch on his laptop. It had become something of a habit in the past few days to check for news of home. As he surfed through the news clippings, it seemed almost certain that Karamveer would win the constituency.

Before logging out, he'd noticed an alert on the Woodsville website. It simply read: *Classes cancelled for the day. Campus closed for non-boarders.*

Rikkhe didn't think twice about the notification. He made a mental note to visit Shyamji at Paranthe Wali Gali. This time he would take Lisa with him, rather than see her there with Dev.

'There's a visitor, sir,' the housekeeper announced. 'A boy your age, won't give me his name.'

Rikkhe frowned. 'Show him to the garden area, please. And tell the staff not to disturb us.'

Not giving his name to the housekeeper had made it seem like the visitor didn't want anyone but Rikkhe to know he was there. Rikkhe would respect those wishes until he learnt the reason behind them.

Something told him he needed to hurry. Without bothering to change out of his nightclothes, he stepped out through the French windows in the lounge and rushed towards the lone, agitated figure sitting in the gazebo outside.

Rikkhe stopped short as he realized who it was.

'Rikkhe,' Aniket said, getting up. He looked terrified. 'I need your help.'

'It's the least I can do after what you did for me yesterday.'

Aniket waved it aside. 'That wasn't for you.'

Rikkhe nodded. 'All the same. How can I be of service?'

'Ramanujam's dead.'

Aniket waited for him to say something, but he didn't. He just stared at Aniket blankly.

'He fell off the roof,' Aniket continued. 'The police think he was murdered.'

'And was he?' Rikkhe's voice was piercing.

'No,' said Aniket.

'You're sure?'

'I was up there with him when it happened.'

Rikkhe had almost known it was coming, but that hadn't made him any more prepared for it.

'You saw it?'

Aniket shook his head, his body shivering. 'I was involved.'

Rikkhe took a deep breath. 'Explain.'

Aniket did.

'I am going to kill you,' Aniket had threatened him.

Ramanujam laughed contemptuously. 'You know what the problem with being a topper is? There's always someone waiting in line to beat you.'

Aniket couldn't control himself. He closed in on the little devil. One hit, to satisfy his ego. One hit, and he would leave.

Ramanujam had other plans. As Aniket got near, he retreated towards the edge of the roof—fast. When Aniket realized what was happening, he grabbed at the boy to stop him.

'What are you doing?' Aniket gasped, panicked. Ramanujam was inching towards a fall, and it took Aniket everything he had to hold on.

'Get off me!' Ramanujam barked. He tugged in the opposite direction, and Aniket's hand tore through his shirt pocket, while the gleeful boy teetered off the edge.

Aniket stood frozen, his hand still outstretched.

The laughter still rang in the air.

Rikkhe didn't say anything for a long time. He just gazed at Aniket, not really seeing him. Then he motioned for him to take a seat and sat down next to him.

'We'd beaten him together,' he asked sharply, leaning sideways towards him, 'so why did you go there to attack him?'

Aniket turned his face away. 'He'd promised to let me top in these exams. If I helped him . . . bring you down.'

Rikkhe sank back in his chair. 'And the results came last night.'

Aniket was quiet.

'Which means his betrayal came much before yours.'

Aniket nodded. He knew he had no moral right to question Ramanujam, but he had stood second in two of the most important things on campus yesterday. He hadn't been thinking clearly.

'How can I help?' Rikkhe asked. He knew exactly how he could help, but he needed to hear Aniket's answer.

'No one will believe me—'

'When you say that Ramanujam killed himself?'

Aniket nodded. 'I wouldn't believe it myself, had I not been there.'

'I would.'

Finally, a little hope on Aniket's face. 'You believe me?'

'I did a little research on Ramanujam. It seems he had a habit of hurting himself whenever threatened with bodily harm.' Rikkhe paused. 'Took it a little too far this time.'

Aniket sighed with relief.

Rikkhe raised an eyebrow. 'You don't seem particularly bothered that you might have prompted him to jump off.'

Aniket met his eyes now, unabashed. 'It had nothing to do with me. He was up there, already planning to jump.'

Rikkhe looked at him closely. 'How do you know?'

Aniket started fidgeting again. 'I just do.'

Rikkhe could see there was no point pressing the issue.

'So you won't grow a guilty conscience and feel the need to confess to the authorities,' Rikkhe was talking to himself.

'No, I won't.' Aniket fell quiet suddenly. 'Wait. You're saying I shouldn't come clean?'

'*I* believe you, Aniket, but your story isn't believable.'

'So what do I *do*?' Aniket stood up, panicking.

'You let me take the blame.'

Aniket stopped moving. 'What?'

'You came to me because you needed to know how to spin the tale to make it believable. I am telling you that you cannot.'

'But *you* can?'

'*Only* I can. The only way this works is if Ramanujam were the one attacking, and then falling by accident. The only person he'd have a reason to attack would be me, because only I have ever beaten him.'

'You'd do that for me?'

'It wouldn't be for you.' Rikkhe didn't know whom it was really for. Maybe himself, maybe Aniket . . . Or maybe himself.

Aniket could finally see getting out of this mess as a possibility.

'Just promise me that you'll keep quiet after I take the blame.'

'It wasn't my fault he jumped, trust me,' Aniket said harshly. 'It was *his* choice to waste a brilliant mind.'

'Tell me the truth, Aniket,' Rikkhe said after some time. 'You said you didn't help me yesterday for any goodwill towards me. So what made you come to me now? What made you think of me?'

Aniket averted his gaze, smoothing a crease on the pocket of his jeans.

'I don't know.'

Rikkhe didn't believe him for one second.

WOODSVILLE'S MAGIC TREE

The Day After, one of the most testing days of Walia's life, was finally over. He'd headed straight to the school after Rikkhe had told the police everything, and had just finished with the press conference he'd called to tell everyone what the police had concluded: a fight between two bright students went tragically awry. It was an accident.

B.S. Walia and his school had dodged a bullet today. B.S. Walia. Those who knew him well enough called him Bull Shit Walia. He had bullshitted his way out of many a tight corner.

Too tired to go back home, Walia left the reporters in the auditorium and trudged to his office. It felt like the early days of Woodsville, when he'd spent countless nights in his office trying to get the place on its feet. And he'd done all that with only one good leg.

It was dark in his office, but he didn't need the light to navigate his way to the luxurious sofa. Sleep claimed him before his head touched the cushions. But he was rattled awake just as quickly, alertness shrugging off sleep in an instant.

'I was watching the conference on your TV, Nanaji,' Himanshu said from the chair near Walia's feet. 'A good performance, I must say. Felt like you almost cared for the boy.'

Walia sat up with a jerk.

'I have been waiting here since evening,' Himanshu said. 'You'd left for the police station by then, I guess. Rikkhe and Ramanujam. Imagine that, eh?'

'What are you doing out of the infirmary?' Walia asked sharply.

'I am here to get the buzz back.'

'What?' Walia was thoroughly bewildered.

Himanshu waved aside his query. 'I am here to tell you that there will be no more elections for head scholar from now on. And the scholarship will go to the student who deserves and needs it.'

Walia snorted. He revelled in a challenge, especially one that questioned his authority in Woodsville.

'I think I need to call your psychiatrist, son,' he said derisively. 'It seems they let you out of observation too soon.'

Himanshu sighed. 'Grandfather, you're ruining the school.'

'I am *running* my school.'

'Into the ground,' Himanshu replied, shaking his head.

Walia stood up angrily. 'Leave now, before your mother hears about this.'

'I am asking you, please don't do this. You created something beautiful, against all odds. It wasn't perfect, I know, but it was still better than this craziness.' Himanshu pointed towards the roof.

'The elections will strengthen the student body and, in turn, the alumni association of this school!' Walia was incensed. 'You know how helpful it is to have a lobby of ideologically like-minded people behind you for the rest of your life? I am giving more power to you students.'

'At what cost?' Himanshu stood up as well. 'By making everyone ethically bankrupt? That won't create an ideology that'll stand the test of time. It needs to be founded on principles to survive.'

Walia turned away, limping towards the window, seemingly realizing the futility of arguing with his fool of a grandson. It was a clear dismissal.

But Himanshu stood his ground, his heart heavy. 'Say, Grandfather, let me give you an example. There's this shy kid. He is naive. He has an imaginary friend who he believes is real. Now this kid is shown that nobody else believes in his friend. Nobody else believes in anything any more, really. What does that do to this kid?'

Walia kept looking out the window, but he was listening intently.

'If nobody else believes in it, his belief ceases to matter. He loses it too. He grows callous, because now he knows that's how the world is. He goes up to his grandfather and threatens to destroy his world if he doesn't comply. He tells him what he'll tell the world if he doesn't comply.'

Walia's breathing had quickened.

'He'll tell the world,' Himanshu spoke slow and low, 'how his grandfather abused his position so that his grandson would become head scholar. How he cheated with the ballots out of love for his grandson.'

'You'd lie.'

'There's nothing like a lie for this kid any more, sir, because he's been taught that beliefs don't matter.'

Walia looked down through the window to the ground shrouded in darkness, where, he imagined, Ramanujam must've fallen. And nodded.

Himanshu saw him nod in the moonlight.

'And, sir, the boy would also appreciate if his grandfather left his mother alone so she could regain some of her own beliefs . . . Or else.'

Himanshu walked out quietly.

Walia grinned. He was finally proud of the boy. He didn't regret succumbing to the threat. It was another one of those days . . . although he had never had two such days in a row. Deals would have to be made, compromises would have to be reached.

Himanshu stopped outside Walia's office. He couldn't believe what he'd done. He couldn't help but feel that while he had tried to change her, Vishakha Sahdev had changed him a little.

*

The nondescript little two-bedroom flat in Shahadra, which the Sahdev family called home, no longer drew any attention. The odd, nosy neighbours had lost interest since the gruesomely wounded woman had passed away. Now it was inhabited by a widower, which was commonplace enough to warrant indifference. There was the brainy daughter, but she was always at that fancy school of hers.

Mrs Kalra desisted from poking her nose into the kitchen, for she now caught the rotten whiff of unwashed dishes whenever she did.

Mr Sahdev himself had never had the time to build friendships, or nurture old ones. The demands of keeping his wife's mutilated body alive took everything he had. And now, even when his days were empty, he didn't put them to much use.

The only sounds that came from the house were from the TV, which Mr Sahdev kept on at all times. When there was no electricity, everything was silent.

When Vishakha finally came back, the house was in one of its silent modes. She didn't know if anyone else was home, or if it even *was* home any more. She remembered nothing of it. The smell of hospital and Dettol was missing, and the place was dirtier than her father would've let it get.

Her father, in deep slumber, hadn't realized that he had company. All those years of hard work and sleep deprivation had made way for a life that had nothing but rest to look forward to. Dreams were few and far between. And they were gentle dreams. Not always, though. Sometimes he had to contend with nightmares. Not that he was complaining.

Even the nightmares were better than being awake in his house. His wife's bed lay untouched. The medicines. The waste. Everything was a memory. And there were too many memories here, memories that pleaded to be acted upon, something Mr Sahdev was too spent to do.

So he slept. Letting his face grow old and his house alien. It was easier. His wife was gone. His daughter was gone. And he had never learnt to live for himself.

It was morning by the time he woke up. He didn't know Vishakha had been home since the night before, and wouldn't have known now either, had his boss not called to interrupt his gentle dreams. The call was to advise him that sympathy for his deceased wife was fast running out, and was being replaced by annoyance at his consistent inconsistency since her death.

Mr Sahdev had been lying on his mattress on the floor, right next to his wife's bed. As he got up, he realized there was no bed any more. Somebody had wheeled it out.

He jerked awake. Rushing into the drawing room, he felt like he was in the wrong house. Everything was different. There was much less *stuff* than he was used to, and it was all spaced out neatly; it all felt so *young*. It was so Vizac.

Suddenly, it didn't feel painful to be in the house.

A mild clang from the kitchen reached his ears, and he glanced in. He couldn't believe his eyes, but there she was! She stood cleaning the dishes.

'Morning, Dad,' Vishakha said. 'I was just going to wake you up. There's milk and toast on the table. You are late for work.'

In the last few weeks, Mr Sahdev had learnt to cry without tears. It proved helpful to him now, as he bawled mentally.

'Right you are,' he croaked.

'And, Dad,' Vishakha said, 'there's a form there I need you to sign.'

Mr Sahdev went over to the table and looked it over. *Application to change status from boarding to day school* . . . He could hear water splash on metal.

He looked at Vishakha working quietly and cried harder. She was finally back home.

Vishakha smiled; she hadn't used those muscles in a while. She felt hopeful.

She felt a little like the shy boy who had stayed in his miserable house for the sake of his mother. Himanshu Pathak had turned her a little into him. And she didn't mind.

*

Dev Bhushan had always been cautious, but that hadn't kept him from losing everything he had. He had been fortunate all his life, but that hadn't prevented months of debilitating bad luck. So as he drove his jeep near the President's Estate now, it was a very conscious decision to drive it at a speed of over 130 kmph.

His dream of becoming a cricketer was over. Following his grandfather's interference, Walia, too, had abandoned him. His grandfather had made it very clear that the two war veterans had struck a deal, sealing his future; he would never make it to the national team. His loyalty to the sport had been spurned. His loyalty to Woodsville had been spurned. His loyalty to the country had been spurned.

So, as his grandfather sat gloating in the drawing room, Dev Bhushan left the house, slamming the door shut so hard the glass broke.

Caution had given him nothing. He pressed the pedal harder.

That imp was dead too. Killed by his own foolishness, it seemed. Another person whom Dev's loyalty had been wasted on. And now Dev was back to being on his own. That's the way he worked best.

He crossed three red lights, driving helter-skelter towards the Rashtrapati Bhavan from India Gate. It got him noticed, first, by the traffic police, then, by the regular police, and after that, by the military guards posted outside the gates.

The last time his life had changed was when he had burnt that place as a kid, back in the States. He needed to change his life once more.

He swerved away from the guards, who hesitated for a split second when they saw him. The car crashed head-on into the reinforced gate, and Dev was thrown forward, smack on to the windshield.

Assault rifles surrounded his bleeding face. He looked up and found himself staring down the barrel of one.

'Down with the President!' he gasped. 'Down with the oppressors!'

'He's just a kid,' Dev heard one voice say.

Someone else whistled. 'You're so screwed, kid,' he said.

Dev smiled. He had broken so many laws that it'd stay on his record forever. A criminal record meant no government job. And *that* meant that try as he might, his grandfather wouldn't be able to get him into the air force. Certainly not after he'd attacked the President.

The one thing that worried him was that they might not let him play professional cricket. He had another wry thought before he passed out. It made him chuckle.

Maybe he could go back to his parents in America and play baseball instead.

*

The passing of Ramanujam had catapulted Woodsville into the national spotlight. The incident instigated numerous debates about the dangers of cut-throat competition in academia. At the forefront of it all was Rikkhe Rajput, who'd somehow managed to garner almost as much admiration, sympathy and love as the poor boy who'd died.

Rikkhe had only helped fuel the issue by admitting how taxing the pressure was on a student's mind. From potentially being the most hated teenager in the country, he'd turned into the most loved one. Editorials in leading newspapers as well as continuous TV coverage only elevated his reputation. What also enamoured the audiences was his royal lineage, which shone through in his every movement. Occasionally, he was joined by Director Walia, who, in order to 'prevent any such future occurrences of undue pressure', had taken the bold step of cancelling elections for the post altogether. His heartbreak and remorse over the loss of his extraordinary ward made the director a valiant champion of education reform, so much so that he was made part of several policy-making commissions instituted by the government.

However, as is inevitable, public interest shifted after a few months. The issue was cast aside, while the individual persisted. Rikkhe became a regular at events, where his voice lent credence to the views of school-going children.

Indeed, a few weeks after completing the boards, Rikkhe once again found himself in a TV studio for a live telecast. It had been a while since he'd been in touch with anybody from school except Lisa, but somehow, the newspeople had still deemed him up-to-date enough to speak about student affairs.

'In there for a quick touch-up,' the production assistant instructed Rikkhe, 'and I'll come fetch you ten minutes before we go live.'

Opening the door to the make-up room, Rikkhe gave a curt smile. 'I know the drill.'

'Oh, and you might know our other panellist for tonight. You're both from the same school, I think.'

Rikkhe entered the room and saw the make-up guy applying the finishing touches to Aniket Jain's face; he looked quite sharp in a tailored suit.

'Hi, Rikkhe,' he said, watching him in the mirror. He'd obviously known Rikkhe was invited.

'Hello, Aniket,' Rikkhe said lightly, taking a seat next to him. 'Forgive me, but I never congratulated you.'

Aniket waved it aside, beaming. 'Oh, it's nothing.'

'I guess that's why they called you, though,' Rikkhe remarked, 'the highest-scoring all-India topper ever.'

Aniket grew sombre. 'I had so much to motivate me this year.'

Rikkhe muttered, 'Didn't we all?'

They sat in silence for a few minutes, as the make-up man shifted from Aniket to Rikkhe.

'How's Lisa?' Aniket asked, turning in his seat to face him.

Rikkhe, who didn't particularly enjoy getting powder in his mouth, mumbled, 'Good. She's going to be studying fashion designing in Mumbai.'

'What about you? You can't just give interviews about school education for the rest of your life.'

Rikkhe smiled. 'I doubt they'll be calling me again, once I join college.'

'Anything decided yet?' A lot of people had been curious about what Rikkhe Rajput would take up, but strangely, no one knew anything.

'I think I'll probably drop a year,' Rikkhe said slowly.

Aniket looked at him incredulously. 'Why?'

Rikkhe didn't say anything until the make-up man was out of the room.

'I guess there's a lot of lost time I have to make up for. I'll go home to begin with . . .' Rikkhe paused. 'There are some matters I need to settle.'

'After that?'

'Mumbai.' There was genuine happiness on his face, so infectious that even Aniket grinned. 'At least for a while. Then I plan to travel some . . . across the country.'

Aniket felt envious, despite having been accepted into Harvard Business School. He wondered if he would ever *not* feel envious of Rikkhe Rajput.

'I heard about Harvard,' Rikkhe said. 'Congratulations! The scholarship came through?'

Aniket nodded. 'Woodsville's got me an apartment in Boston, can you believe it?'

Rikkhe could. He was the one who'd handed the brochure for the place to Walia.

'I was a bit surprised, though,' Aniket continued. 'I thought the scholarship would go to the head scholar, as per the conditions of the election.'

Rikkhe knew Himanshu had somehow convinced Walia otherwise.

'Well, as you now know, I didn't need it,' Rikkhe explained, 'and Himanshu wasn't eligible for it any more. I guess the director took the logical decision.'

'Yeah, I heard Pathak joined some wildlife photographer as an intern,' Aniket said, lowering his voice. 'Imagine that!'

'Yeah,' Rikkhe said thoughtfully, 'he's going to be doing his fair share of travelling as well. Maybe we'll run into each other.'

'Maybe I'll run into Bhushan,' Aniket said menacingly. 'He's gone to the United States as well. After the stunt he pulled here, I think leaving the country was the best option available.'

'I heard,' Rikkhe said darkly. 'I hope it does him some good.' He didn't think it would.

'Speaking of scholarships,' Aniket said brightly, 'did you know Vishakha got offered one from MIT, for economics?'

'She turned it down,' Rikkhe informed him. 'She'll be studying commerce at SRCC.'

Aniket couldn't believe his ears. 'But why?'

Rikkhe shrugged. He'd guessed it had something to do with her father, but he wasn't sure.

'Maybe she's angling for the Planning Commission,' Aniket said to himself. 'Professor Dheer had said he needed research assistants for his work there.'

'Where do you think Ramanujam would've gone?' Rikkhe asked abruptly.

Aniket didn't hesitate. 'Probably on to ruin someone else's life.'

This callousness nagged Rikkhe. It didn't fit with who Aniket was.

'Sometimes,' Rikkhe began, 'when I'm speaking on these shows—about him—'

'You feel guilty.' Aniket had seen Rikkhe falsely confess to the public about his involvement in Ramanujam's death a number of times. The regret was always genuine.

'And a fraud,' Rikkhe whispered. 'He'd accused me of being a fraud. He was right at the time. Maybe he still is.'

Aniket chuckled. 'I thought you were a fraud for the longest time. You know when it was that I realized you weren't one?'

Rikkhe didn't speak.

'The day you took the blame for me. You didn't have to, but you did. And I knew what everyone said about you was true.'

'What's that?'

'"He's a good guy."'

Rikkhe didn't look convinced.

'You know what the problem is, though?' Aniket went on. 'It's that you unknowingly shouldered the blame that rests solely with Ramanujam. That's why you started believing it.'

Rikkhe looked up. 'Ramanujam's blame?'

'Remember how I told you he went up there intending to jump off?' Aniket said fiercely.

Rikkhe did. 'I asked you what made you so sure of it.'

'What does, in cases like these?' Aniket asked pointedly.

Rikkhe was confused for a moment. Then it struck him. 'A suicide note!'

Aniket got up to leave. 'He *wanted* people to hate you. He *wanted* you to doubt yourself.'

'How—?'

'My hand tore through his shirt pocket,' Aniket spoke through gritted teeth, 'and it wasn't empty.'

Aniket threw something on the table in front of Rikkhe. 'I brought this for you. Just stop feeling guilty already.'

Rikkhe's hand was steady as he picked up the note, but he shivered inwardly. It was Ramanujam's neat scrawl.

It's become too much for me. With the constant bullying, the threats and the social alienation, Rikkhe Rajput has done everything he can to prevent me from realizing my goals at Woodsville. The only person responsible for my death is Rikkhe Rajput. He's not the saint everyone thinks him to be. He's a fraud. Maybe after me, others will speak up. For now, though, screw you, Rikkhe.

'That's how he planned to beat you,' Aniket hissed. 'Unfortunately for him, I got the note.'

For the second time in his life, Rikkhe was struck by how far Ramanujam could go to win.

'He *was* the very best of us, then,' Rikkhe breathed, realizing how sheer dumb luck had saved him.

'Or the very worst,' Aniket retorted, his back to Rikkhe. 'You know how I can say everything he wrote there is wrong, though? It's because you didn't need to see this before you decided to help me.'

It was as though a cloud had been lifted from their midst. Rikkhe beamed.

'You aren't as bad as everyone thinks, Aniket. And you know how *I* can say that? You didn't use this,' he held up the note, 'to pressure me into doing what you wanted. You let go of your pride so I could hold on to mine.'

A mischievous smile played on Aniket's lips as he left. 'Don't be so sure of that, Rajput, I would have used this had you not volunteered to save my ass!'

Alone in the room, Rikkhe laughed lightly, shaking his head.

'I know better than to believe you, my friend.'

EPILOGUE

*T*he tumultuous academic year hadn't left any tangible mark on Woodsville, save for one thing. In the farthest corner of the campus, behind the student residences, a patch of wild grass had been cleared. A prodigy lay buried beneath, along with a single seed.

As the seed grew to live for much longer than its symbolic counterpart, the clearing became a sort of shrine for the students of Woodsville. No one remembered having planted anything in his grave. The tree that sprang forth seemed to have done so of its own accord.

Thousands of students would flock to Ramanujam's grave in the coming years, praying for love and success. It was believed that the spirit of the innocent young boy listened to all.

The first visitor to the grave, however, had walked up long before the superstition started. He was different from the others. He didn't come to pray to a saint, but to talk to a friend.

Sid 'Charsi' Malhotra was the only one who had told that patch of earth that it was finally home.

He was the only one who had gone to that enclosure and cried for the boy buried there.

He was the one, in the unlikeliest of realities, who had gone in there with a seed in his pocket.

ACKNOWLEDGEMENTS

Words are precious, and as I employ a few on something as selfish as acknowledgements, I'll save some on the dedication. This book is dedicated to all those I must acknowledge for its existence.

My sister. For reading and reviewing each newly formed paragraph (yes, I'm that slow) and giving me the perseverance to write (also for teaching me the word perseverance).

Ma. What do you thank Ma for? Just everything.

Pa. For telling me to trust my judgement, when I clearly trust his more. Oh, the irony.

Sohini Mitra. The person responsible for making sure that *Toppers* didn't remain a DOC file on my laptop, and for being there every time I needed her.

Purnima. Who's polished my amateurish writing so much that it looks like it came from a real author (she'll be the first person I send this to).

Anupam Verma. The man who's put in more effort into this book than the rest of us combined, relentlessly fighting to get it to its best possible form (*stellar* form, he'd say) before it reached you.

And you, reader. You're the reason for it all.